I0628659

Stealing a Country

A Rory Mack Steele Novel

Eugene Lloyd MacRae

Published by Eugene Lloyd MacRae, 2012.

This is a work of fiction. Similarities to real people, places, or events are entirely coincidental.

STEALING A COUNTRY

First edition. November 10, 2012.

Written by Eugene Lloyd MacRae.

Special thanks to Jazz, Smoky, Maxi and Suki who kept me company while I worked on this book

Chapter 1

HUNTSVILLE, DISTRICT of Muskoka, Ontario, Canada
TWO MEN IN BLACK LEATHER JACKETS and dark, denim jeans crept slowly towards the two-story vacation cottage of their target. It was a chilly December evening but the lack of snow had made their trek through the stands of dense pine trees surrounding the acreage easy and hid their movements. But now they were out in the open and had to be careful. Very careful. They moved cautiously as they crossed the distance from the tree line to the edge of the driveway where they knelt for a moment, listening and watching. The men worked in tandem as they scanned the windows and the edges of the cottage for any signs of movement. Everything was still and quiet. A single, soft light on the second floor and the faint scent of a wood burning fire were the final nails in someone's coffin. The men now knew their target *was* there.

Satisfied they wouldn't be seen, the two men made the final sprint to the large, silver Mercedes sitting in the darkness of the driveway. The larger of the two men squatted near the back wheel and kept an eye on the cottage.

The smaller man got down beside the car and rolled over onto his back. He gripped the bottom edge of the Mercedes and slowly pulled himself underneath. Reaching into a pocket of his leather jacket, he pulled something out and began to work under the car.

After a few minutes, the porch lights on the vacation cottage lit up. The larger man tapped the smaller man on the foot several times, urging him to hurry up.

The smaller man under the Mercedes was startled and his body jumped. He cursed, "No hagas eso."

The larger man tapped the smaller man's foot again and whispered, "Silencio."

The smaller man cursed under his breath as he went back to work.

"Dar prisa."

The smaller man grumbled as he finished his work and then hustled out from under the silver Mercedes.

The front door of the two-story cottage opened and light spilled out into the night.

The two men made a run for the tree line, keeping as low as possible.

Two young children, dressed in snowsuits, burst through the open doorway. Laughing and giggling, they headed across the front porch and ran down the steps towards the Mercedes. A tall, handsome man wearing a light green parka walked out behind the children. A beautiful, redheaded woman appeared in the doorway behind him. The man turned, held the woman's face tenderly and planted a firm kiss on her red lips. Then he put his arms around her and tried to draw her close. The woman pushed him back playfully, gesturing for him to get going. He smiled at her as he pulled on leather driving gloves. Turning, he walked down the stairs, heading for the silver Mercedes.

Cassandra Glynn stepped out on the front porch of their Muskoka vacation cottage and leaned her hip against the stair railing. Dressed only in a blue pantsuit, she crossed her arms against the night chill. Her husband was trying to get Connor and Alanna into the Mercedes but they were too busy throwing small snowballs at each other.

"Let's go you two," urged their father as he grinned at their antics, "grandpa and grandma are waiting." Bryson Glynn looked back at Cassandra and winked.

The gleam in his eye told Cassandra he was obviously anticipating having a long weekend all alone with his wife. Cassandra was 5 foot 10 inches tall, with long legs, shoulder length red hair, a freckled complexion and a gleam in her own green eyes. She jutted her chest out and winked back at him.

The children finally climbed into the back door of the silver Mercedes and Bryson closed the door behind them. Then he walked around to the other side of the car and got into the driver side door. He started the car and the low rumble of the diesel engine filled the night air. Bryson Glynn rolled down his driver side window and waved back at his wife as he pulled away from the cottage. Connor and Alanna appeared in the back window of the Mercedes, laughing and waving goodbye to their mother.

Cassandra walked down a couple of steps and waved back at them as long as she could. She continued to wave as she watched the red tail lights of the Mercedes get smaller. Then she quickly turned and bounced up the steps towards the open door to get out of the chilly, night air. Cassandra Glynn was already planning on surprising her husband with some new, sexy lingerie she had bought before they had left home.

Crack! Crack!

Cassandra Glynn turned at the sounds. The small, red taillights in the distance swerved to the left. Cassandra's heart went into her throat as she realized the car had swerved left towards the lake. It was a steep drop over the black rock into ice-cold water. She screamed at the top of her lungs as she ran down the long driveway. The red taillights disappeared beneath the frigid surface.

The two men in dark clothing slipped into the night.

Chapter 2

CBC NEWS FLASH

"**GOOD EVENING**, I'm Bryer Taylor-Johnson. Tragedy struck last night in Muskoka vacation land. Bryson Glynn, Member of Parliament for Toronto Rosedale was killed in a tragic accident along with his two children, Alanna and Connor. Glynn's car plunged into the icy waters of Lake Corsair where his vacation home is situated. Police sources say Glynn's Mercedes swerved off the road as he and the children were leaving their vacation home to visit his wife's parents.

Bryson Glynn was a rising star for the Canadian Federal Party. He had won the Toronto Rosedale riding in the last two elections and was instrumental in the push to coordinate police efforts across the country in cases of missing children and to create a national database. He recently met with American officials to try and create a joint effort across North America.

Glynn is survived by his wife, Cassandra Glynn."

SIX MONTHS LATER
    CBC News Flash

"Good evening, I'm Bryer Taylor-Johnson. Cassandra Glynn was overwhelmingly chosen as the riding's candidate for the parliamentary seat in Toronto-Rosedale this afternoon. Ms. Glynn is the widow of the late Bryson Glynn, who held the seat for the Canadian Federal Party in the last two federal elections. Bryson Glynn and his two children were drowned in a tragic accident last December when their car plunged into Lake Corsair at their Muskoka vacation home. Ms. Glynn had kept in the background, raising their two children while her husband worked diligently for causes they both believed in. She stated publicly that she wanted to continue on with those good works and made a decision to run for her husband's old riding seat. Canadian Federal Party riding spokesperson, Mavis Beachmont-Montgomery said that Cassandra Glynn was a clear-cut favorite from the beginning. Ms. Glynn had little opposition in the democratic voting process to elect the Toronto-Rosedale riding candidate to run in the next federal election."

TORONTO CONVENTION Center, Toronto, Ontario, **Canada**

Cassandra Glynn left her room on the first floor of the Toronto Convention Center and hurried down the hallway. She had wanted to get to the All Candidates Meetings for the Canadian Federal Party much earlier this evening but the CBC interview had gone a lot longer than planned. But she had no one to blame but herself. She was so passionate about discussing the political platform her husband had used in winning two elections that she could easily get carried away. But more importantly, she always made sure to discuss all the causes she and Bryson had talked about. She felt it was his legacy and she had to make sure it carried on.

Heads turned as Cassandra and the scent of her delicate perfume passed by. Most of the men took extra time to admire her long, shapely legs and the hourglass figure. Cassandra Glynn had spent the last two weeks picking out her outfit. She wore a red, A-line dress that floated around her knees, sheer pantyhose and red, high heeled shoes that brought her height to just over 6 feet tall. She looked like an Irish Amazon. This was the woman her husband had loved to see. This part she was doing for him.

Friends and acquaintances greeted her and wished her well as she strode confidently across the lobby and headed towards the wide hallway leading to the York Room. Reporters and television news crews with cameras were everywhere, interviewing any candidate willing to stop and talk. And there were plenty of those. Updated news reports were constantly feeding information out to the political junkies around the country.

"Mrs. Glynn, can I get a moment?" asked one of the reporters. She thrust a microphone in front of Cassandra.

"I don't have too much time Wendy," Cassandra said as she continued her march. The reporter hustled to keep up with her.

"Are you going to continue with your husband's policies for the riding?" the interviewer asked, "or will you have your own platform when the election comes?"

Cassandra Glynn stopped in her tracks. "I plan on continuing on with my husband's work," she said, "that's the only reason I'm here. He worked so hard, not only for the people in his own riding but across the country. I'm sure you remember all the work he did with missing children and with homeless children. Those issues concerned him greatly once our own two children were born. I want to continue on with that work, to continue on with my husband's legacy. For him *and* my children. I'll talk about things more specifically once election time rolls around, Wendy. You'll be my first call."

"I'll hold you to that," the interviewer said with a smile, "thank you so much for your time, Mrs. Glynn."

Cassandra Glynn was almost skipping in anticipation as she moved down the hallway again. She approached a large group of people milling outside the open York Room double doors. She could hear someone inside the room testing the sound system. There was a buzz of excitement in the air. She caught sight of Clarke Navarro, the Chief Party Whip of the Canadian Federal Party and she headed directly for him. He was talking with a group of people that included Mavis Beachmont-Montgomery, the spokesperson of her riding. Beside Mavis was a tall, sandy-haired man Cassandra thought she recognized but couldn't quite place. A step behind him was a beautiful, young Latino woman in a dark pantsuit. She had short, black hair, dark, hard eyes, and when she turned her head, a thin black wire was visible behind her ear.

Cassandra approached the group with a brisk step, "Hello everyone."

Clarke Navarro turned to her with a mild look of surprise on his face, "Cassandra? What are you doing here?"

Cassandra stopped dead in her tracks as she looked at Navarro. She was a little bewildered at his unexpected comment. She pointed to the open doors just behind him. "I'm here for the All Candidates Meeting." Navarro's facial expression told her something was wrong. She looked over at Mavis Beachmont-Montgomery, who suddenly looked very embarrassed. No one else in the group said a word for a moment.

"What's going on here?" Cassandra asked.

There was no answer as other members of the small group started walking away.

Cassandra noticed the retreating group began talking in quiet tones as they looked back at her. She turned her attention back to the ones still standing there - Clarke Navarro, Mavis Beachmont-Montgomery, the tall, sandy-haired man, and the short, dark-haired woman - all waiting for an answer.

It was Clarke Navarro who finally spoke in a low voice, "Cassandra, the Prime Minister did not sign off on your candidacy. I thought you knew that?"

"What do you mean? I won the nomination. Tell him, Mavis."

Mavis avoided Cassandra's gaze and her face blushed a cherry red.

"Cassandra," Clarke Navarro said, "you know the party rules. The Prime Minister has to sign off on the candidate, no matter what." He indicated the tall sandy-haired man standing beside him, "The Prime Minister has chosen Demario Gomez here to run in that riding."

Cassandra looked at the man and realized where she knew him from, "The retired hockey player? You're kidding?"

Demario Gomez sneered at her.

"But I was *democratically* elected by the riding association," Cassandra countered. "Tell him, Mavis."

Mavis frowned, "Democracy seems to have *nothing* to do with it."

Navarro scowled at her.

Mavis put her head down and emitted a small apology, "I'm sorry, Cassandra, I really am." Then she quickly turned tail and disappeared through the open doors and into the crowd of the York Room.

Cassandra was totally stunned and embarrassed as she stood there.

A number of people in the hallway were looking at her and talking in hushed tones.

Clarke Navarro took Cassandra by the arm and walked her away from the York Room.

The young Latino woman followed just behind them.

"I'm sorry you've been embarrassed like this Cassandra," said Navarro, "I thought Larrise would've told you."

"Larrise knew!" Cassandra yelled. She jerked her arm away from Navarro's grasp.

Navarro indicated with his hands to keep her voice down. "Larrise and I talked earlier," he said, "she accepted a post in the Prime Minister's office and–"

"She what!" Cassandra yelled instantly, "I'll kill her!"

"Keep your voice down," Navarro urged her again as he turned and gestured back towards the York Room to a young blonde woman.

The young blonde moved quickly past the dark-haired Latino woman to Navarro's side.

"Ellen, please get Mr. Tillman out here," Navarro said.

The young blonde nodded and headed for the York Room.

The dark-haired Latino woman moved discretely closer to Navarro and Cassandra.

"It's nothing personal Cassandra," Navarro continued. "And I assure you the party takes care of its people. Larrise accepted the position and we have a position for you as well–"

"You can shove your position!" Cassandra yelled, "You *know* I'm doing this for my husband."

"I'm sorry Cassandra," Navarro said. He spread his hands out in helplessness, "You know my hands are tied–"

Cassandra Glynn whirled around on her heels, her red dress flaring, "Wait until I find Larrise. I'll kill her! I'll kill her!" With her red hair flying behind her, Cassandra marched in full stride back down the hallway. Everyone in the hallway was now watching this tall, fiery redhead who appeared headed for a confrontation. They made sure to stay out of her way.

Navarro had a smug, dismissive smile on his face as he watched the volatile woman in the red dress march down the hallway. He turned and walked back towards the York Room.

Cassandra Glynn tore across the lobby and down to the hallway towards room number 29 with a deadly purpose. She was mad and the people she passed along the way knew it. Normally very polite, Cassandra pushed her way through a crowd of people and continued her assault down the hallway. She headed directly for Larrise Abbatiello's hotel room.

She found the door to room number 29 was slightly ajar and she barged right in, banging the door back against the wall. "Larrise!" she yelled. "Larrise Abbatiello, you show yourself right now. Where are you?" She marched across the carpeted floor.

"Larrise!" she yelled again at the top of her lungs. To her right was a small kitchenette with a tile floor.

And lying on the floor, in a pool of blood, was Larrise Abbatiello!

Cassandra Glynn let out a cry of shock and moved to the body without hesitation. Her anger was gone and concern for her friend replaced it instantly.

As she neared the bloody body, a strong arm grabbed her around the waist from behind. A cloth was placed over her nose and mouth in one swift movement.

Cassandra Glynn felt the strong body behind her lift her firmly off the floor.

She struggled to free herself. She tried to scream but she only succeeded in inhaling fumes that assaulted her senses.

After a brief struggle, Cassandra Glynn passed out.

CASSANDRA GLYNN HEARD faint voices behind her. The world was coming back into focus. She was lying face down. Shaking her head to clear the cobwebs, Cassandra slowly got up onto her hands and knees. That's when she realized she was holding a pair of scissors in her right hand. The scissors had blood on them. There was also blood on the side of her hand and on her wrist where her arm had been laying in the pool of blood!

"She killed her!" a panicked female voice said behind her.

Cassandra turned on her knees quickly. A small crowd of people was standing in the room, looking down at her. Still holding the bloody scissors, Cassandra Glynn looked every inch a murderer!

"Someone call the police," urged a male voice in the crowd.

Cassandra looked down at the scissors and then at the body of her friend. She realized what it looked like. To everyone else in the room, it looked like she had just walked in and stabbed

Larrise Abbatiello. She stood up on shaky legs and slowly turned around, her head spinning at the turn of events. Everything was happening so fast.

Another female voice in the crowd called out, "The police are on the way."

"I didn't do it," Cassandra mumbled. She looked back at the bloody body of Larrise Abbatiello and realized she would be charged with murder. She moved towards the crowd. She had to get away, she had to leave.

One of the men in the crowd stepped forward, hands out, "Don't move lady. Stay right there."

Cassandra thrust the scissors at him and he jumped back.

A woman screamed. Another yelled, "Get out of the way Cal. She's crazy. Let the police take care of her."

Thrusting the scissors out again, Cassandra parted the crowd, frantically making her way to the open doorway. Once outside the room, Cassandra looked for escape - saw only a few people to the right - threatened them to move to the side - then dropped the scissors and began to flee blindly from the scene of the murder.

Chapter 3

CASSANDRA REALIZED IN HER PANIC she had been running without any specific direction. She didn't even know where she was in the sprawling convention center now. She slowed to a walk. Running in high heel shoes was not easy and she was out of breath. She forced herself to focus. She realized escape was going to be extremely difficult. Because of the All Candidates Meeting, there were a lot of extra security guards roaming the convention center. There were also a number of police officers who had been outside directing traffic. And there were probably Royal Canadian Mounted Police here as well because the Prime Minister was in the convention center. They would all be alerted by now and joining the chase. They were all going to be chasing her. Chasing Cassandra Glynn, the murderer.

She heard some voices up ahead. Stopping dead in her tracks, she listened. Voices now sounded behind her and she turned, listening intently. The hallway was curved and she couldn't see anyone yet, but the voices were coming closer. She was about to be trapped between two sets of searchers. She felt a tightening in her chest and she desperately looked around for a way out. Cassandra spotted a door up ahead on the left. It didn't look like a hotel room door. But was it a place to hide? She ran forward, toward the voices. She prayed she would make the door before someone saw her. Reaching it, Cassandra slowly turned the round, aluminum doorknob. The door was unlocked. She opened it and looked inside. It was a large laundry room. She moved inside, quietly closing the door behind her and leaning back against it. Listening intently, she heard the voices coming closer in the hallway outside. Turning around slowly, Cassandra reached down to lock the door – there was no lock! She looked desperately for a hiding place – there were none. She looked for other doors – there were none. That meant no other exit. She had trapped herself.

No, there *was* a way out. There were a set of tall, French windows dead ahead. She ran for them. As she reached up to the center latch, Cassandra realized there was still blood on her hand. She turned back to a sink she had passed and washed her hands quickly. She fought back hot tears as she realized it was Larrise Abbatiello's blood she was washing off. Her long-time friend was dead and she was going to prison for it. Cassandra dried her hands and moved back to the French windows. Looking through the glass, she realized they opened into the large garden area at the side of the convention center. Reaching up, Cassandra undid the latch and pushed the two windows wide open. She lifted her leg, setting it on the lower frame and pulled herself up. The outside wall below the French windows was very wide and sloped downward and then there was a drop. Cassandra started to walk gingerly down the slope. Then she started sliding down. Her high-heeled shoes were betraying her! She let herself go and slipped over the edge, holding her breath as she dropped. Then her feet hit the ground.

Cassandra couldn't move! She felt a sudden breeze around her exposed lower body. Her red dress was caught. The hem had caught itself in a crack on one of the open window frames when she'd dropped. Her red dress was now yanked up around her arms and shoulders. Cassandra fought desperately to loosen the dress from the window frame. She tried to turn and reach up. That was a stupid move. The dress was now twisted tightly around her. And her extended arms were pinned to her body by the twisted material. She couldn't fully lift and extend her arms to reach the window frame now. Cassandra heard voices.

The police were in the laundry room. They were going to see her if they came over to the window!

Cassandra almost laughed. Her first thought had been the embarrassment at being caught with her dress up around her ears. That was the least of her worries right now. She tried to calm herself. She had to think. As a last-ditch effort, Cassandra jumped up and down in her high heels. She did it again and again, trying to jump up and down quietly but desperately trying to unhook the hem. There! She finally freed the dress. She pushed it back down around her body and slipped away into the shadows of the garden. Cassandra looked back as she crouched low in the darkness.

Several security guards suddenly appear at the open French window. Two of the guards shone flashlights around the outside garden.

Cassandra shuffled over behind a few larger bushes.

The flashlight beams crisscrossed right over her. The two security men quickly closed the French windows and disappeared.

Cassandra waited for a few moments and then kept low as she moved further away into the garden, the rich fragrance of rose beds and lemon-scented geraniums barely registering. She figured she could escape by heading in the direction of the building next door. But she didn't get very far before she ran up against a tall, iron fence. There was no way she could climb it. Cassandra could hear voices far over to her right. They were looking for her at the back of the conventions center now. Cassandra headed in the opposite direction, towards the front of the convention center. She kept close to the iron fence and as far away from the windows of the convention center as possible, trying to avoid the patches of light spilling out through the glass. Her only hope of escaping now was to slip out into the street and blend into the crowd.

But as Cassandra approached the front of the convention center, she realized that escape in this direction was going to be impossible. The entire street in front of the convention center was a zoo and people were everywhere. But all the police officers standing in the street and on the sidewalk meant she would be spotted as soon as she stepped out of the garden area. There was no way she was going to be able to escape this way. And she knew it was only a matter of time before those behind her caught up with her. Once they started searching the garden it would be all over. She felt panic.

The screech of a microphone sounded out in the street. Cassandra realized all the media, who had been present to cover the All Candidates Meeting for the Canadian Federal Party, were now setting up in the street in front of the Toronto Convention Center. They would soon be sending out news flashes across the country about her and the sensational murder. It was all happening at the speed of light because of the political convention. Cassandra noted a large television monitor mounted on the front wall of the Irish pub across the street. It normally showed sporting events to attract patrons but it had been switched to the breaking news. The news media here were already broadcasting breaking news banners and video from the scene.

Several microphones were clumped together in the middle of the street in a makeshift news podium. A uniformed police officer strode to the podium. Questions were fired at him from every angle by dozens and dozens of reporters. It was a media frenzy. The officer held his hand up for quiet and started to speak, "I can't say very much right now because we are in the middle of a criminal investigation. But I can confirm that there is one individual who was found dead in a room on the main floor. No, I can't name the victim until we contact the next of kin."

Dozens of questions were fired at him again. "Do you know who committed the crime?" asked one reporter.

"I'm sorry, I can't say much more at this time since this is an ongoing criminal investigation. We are interviewing witnesses, that's all I can say at this time. The reason I'm here right now is that we need help from the public to find a person of interest. We are presently looking for Cassandra Glynn. That's right, Cassandra Glynn."

"One of my sources says she was seen fleeing the scene," yelled out one of the reporters. "Is that true?" That comment stirred the crowd of reporters even more and they all began shouting questions, looking for answers.

The officer held his hands up to quell the frenzy, "All I can say right now is, Cassandra Glynn is a person of interest. If anyone has seen her or knows where we can find her, please contact Toronto police services." The officer proceeded to give out her complete description, including the clothing she'd worn when last seen.

Cassandra looked up and realized a large picture of her was now being flashed on the television monitor on the Irish pub across the street. Cassandra was angry and she stood up. She was going to set them all straight. "I didn't do anything," she said in a loud voice as she took a step ahead.

Suddenly, an arm went around her waist and a hand clamped over her mouth. She was pulled back into the darkness of the garden. Cassandra Glynn began to kick out her feet, trying to fight and wrestle herself away from the person pulling her backward.

Chapter 4

A VOICE SPOKE into her left ear, "It's okay. I'm a friend."

But Cassandra continued to fight.

"Sebastyen Pipes sent me," the voice added.

After a moment, Cassandra stopped fighting. The person behind her paused for a moment and then released his hand from her mouth and from around her waist. Cassandra spun around, her red dress flaring out. She was looking at a tall man with black hair and intense, silver-blue eyes.

"My name is Rory Mack Steele. We don't have much time." He held a hand out to her.

Cassandra Glynn looked down at his extended hand.

"We need to go," Rory said. "You're in danger."

"I know," Cassandra said. "The police are looking for me. But I didn't do it–"

"I believe you. But that's not the real danger."

Cassandra blinked at the comment but was still unsure.

Rory glanced past her shoulder, making sure no one was coming from the chaos in the street. Then he wiggled his fingers, "Trust me. We need to go. Now."

Cassandra tentatively reached out.

Rory took Cassandra's right hand, gave her a nod of assurance, turned and led her back through the garden.

"Where are we going?" Cassandra asked as they weaved between the bushes, plants, flowers and small trees. There was no answer. A moment later, Cassandra blinked as they passed the dark forms of two men lying face down on the ground. They were dressed in dark jeans and leather jackets. "Who...who are they?"

Rory kept going. "I was hoping you could tell me."

Cassandra looked back at the dark forms. "Me?"

"Yeah, do you know them?"

"I...I don't think so. I could only see the sides of their faces...but...no, I don't think I recognized them."

"You're sure?"

"Pretty sure," Cassandra said. "What happened to them?"

"I knocked their heads together," Rory said casually.

"You did? Why?"

Rory led her at an angle through the garden toward the iron fence. "They were speaking a mixture of English and Spanish—"

"You knocked them out for that?"

"No. Unless I miss my guess, they sounded like they're Colombians. You still sure you don't know them?"

"Colombians?" Cassandra looked back and shook her head, "No, I'm pretty sure I don't know any Colombians. What were they doing back here?"

"They were going to kill you," Rory stated simply.

Cassandra's voice was a squeak, "Kill *me*?"

"Yeah," Rory said, "I heard them talking about taking you up to the roof of the convention center and throwing you off."

Cassandra's complexion went white, "T-throw me off the roof? Why would they do that?"

"I imagine they intended to make it look like suicide."

"I don't understand," Cassandra said, now starting to shake, "I don't even know them. Why would they want to—?"

"I imagine it would be made to look like you committed suicide after you killed your campaign manager."

"I didn't do that," Cassandra insisted.

"Like I said, I believe you. But someone wanted to make it look like you did. You kill your friend and then you kill yourself because you were remorseful. It would be an open and shut case. No need to run an in-depth investigation." Rory stopped at the black iron fence and looked it over.

A confused Cassandra put a hand to her forehead, "I don't understand what's happening. This whole thing is turning into a nightmare."

"I know how you feel," Rory said as he turned to look at Cassandra. "But I'm afraid it gets worse. One of the men I knocked out had a Toronto Police Services Detective shield hang around his neck."

"T-they're police...?"

"I think they just inserted themselves into the search to find you, but we can't rule out the possibility. Maybe they're undercover detectives who are on the take with someone who wants you dead. Either way, right now we don't know who's a good guy and who's a bad guy. We'll need to avoid *everyone* until we can figure out what's going on."

Cassandra Glynn was in total shock. Her whole world was turned upside down in such a short span of time that it was mind-numbing.

Rory turned to look at the iron fence again.

"I was already here," Cassandra mumbled in a faraway voice, "And I can't climb that fence."

"I know. And I don't plan on it," Rory said. He took Cassandra's hand and moved further down along the iron fence. Coming to a stop, he began to feel around the thick iron bars.

"What are you doing?" Cassandra asked in an urgent voice. "We can't squeeze through either. We should be looking for another way out or they're going to catch us. I can hear more voices at the back of the convention center. And it sounds like they're coming this way."

"There should be a gate," Rory said as he ignored her increasing panic. He moved down a few more bars along the fence.

"I don't see anything," Cassandra said. She looked up and down the bars and began to panic, "Please, if we stay here–"

All of a sudden a section of the fence popped open and the section swung away like a gate.

"How did you do that?"

"It's a utility gate for maintenance people. It's built this way in case maintenance men have to work on either side of the fence," Rory explained. "That way they don't have to go all the way down and around a long stretch of fence." Rory took Cassandra's arm and moved her through the gap in the fence, closing it quietly behind them.

"Now what?"

Taking Cassandra's hand, Rory led the way across a stretch of grass towards the next building. Looking to the left, Rory saw the figures of police mixed in with the crowd at the front of the building. He wouldn't be able to get her to safety in that direction. He angled towards the back of the building, figuring they could go through the parking lot behind the building and escape through the back entranceway. But a few moments later, all he could see was a tall cement wall at the back of the parking lot. There *was* no back way out. Rory now led Cassandra across the semi-darkness of the parking lot, heading for the far side of the building. He stopped dead after twenty feet. Beams of light speared the darkness ahead and told him a vehicle was moving slowly down the far side of the building. It wouldn't be long before they reached the corner. And once they turned this way, it was game over. Voices sounded far behind him. Rory turned and realized someone was skirting the far end of the fence and headed this way

"Do you think they saw us go through the fence?" Cassandra whispered in a worried voice. She was looking where Rory was looking as well.

Rory wasn't sure, but it did look like they were about to be trapped. There was no way out.

Chapter 5

THINKING QUICKLY, Rory moved towards the back of the building, looking for a way inside. He found a door but it was locked. He pulled Cassandra to the left, looking for another door when he spotted a steel ladder just above his head. He stepped back and looked up. The ladder went to the top of the roof, 10 floors above them. He gave it some thought and came to the conclusion that they had no choice. Rory stepped forward, jumped up and pulled down the lower section of the ladder.

Cassandra realized what he was going to do. She stepped back and looked up, "A-are you crazy?"

Rory let the ladder slide back up and stepped over to Cassandra, "We have no choice. Remember, we don't know the good guys from the bad guys."

Cassandra looked up again, "But...I can't climb up that. I'm afraid of heights!"

Rory firmly took her elbow and escorted her back to the ladder, "In that case, don't look down and I'll be right behind you." He jumped again and pulled the section down, "You go up first. Hurry, before we're spotted."

"In this dress?" Cassandra exclaimed as she put her hands on her hips.

"I won't look," Rory said with a shake of his head.

"Yeah, that's what they all say," Cassandra complained as she crossed her arms over her chest.

"Your choice," Rory said. "Jail or modesty. Take your pick."

Cassandra grumbled, "The man has a point, I guess." She hesitated for a moment and then stepped over to the ladder and put her right foot on the first rung.

"Remember, just don't look down," he reminded her.

"Okay. And *you* don't look up!" Cassandra countered as she stabbed a finger in his face.

"It's a deal," Rory said. "Now start climbing." He shook his head again. This woman was worried about the stupidest things despite the fact that her life was in danger.

Cassandra climbed up three rungs.

Rory stepped on the lower rung and pressed his chest against her lower legs as he gripped the side rails.

"Excuse me," Cassandra complained. "What exactly are you doing?"

"As you climb, I'll stay against your legs. That'll make you feel safer as we climb," Rory explained.

"Yeah, well, you're a little fresh for a hero," she complained. She started to climb the ladder again.

The climb was slow but steady. The aroma of fish and chips from a nearby restaurant floated across the air.

Once they reached the halfway point, Rory paused and looked down to the left. He could see flashlights moving towards the back of this building. They were getting close.

The slight breeze higher up along the building lifted Cassandra's red dress as she continued climbing, flaring it out slightly.

When Rory stopped looking down, he moved up two rungs quickly to get back against her legs...and the red dress settled down over top his head.

Cassandra stopped climbing and, squeaked"Eeeek! Get out from under there. Get out from under my dress."

"Just move up another rung," Rory instructed her.

"Just get your head out from under there!" Cassandra protested.

"I *will* if you just move up. I'm *not* looking," Rory grumbled.

"You better not be!" She started climbing again.

As she climbed, Rory dipped his head and he was out from under the hem of her dress. "I didn't look," Rory assured her.

"That's what they all say," Cassandra grumbled.

Rory climbed a little faster behind Cassandra and was now holding her dress down with his body.

Halfway up, Cassandra complained, "Will you stop butting into my bum with your head?"

"Yeah, well it's not too great for me either," Rory complained.

"Oh really?"

"Yeah, I just hope you didn't have beans for dinner."

"I don't do that. I'm a lady," Cassandra replied.

"That's what they all say."

Cassandra responded with the sound of irritation.

As they neared the top of the building, Rory looked down to the right. Car lights were illuminating the back parking lot now. He could see flashlights and dark figures milling around the corner at the far side of the building. He looked down to the left and saw several figures were moving in a hurry to the spot below them. Had they been spotted? "Hurry up," he urged.

"I'm going, I'm going," Cassandra complained as she reached the top of the ladder. She bent over and her red dress flared out in the breeze again, revealing the back of her thighs as she took a long stride onto the roof. Cassandra quickly pulled the red dress back against her legs as she whirled around, glaring at Rory.

Rory jumped from the ladder onto the roof and held a hand up, "I didn't have *anything* to do with that."

"Yeah, right."

Rory turned and peered down over the edge of the roof. He watched the figures below moving away from the back of the building. It looked like they hadn't been spotted after all. Rory turned and took Cassandra by the hand leading her towards the center of the roof as he looking for an exit. They skirted the larger rooftop air conditioner and spotted a rooftop door. Rory moved quickly to the door and found it was unlocked. He guided Cassandra through the door and down a flight of stairs. At the bottom of the stairs was another closed door. This one was unlocked as well. Rory opened it slowly. It led out into a hallway that was empty. Taking Cassandra's hand again, he led her through the doorway and down the hallway, where they stopped in front of an elevator.

"Shouldn't we be taking the stairs?" Cassandra asked. "You know, like in the movies, stay out of sight and all that?"

"Quit complaining. Do you really want to climb down all those flights of stairs in those shoes?"

Cassandra crossed her arms and frowned, "Okay, fine. You have a point."

The elevator doors chimed and opened. It was empty. Rory hustled them inside. He pressed the button for the main floor and they stood in silence side-by-side.

Cassandra maintained crossed arms, nervously watching the floor numbers count down, "You think the police will be waiting for us at the bottom?"

"I doubt it."

"You doubt it but you don't know for sure."

"I would think they would be looking for you to run *into* the front of the building and go up the elevator, trying to escape."

Cassandra nodded and looked relieved, "Right. They wouldn't be expecting us to climb up the back ladder and come down the elevator. So they *won't* be waiting for us at the bottom."

"At least, that's the theory," Rory said as the elevator stopped at the bottom floor.

Cassandra turned her head quickly and looked at Rory, "The *theory*?"

Rory shrugged his shoulders.

Cassandra Glynn looked back to the front as the elevator doors slowly opened. She closed her eyes and licked her red lips. When she opened her eyes again it was fine. No police were standing there waiting for them.

Rory took her hand again and they stepped out into a lobby that was packed with people. They were all talking about the events that had occurred next door. Nobody seemed to notice the woman the police were looking for standing in their midst. Rory guided Cassandra through the noisy crowd to the front of the lobby and looked out the wide expanse of glass windows. The street out front was filled with all kinds of people as well, all milling about and talking about the sensational crime. Rory could see far enough down both ends of the street to see uni-formed police officers moving slowly through the crowd, obviously keeping an eye out for the murder suspect. He took a deep breath, trying to figure out what his next move should be.

Cassandra shifted from foot to foot as she stood beside Rory. "It's like being in a fishbowl in here," she whispered. "What if they recognize me?"

"People usually don't if you hide in plain sight," Rory said as he chewed on his lip, thinking.

Cassandra looked at him with one eyebrow raised, "What does that even mean?"

Rory didn't answer, He was too busy thinking over the situation. After a moment, he noticed a number of people in the street wearing Blue Jays' hats and T-shirts. Rory snapped his fingers, "There was a Blue Jays baseball game tonight."

"Pardon?" Cassandra asked.

"I have an idea. Just wait here," Rory instructed as he left Cassandra.

Cassandra squeaked in surprise as Rory left her side. She crossed her arms and glanced around at the crowd, half expecting them to descend on her, carrying her off to jail.

Chapter 6

RORY MOVED OUTSIDE and headed directly for a young boy he had spotted, "Hey kid? I love your ball cap. Where can I get one? Is there a vendor nearby?"

The kid just shrugged his shoulders, "I dunno. I got mine at the game."

Rory took a quick look around. He couldn't see a vendor or anyone hawking Blue Jay gear nearby. There was no time for haggling, either. He reached into his pocket and pulled out five $20 bills as he turned to the kid again, "Look, I'm from out of town. I'll buy your cap. How's a hundred bucks?"

The kid's eyes went big and he grabbed for the cash, handing over the Blue Jays cap before the country clown could change his mind.

Rory turned to go back inside and stopped dead in his tracks.

A man in a black leather jacket was staring into the building at Cassandra.

Rory thought he looked like one of the men he had knocked out back at the convention center. He had been behind them - and it was dark - but he looked familiar - especially the clothing. Rory scanned the crowd quickly, wondering if the other one was nearby as well. He didn't spot anyone, but that didn't mean he wasn't there. Rory moved slowly to the side and spotted the bulge of the weapon in the man's jacket. A strike to the man's kidneys might incapacitate him, but probably not long enough for Rory to grab Cassandra and run without being shot to death. Especially if the man had a partner - or partners - somewhere in the crowd. Rory looked for another answer out of the predicament. The problem was, there wasn't any–

The man put a cell phone to his ear and turned quickly, threading his way in a hurry through the crowd, looking back once to make sure Cassandra was staying in place.

That solved Rory's immediate problem, but this couldn't be good. More than likely the man would be returning with reinforcements. Rory quickly headed back into the building while adjusting the kid's ball cap to be as big as possible. It would barely be a fit but it had to do.

Cassandra looked immensely relieved to see him.

Rory handed her the ball cap, "Pile your hair up underneath this ball cap."

Cassandra looked at him like he had two heads but complied. When she was finished, Cassandra pulled the baseball cap low over her eyes as best as she could.

Rory grabbed her hand and pulled her toward the front door.

Cassandra readjusted the ball with her other hand and grumbled as they stepped out onto the street, "Yeah right, great disguise. A Blue Jays cap, a fancy red dress, and high-heels. That'll work really well, Sherlock!"

"Hide in plain sight," was all Rory said. He was more preoccupied with the man in the black jacket who was coming back.

And he had a friend in a black leather jacket. Rory was convinced now. They *were* the two men who had wanted to throw Cassandra off the roof.

"What do we do now–?"

Rory grabbed her elbow and hustled her off to the right quickly.

Cassandra squeaked in surprise and she had to make quick, tiny steps in her high-heeled shoes.

Rory led the way, weaving his way in and out of the crowd. But it seemed more and more people were heading for all the commotion that he and Cassandra were trying to leave behind, making headway nearly impossible.

Rory glanced back to see the where the two men were.

They were both looking through the front glass of the building where Cassandra had been standing. One of the men hustled inside the building while the other one turned in circles, scanning the crowd.

Rory could only hope Cassandra's red dress didn't stand out as a beacon in a sea of blue jeans and Blue Jays shirts.

Chapter 7

RORY AND CASSANDRA threaded their way through the Blue Jays' fans, trying to blend in as best they could. At the first cross street, Rory turned left and headed northward. He glanced back a few times as they walked.

"Why do you keep looking back?" Cassandra asked. A moment later, alarm registered in her eyes.

"Yeah. I think our two friends are back. I think one of them spotted us before we got too far from the building."

"Our two friends?" Cassandra's eyes went big, "You mean someone is following us?"

"Yeah, one of them spotted you back there."

"Why didn't you say something–?" Her eyes blinked, "You...you don't mean two of those Colombians from back at the convention center, do you?"

Rory didn't reply.

Cassandra looked back in panic and stumbled.

Catching her, Rory held her steady as they moved through the crowd, "It's okay. Don't panic."

Her voice a strained whisper, Cassandra said, "Too late to tell me that now."

"You're doing fine." Rory glanced back, gauging the distance between them and the two men in black jackets. They were getting closer so he started moving a little faster, pulling Cassandra along by the hand.

"What do we do now?" Cassandra asked desperately.

Rory veered to the left, "Let's try hiding in plain sight again."

Cassandra held onto the ball cap as she was pulled into a restaurant. The sounds of clinking cups and cutlery punctuated the succulent smells of coffee, fish and chips, and roast beef.

A purple-haired young woman standing next to the restaurant podium greeted them. "For two?" she asked.

Rory nodded and fidgeted while the young lady casually picked up a couple of menus from the podium. Then she slowly led them over to a booth. Rory saw a problem right away. The only seating available in the crowded restaurant was against the long line of windows looking out onto the street.

Cassandra slid into the seat on the far side of the table. When she turned her head, she realized they were exposed to the entire world walking by on the other side of the window, "Oh, crap. Another fishbowl."

"Yeah, maybe not such a good plan," Rory admitted as he slid in on his side.

The young woman set the two menus down and disappeared.

Another young lady appeared holding a carafe, "Coffee to start?"

"Yeah, that would be good," Rory said with a nod.

Cassandra fidgeted as the young girl poured two coffees.

"Do you know what you want?" the young lady asked.

"Uh, no, give us a minute," Rory told her.

Rory reached for the sugar when the young girl left and–

The two men appeared in the crowd on the sidewalk, just outside the restaurant window.

Cassandra started to slink down in her seat.

Rory subtly shook his head no.

She stopped sliding but Cassandra turned her head slightly away from the window and looked down at a menu.

As nonchalant as possible, Rory pulled the sugar back to his cup. Picking up a spoon, he dropped two spoonfuls of sugar into his coffee and then added creamer. All while he kept one eye on the two men just on the other side of the glass.

The two men stopped and looked up and down the street, trying to figure out where their quarry had disappeared to.

Cassandra sat perfectly still, not moving a single muscle as she stared at the menu.

After a few minutes, one of the men gestured across the street and said something. The other man nodded. The first man stepped into the street and dodged through the traffic, heading for the other side. His partner continued on up the street.

Rory watched for a moment and then said, "Okay, they're not on the other side of the window now."

Cassandra let out a breath of relief. Her eyes moved to look outside, and then she leaned forward and whispered, "S-shouldn't we go?"

Rory shook his head, "Not yet. I can still see one of them on the other side of the street." He reached across and opened her menu, "It looks better that way."

Her hands trembling, Cassandra straightened out the menu, her voice weak and shaky, "Yeah, I guess it does."

Glanced around at the crowd, Rory didn't see anything to be worried about in here and he returned his attention the street just on the other side of the glass. He gestured to Cassandra's cup, "Drink a little. It should help."

"I already got enough jitters but okay." Cassandra did her best to look natural as she put sugar and creamer into her coffee, stirred and then lifted the cup to her lips.

Rory reached out and gently placed his hand on hers to reassure her.

Cassandra lifted up her other hand to steady the cup and took a sip.

Rory understood her nervousness. He sipped his own coffee as he kept an eye out for their two friends to return outside.

After a few moments of nervous silence, Cassandra asked him, "You said Sebastyen Pipes sent you to help me?"

Rory nodded yes as he eyed the crowd and the street.

"How did he know about this so quickly?" Cassandra asked.

Rory continued to monitor the scene outside the restaurant window as he talked, "He didn't. He actually called me yesterday. Sebastyen referred to your family's accident and said he had found something that told him you might be in danger."

Cassandra stared at Rory for a moment, "My family's accident? What do you mean? What did he find?"

"He didn't say. But he was very worried and very firm about me going down to the convention center and making sure you were safe. He said he had worked with your husband a lot and he felt he owed it to him. That was how Sebastyen put it."

Cassandra nodded as her eyes focused internally, "Yeah. After our two children were born, Bryson became very interested in missing children. He met Sebastyen Pipes when he was trying to set up a DNA database for missing children cases. As I understand it, Mr. Pipes had lost a daughter when she was very young and he stepped in to do a lot of the work. I'm even told he paid for a lot of the work out of his own pocket. After that, my husband and Mr. Pipes helped each other out as much as they could. Mr. Pipes had a lot of clout in certain government circles and helped push for my husband's initiatives. In turn, Bryson helped the forensics lab get a lot of funding. I never met Mr. Pipes myself but Bryson thought a lot of him."

Rory nodded as he kept a steady watch out the window.

"How do you know Sebastyen Pipes?" Cassandra asked.

"My family runs a private investigation business, Highlander Investigative Services. We helped Sebastyen with some of his cold cases over the years."

Cassandra nodded, "According to my husband, Sebastyen Pipes went above and beyond the call of duty. Whenever a case went cold, he kept on working on it in his spare time."

Rory nodded in agreement, "When the police were actively working on a particular case, he would call us."

"So he hired your company?"

Rory shook his head, "No. We always donated our time and resources."

Cassandra lifted her eyebrows as she considered the man who had come to her rescue. After a moment, she took another sip of coffee and looked around. Then she looked at Rory and asked, "What are we going to do now?"

"Considering what's happened, I think it's best if we go see Sebastyen Pipes. The Center of Forensic Sciences is not far from here." Rory then turned around and spotted a restroom down a hallway past the front entrance.

"Is something wrong?

Rory shook his head, "No, everything is fine. I'm just going to use the restroom and then we'll head out. I'll be right back, okay?"

Cassandra nodded yes, but her face told a different story.

Cassandra felt extremely exposed as she sat alone in the booth. She kept looking out the window. Suddenly, her eyes shot wide open as the two men trailing them entered the restaurant. Cassandra started slumping down in her seat and then thought better of it. She sat up a little taller.

The two men were taken to a table just three booths down to her right and nearest the front door of the restaurant. They ordered coffee. The man facing her pulled out a cell phone and made a call.

Rory came out of the restroom. He was about to walk out of the hallway and past the front door when he looked up.

Cassandra's eyes met his. She shook her head no.

Hesitating for a moment, Rory discreetly checked his zipper, figuring it must be down. No, it was fine and he kept walking.

Cassandra shook her head - discreetly but more frantically - then tilted her head, using her eyes to convey a message - look at the booth.

Still unsure of the problem, Rory took another step, looking in the direction she indicated - and froze in his tracks. He saw the black leather jackets Holding his breath, he took a slow step back into the hallway.

Somewhat relieved, Cassandra slowly glanced around, searching for a way out of a bad situation. Licking her lips, she looked back at Rory, raising her eyebrows in question.

Rory had no answer.

He considered every possibility - but there was no way for Cassandra to get out without passing the two men - and if they realized who she was - it was probably a fight to the death. And at least one of them had a gun so the deaths would be Rory, Cassandra, and who knew how many others.

The man on the cell phone casually glanced around as he talked.

Cassandra squeezed her eyes shut.

Rory knew how she felt.

They were trapped.

Chapter 8

AFTER A FEW TENSE MOMENTS, Cassandra put her hands to her lips, prayer-like, and closed her eyes. Then she opened her eyes, removed the Blue Jays' ball cap and set it on the table. Blowing out a number of small breaths, Cassandra seemed to compose herself.

Rory watched her, his eyes narrowed.

Cassandra's attention went to two elderly ladies just one booth down. One of the ladies had placed her purse on the out-side edge of the table and Cassandra eyed it. She took another deep breath. Rocking her upper body very slightly in anxiety, her red lips counting off - one- two - three. She slowly slid over to the edge of her bench seat.

Rory went on alert and he shook his head no. He didn't want her trying to sneak past the men.

But Cassandra stood up quickly, stepped confidently ahead and put her hand on the woman's purse. She tipped the purse sideways and pulled it over the edge of the table, spilling its con-tents on the floor. The clatter of the bouncing items from the woman's purse made everyone in the restaurant turn to look in her direction.

Rory held his breath.

"Oh, I'm so sorry," Cassandra said loudly as she squatted down and pulled the hem of her red dress back to a point just above her knees. But instead of leaving her knees together, Cassandra Glynn spread them wide open.

From his vantage point, Rory could see right up her red dress.

And so could the man on the cell phone facing Cassandra. He kept the phone to his ear as he reached across and tapped on his partner's arm. When his partner looked at him, the man smiled and indicated Cassandra behind him. The man turned and both were now looking up Cassandra's red dress.

And so was Rory - still - her actions had taken him by surprise. Like the two men, his eyes were now glued to Cassandra's white panties underneath the sheer pantyhose.

After a few seconds of staring between her open legs, Rory glanced up at Cassandra's face.

Cassandra Glynn shot him an angry look - her green eyes boring into his. She dipped her head several times to the left, her expression intense.

Rory glanced in that direction, his eyebrows pushed together. His attention turned to the sight between her open legs again - he opened his mouth to say something - looking up into her green eyes–

Cassandra continued to pick up the items but her jaw was clenched hard as she glared at Rory - her eyes daggers - if looks could kill, he was dead.

Tearing his eyes away, Rory finally understood what she was doing. He left the hallway, striding to the door - taking one last look.

Cassandra kept her legs wide open, allowing Rory the opportunity to get outside without being seen. Then she quickly finished putting the items on the floor back into the purse, closed her legs and stood up, apologizing profusely to the elderly ladies. Cassandra Glynn then walked tall in her red high heel shoes past the two Colombians.

The pair kept their eyes glued to her long, shapely legs until she disappeared out the door.

Cassandra was shaking by the time she joined Rory outside on the sidewalk.

Rory took her arm and they kept their heads turned away from the restaurant window as they moved northward. After a few moments, Rory glanced back over his shoulder. The men were still inside the restaurant and since they couldn't see them now, Rory moved Cassandra along at a little faster pace.

Cassandra's voice was filled with indignation as she glared at him, "What *exactly* were you doing back there?"

Rory looked at her in innocence, "What do you mean?"

"*They* were supposed to be looking up my dress *as a distraction! Not* you."

"Oh, sorry," Rory said. He shrugged, "You took me by surprise. But nice play on hiding in plain sight. And here I thought you didn't understand the concept."

Cassandra growled through clenched teeth.

Rory turned his head to the right and an amused grin flashed across his face.

Chapter 9

CASSANDRA STAYED MIFFED with Rory as she walked on in stony silence.

Rory glanced back a few times, checking for any sign of the Colombians. He couldn't see them, but the street was full of noisy, talkative people and they could be in the crowd somewhere back there. Rory decided to take a little shortcut. He took Cassandra's elbow and guided her eastward into a small, quiet park. They exited the other side the park and crossed the street before heading north for a few more minutes. The problem was the street had far fewer people here and they would be easier to spot. Rory glanced back. No one came out of the little park behind them. He felt a little more confident that they had given the two Colombians the slip.

Reaching the corner, Rory turned Cassandra Glynn right. A few minutes later, they were approaching the Center of Forensic Sciences on the north side of the street. This street was completely vacant of people and traffic and the building looked totally asleep. Rory and Cassandra approached the glass front doors as they kept their eyes open and alert for any movement around them. Rory pressed the buzzer.

A stout security guard appeared around a corner and came strolling across the foyer of the building towards them. He definitely wasn't in any hurry.

Rory and Cassandra tried to stay calm but it wasn't easy. Both of them discreetly kept looking up and down the sidewalk, half expecting their Colombian friends to appear suddenly out of the dark. There was also the fear that the police could swoop in at any minute as well.

The security guard finally reached the glass doors inside. He fumbled with a large key ring until he found the right one. Then he unlocked the front doors, "Mr. Steele, nice to see you again. I imagine you're here to see Mr. Pipes?"

Rory slipped through the doorway, pulling Cassandra with him, "That I am, Ernie."

"Well, he is upstairs as usual." Ernie politely tipped his security cap to Cassandra as she passed, "Ma'am."

Cassandra nodded and returned a little smile of relief. It appeared he hadn't recognized her. Once past him, she turned her head away, pretending to look around; wanting to make sure he didn't have a second chance to identify her.

Rory guided Cassandra across the foyer towards the row of elevators, looking back over his shoulder, "Sorry it's so late and we woke you up from your nap, Ernie."

Ernie locked the doors again, his voice filled with mock indignity, "Oh sure, you know I'm always asleep." The keys jangled as he returned them to the hook on his belt and then he began walking behind Rory and Cassandra, "It's a well-known fact, Mr. Steele, that all kinds of criminals get in here when *I'm* on duty. They even time their break-ins around my shifts."

Rory pressed the up button on the elevator as he winked at Cassandra. The elevator dinged, and the doors immediately began opening. Rory slipped inside, pulling Cassandra with him, punching the button for the 4th floor.

Ernie stopped, thumbs in his belt, "Ma'am, knowing Mr. Steele as I do, I bet this is his idea of a date." He cackled at his own comment.

At the back of the elevator, Cassandra smiled.

Rory gave Ernie a smile and two thumbs up as the doors closed. The elevator moved up smoothly and silently. It stopped and the doors opened. Rory stuck his head out to check the hallway, holding his hand against the door to make sure it stayed open. When he was finally satisfied the hallway was clear, he gestured for Cassandra to follow him. They turned right and walked down a long white hallway, their footsteps echoing lightly off the walls. They approached the door on the left marked Lab 4A. Going inside, Rory led Cassandra passed a few offices towards a pair of swinging doors. They passed through them into a large laboratory. The faint scent of alcohol wipes and cleaning solution carried on the air.

A large man on the other side of the room, dressed in a white lab coat, turned as soon as they entered. He had curly salt-and-pepper hair and a large white beard, and his brown eyes opened wide, "Rory!"

"Hi, Sebastyen."

The man hustled across the room, grasping Rory's hand and shaking it vigorously, "I heard about the goings-on at the convention center on the police scanner. I imagined you would be in the middle of it and I was worried about you."

Rory allowed his hand to be pumped up and down, "I know Sebastyen, I was a little worried about me too. But I'm fine." He turned to look at Cassandra, "Sebastyen, this is Cassandra Glynn. Cassandra, this is Sebastyen Pipes, the man who called me to check on you."

Sebastyen took Cassandra's hand and shook it politely, relief obvious in his eyes, "Yes. Of course, of course. Your pictures don't do you justice, Mrs. Glynn."

A slight blush crept across Cassandra's cheeks, "Thank you, Mr. Pipes."

"Call me Sebastyen, please."

"And you can call me Cassandra. And I just want you to know that I didn't do what they said I did."

Pipes nodded, "I know, I believe you."

Cassandra appeared to be relieved.

"I'm just so glad you're safe."

Rory took a breath and let it out, his voice serious, "It's a good thing you sent me down there, Sebastyen. Your instincts were correct. What you didn't hear about on the police scanner was that two men were trying to kill Mrs. Glynn not long after the murder of Larrise Abbatiello. I overheard them talking about throwing her off the roof."

Pipes blinked, "Seriously?"

Cassandra turned white again at the mention of her possible death at the hands of two unknown men.

Rory put a hand on the small of Cassandra's back, "It's fine. You're safe now, keep that in mind."

Nodding, Cassandra said, "I know. It's just...."

Rory looked at Pipes, "I think they were trying to cover over the murder of Cassandra's campaign manager, by making it look like Cassandra committed suicide in remorse."

"I thought she could be in trouble," Sebastyen Pipes said as he stroked his beard thoughtfully, "but this...this is a bit of a surprise."

Cassandra reached out and touched his hand, "I want to thank you so much for sending Rory to help me. He's been a real lifesaver, in every sense of the word."

"You're very welcome dear," Sebastyen Pipes mumbled. He seemed to be still lost in thought.

Rory watched Pipes stroking his beard for a moment, then he prodded him, "Sebastyen, you sent me down there in the first place because you said you had some evidence about her husband's accident. That's why I'm here. To find out what it was."

Pipes glanced at Cassandra. "Yes, But...maybe we can talk about that later...?"

Cassandra glanced at Rory and crossed her arms over her chest, "I can understand your reluctance Sebastyen. But...if there is more to what happened to my husband - and my children - I need to know it. I know it might not be easy for me but....I need to know."

Sebastyen Pipes scratched his beard for a moment. Then he turned around, hustling back to where he had been working, "Alright, this way."

Cassandra took a deep breath, gave Rory a nod and then they joined Pipes at his laboratory work bench.

Pipes wrung his hands together, held them to his face for a moment, and then began, "Alright. Right from the beginning, everyone involved in the investigation concluded it was just an unfortunate accident But we always investigate, just in case. And since I knew Bryson very well, I insisted I take the lead in his case. I didn't want to leave it to anyone else. I wanted to go over everything with a fine-tooth comb, just for my own satisfaction. Unfortunately, I had to could come to the conclusion that it was simply a tragic accident. Nothing in the evidence told me anything different. But...there was *something* that puzzled me for quite some time."

"What was that?" Cassandra asked.

The forensic scientist paused for a moment again, "Well... I was very puzzled at something we had found on the undercarriage of your husband's car."

Rory cocked his head, his interest piqued, "The undercarriage?"

Sebastyen nodded.

"What was it?"

Turning to a computer keyboard, Sebastyen typed something rapidly on it and an image popped up on a large computer screen. On the top portion of the screen were a number of lines that look like a variety of mountain peaks. On the lower part of the screen was a series of octagon shapes, joined by various lines.

Cassandra had her arms crossed and she looked closely at the image on the screen.

Rory did the same, looking over the lines and shapes, "If I remember correctly from my old science classes, those are symbols for compounds."

Sebastyen nodded and tapped his knuckle against the screen at one of the compounds, "They are. And *this* is the one that puzzled me."

Rory looked at the screen and then at Sebastyen, "And that compound would be...?"

"Picric acid."

Chapter 10

CASSANDRA'S EYEBROWS were knit together as she looked at the series of octagon shapes on the screen, "What exactly is this...picric acid?" She looked at Rory.

Rory only shrugged his shoulders, "I've never heard of it either." He looked at Pipes, "Sebastyen?"

Sebastyen raised a finger, "Picric acid - or Trinitrophenol - is a very dangerous chemical."

"Okay. But if it's such a dangerous chemical, why was it under her husband's car?"

"Ah, the same question I asked myself," Sebastyen replied. "Over and over again, I kept asking myself the same question. You see, at first, we thought it was simply contamination from the lab. Picric acid doesn't have a lot of use in a lab setting these days but it still is present in many laboratories. The problem is the compound is very toxic and very dangerous. You have to be careful when you handle it. *Extremely* careful. Because of that very factor....it really has very little use today in any capacity."

Rory shook his head, "I'm sorry, Sebastyen, but that still doesn't explain why it was under his car."

"Let me give you a little history lesson and see if you can figure out what I'm driving at. Back in the late 1800s, it was used as an explosive. It's actually much more explosive than TNT but it's very unstable by comparison. For example, they used to use Picric acid in artillery shells." Pipes held up a finger to make an important point, "*But* if the substance starts to react with the metal casing, metal picrates are formed which are even more unstable. It's one of the reasons why they stopped using it. Vibrations, frictions or a bump could easily make it go BOOM!"

Rory nodded in understanding. Then it struck him. He narrowed his eyes and cocked his head, "Are you saying you think someone used this as an explosive element on her husband's car?"

Sebastyen nodded eagerly, "Yes, yes, you got it. I found traces on the brake line. It reacted with the metal. It blew a hole through the brake line and it looks like it also took out the tire. They did something to the steering as well but I'm not sure exactly how–"

Cassandra gasped, "So someone sabotaged his car? They use this explosive and killed my husband? And my children? It wasn't an accident?"

Sebastyen closed his eyes for a moment, then frowned, "I'm so sorry Mrs. Glynn. I shouldn't have come out with it like that. I'm afraid I get carried away."

Holding a hand to her mouth, Cassandra closed her eyes for a moment and then said, "No, it's not...I'm not blaming you. I wanted to know and...it's just the shock."

Rory pushed through the awkwardness, "Okay. If we know the explosive that was used, then we should be able to trace it back to where it was purchased. And if this chemical isn't used that much, it should be easy–"

Sebastyen shook his head, "No, I'm afraid it's not that easy." He turned and picked up something, tossing it to Rory.

Rory caught it and took a look at it. Rory looked at Sebastyen in confusion, "A bottle of aspirin? I don't get it?"

Cassandra looked at the bottle and then back at the forensic scientist, "I don't get it either. Are you saying they used aspirins to kill my family?"

Sebastyen grimaced, "Yes and no. They created the Picric Acid from common aspirins."

"Are you serious?"

Nodding, Sebastyen reached over and picked up a glass beaker, tapping it with a finger, "All I have to is fill this glass beaker with warm sulfuric acid. Then I dump that bottle of aspirins - which is simply acetylsalicylic acid - into the beaker. Then I add sodium or potassium nitrate - stir it - then put the whole mixture into water. When I filter that...I'm left with the explosive chemical Trinitrophenol. That's it in a nutshell. It would take about three hours to create."

"Then they would need a lab like this," Rory countered.

Sebastyen shook his head, "No, I'm afraid not. If you've got a lot of guts, all you need is a place with a very good ventilation system. Crack houses perform this kind of dangerous chemical conversion all the time. Tin and aluminum are the only metals it won't react with. But they probably stored the final compound in a glass container or maybe even a test tube. Using a test tube with a stopper - they could carry around a very highly explosive compound in a very small package in their pocket - easily enough to do the job."

Rory and Cassandra looked at each other - stunned.

It was Cassandra who asked the inevitable question, "But why would someone want to kill my husband? Or my children?"

Sebastyen only shook his head as he set the beaker down. He had no answer for that question.

Rory stared at the floor for a moment, thinking. Then he asked Sebastyen, "Have you told the police about this?"

Scratching his beard, Sebastyen said, "Well, I put it into the database."

Detecting something left unsaid, Rory asked, "What is it, Sebastyen?"

Looking discreetly around, Sebastyen lowered his voice, "Like I said, I put it into the database. But...before I could talk to someone specifically about my findings, a little over one hour later, I had two men from CSIS down here flashing their credentials. They collected my notes, purged the database and told me to keep my mouth shut. They spouted their national security crap and left."

Cassandra pulled her head back, "CSIS? The Canadian Security Intelligence Services? This is the first I've heard of this. Why would they be involved in my husband's death?"

Sebastyen shrugged his shoulders, "I have no idea. I wondered the same thing myself."

"Maybe foreign terrorists are involved?" Rory asked.

Cassandra's voice was firm. "Absolutely not. My husband had nothing to do with foreign affairs."

"You're sure?"

"Yes. He was never involved in any government business or policies that pertained to anything outside the country. We talked all the time and there was nothing he was involved with that would cause foreign terrorists to kill him or my children."

Rory went in another direction, "Okay. But your husband did work with Sebastyen to find missing children. Maybe he was getting too close to something? To some group kidnapping children or...?"

Sebastyen scoffed at that, "How would that involve national security? That would be the domain of the Royal Canadian Mounted Police and NCMPUR, the National Centre for Missing Persons and Unidentified Remains. That doesn't make any sense either."

Everyone looked at each other.

No one had an answer.

Sebastyen broke the silence, his voice lowered again, "Now you see why I contacted you, Rory. I knew in my heart it wasn't an accident. And when I see CSIS become involved...well...I guess I'm getting more and more suspicious in my old age."

Rory stroked his jawline as he looked down, "Yeah. Considering the circumstances, I can understand your feelings."

Cassandra crossed her arms over her chest again, her eyes focused internally.

After a few moments of silence, Rory seemed to come to a conclusion and looked up, holding his hand out, "Okay. Thanks for the information, Sebastyen. I know you're putting yourself on the line here."

Sebastyen shook his hand, "I'm not worried about that. I'll continue to analyze the steering and the other parts of the car. Maybe something else will pop up."

"Good. Cassandra? We should get going. Those CSIS guys could come back at any moment."

Cassandra nodded and turned to Sebastyen, giving him a big hug, thanking him for his help.

Sebastyen gave her a big hug and a smile in return.

Rory and Cassandra Glynn headed back to the front doors of the building.

They had a lot more information.

But they also had a lot more questions.

Chapter 11

10 DIVISION POLICE STATION, Toronto

DETECTIVE CAMRON MACKINNON sat at his desk, reading a part of the preliminary report on the murder of Larrise Abbatiello. MacKinnon was husky, barrel-chested man of Scottish descent, with curly black hair, a thick, bushy mustache and was a thirty year veteran of the force. He set the preliminary report down and picked up a section of the crime scene report. Something didn't quite make sense. He laid the report down, took off his glasses and began to swivel his chair back and forth.

Across from him, at her own desk, his partner Jeanette Sepulveda, stopped typing at her computer and sat back, considering her partner. The short, athletic Hispanic woman with the piercing eyes had worked with MacKinnon for the last ten years of her own twenty-five years on the force and she knew him well. "When you start chewing on your glasses like that," she said at last, "that means an open and shut case like this gets complicated."

Detective MacKinnon grunted as he stopped swiveling.

"Let's have it, Cam," Sepulveda said as she sat forward in her chair.

MacKinnon simply shook his head, "I don't know yet. Something just doesn't seem right. But I'm not sure what." He began to swivel back and forth in his chair again.

Sepulveda reached over and picked up the part of the crime scene report her partner had been reading. She shuffled through the pages. After a few minutes, she put the report down and reached for the telephone. "You want Chinese or Thai?" she asked.

MacKinnon looked over at her, then up at the clock, "It's getting pretty late. Our shift actually ended hours ago."

Sepulveda simply shook her head and complained, "When you get like this, we ain't going home anytime soon."

MacKinnon grunted again, "Well, what else have we got to do?"

"Hey! I got a love life," Sepulveda complained as she listened for someone to answer on the other end of the phone.

"You talking about some dog you got at home?" MacKinnon teased.

"Better than some of the dogs I've seen you with," Sepulveda countered.

"Ain't that the truth," MacKinnon admitted as he swung back to pick up the autopsy report.

CHINESE DINNER FOR two arrived 20 minutes later and the two Toronto Police Detectives ate quietly. They drank Tim Horton's coffee and sifted through the piles of reports they had on their desks. Something continued to bother Detective MacKinnon but he couldn't put a finger on it. He began to wear out the casters on his chair as he swiveled back and forth.

TWO HOURS LATER, SEPULVEDA stood up like a shot. She had a part of the crime scene report in her hand.

MacKinnon had been leaning back in his chair, reading another part of the preliminary report again for the umpteenth time. He leaned forward, anticipating his partner's words.

"Son of a bitch," Sepulveda whispered.

"What is it?" MacKinnon queried.

Sepulveda handed the crime scene report over to her partner.

MacKinnon took the report and looked at the page she had been reading. He shrugged after a moment, "What exactly am I looking for? What did you see?"

Detective Sepulveda moved swiftly around the desk to her partner's side. "Take a look at the blood evidence. And keep in mind what all the witnesses said. When they came into the room, they found Cassandra Glynn getting up on her knees with the scissors still in her hand."

"All right," MacKinnon said, nodding his head as he reread that section of the crime scene report.

"Think about what they said, Cam. Cassandra Glynn had passed them in the hallway a few minutes *before*, heading for the room. They all said the same thing. She was steaming mad when she passed but it was *only a few minutes* before. They heard brief yelling in the room and then a cry that caused them to rush inside to investigate. The door was wide open. They didn't see anyone else go in and nobody left."

"Okay," MacKinnon replied, still not sure where this was going.

Sepulveda repeated slowly as she looked down at her partner, "A few minutes *before*, Cam."

MacKinnon looked at the page, still not comprehending. Then he suddenly slapped the page. "Son of a bitch!" He looked up at his partner.

Nodded her head, Sepulveda said, "Blood begins to coagulate immediately. Remember that seminar we took last year? The coagulation factor can depend upon the surface where the blood lands, on the humidity factor or on the heat in the room. But the witnesses said it was only a few minutes...."

"She'd been dead almost an hour before Glynn arrived," concluded MacKinnon. He scanned with his finger through the report. "It's here - plain as day - the area on the floor, where Cassandra Glynn was seen kneeling by the witnesses, had traces of smeared, coagulated blood."

"There was no way she could've done it," Sepulveda continued as she headed back over to her side of the desk. She leaned over her desk and ran her finger down another report, "And there were traces of a second layer of coagulated blood on the scissors."

"So the scissors *were* the murder weapon," MacKinnon said, "but used by someone else first."

Sepulveda nodded, "Right. The second layer must have come from someone placing the scissors in her hand, and then she touched the blood pool with them when she was getting up."

"That would fit," MacKinnon said with a nod.

Sepulveda held a finger up, playing devil's advocate,"Or...she *did* kill her campaign manager....and she went back later to throw everybody off."

MacKinnon rocked a moment, thinking about it - then shook his head, "No. The timeline doesn't bear that out. She was doing a CBC interview that took a little over two hours to complete. There was the interviewer, the cameraman, a couple of grips and Larrise Abbatiello's assistant present and they all give her an alibi. Cassandra Glynn was seen leaving her hotel room right after the interview, going down to the all candidates meeting and then heading right to Abbatiello's hotel room in a fit of rage."

"So that leaves us with only one conclusion," stated Sepulveda.

MacKinnon nodded his head as he looked at the report again, "She was set up."

The two detectives looked at each other - stunned at this revelation.

Sepulveda spoke up after a moment, "Maybe the whole crowd of witnesses who saw Glynn with the scissors are in on it."

"Possible," MacKinnon admitted, "but I don't see any motive."

"Maybe one of the witnesses did it," Sepulveda speculated. "And the rest are helping them to cover it up?"

"We can follow up on each one of them, dig deeper for a motive," MacKinnon suggested. "I doubt we'll find anything though."

Sepulveda slowly nodded her head in agreement, pondering the information. Then she looked across at her partner, "That leaves just one other possibility, Cam. Someone else was in that room an hour before. And that someone else set up Mrs. Glynn to take the fall."

MacKinnon scratched his jawline slowly, giving that theory some thought. Then he looked down at the pile of reports on their desks, "Correct me if I'm wrong, but I don't think they processed all the rooms at the crime scene."

Sepulveda shook her head, "No, I don't think so. They didn't touch the bedroom or the bathroom if I remember correctly. Everything looked too cut and dry. They had another case to get to right away and headquarters told them to get moving."

"Stupid budget cutting and corner cutting," MacKinnon complained. "I told them it would catch up to us, sooner or later. And this might be the one."

Sepulveda reached for her phone, "Everything is still roped off. We can get the other rooms processed and see if something pops up. I'll call Tiny at Toronto Police Services right away and get another team of Forensic Identification Officers down there right away."

MacKinnon nodded in agreement as he reached into his desk and pulled out a set of car keys. "And ask him to send all the reports he has now over to Sebastyen Pipes at The Centre of Forensic Sciences. Pipes can do stuff fast and he sees details others miss. If we act fast, maybe the perp is still at the convention center drinking stupid lattes. We'll grab a couple of large, double-double coffees and some donuts at Tim Horton's on the way over to bribe Pipes."

"You should be arrested yourself," Sepulveda said. "You keep bribing that man with coffees and donuts. He's probably put on fifty pounds, thanks to you."

Chapter 12

RORY AND CASSANDRA left the Center of Forensic Sciences and crossed the street. As they stepped onto the sidewalk, Rory suddenly took Cassandra by the elbow. He moved her behind one of the large columns at the entrance to the building in front of them.

"What's wrong?" Cassandra asked in fear.

Rory was silent for a moment as he peered westward down the street, "It looks like our two friends again."

"How did they find us?" Cassandra asked.

Rory shook his head. "I don't know. I don't like this. We can't seem to stay more than a step ahead of them."

Cassandra leaned forward slightly, trying to peer around the column.

Taking Cassandra's elbow again, Rory said, "Come on."

Squeaking a bit as she moved in quick steps in her high heels, Cassandra continued looking back over her shoulder.

Keeping the large columns between them and their two friends, Rory led her eastward to the street corner. From there, they hustled them southward.

After a block and a half, Cassandra asked, "What now?" She glanced back.

"I'm not sure," Rory answered. The whole situation swirled through his mind as he guided Cassandra down the street. He needed more information. Especially more information on what had happened back at the convention center. And there was one question he could start with. He wondered what Cassandra Glynn would say. He mulled it over for a few moments and then decided to bring the subject up, "One of the reporters said you were seen fleeing the murder scene. Is that right?"

Cassandra didn't hesitate and nodded. As they walked, she explained the sequence of events that led up to her finding Larrise Abbatiello's body and eventually fleeing the police.

Rory listened to her story quietly. Everything sounded plausible and made sense.

Cassandra lifted a hand to her cheek and wiped a tear away.

"Sorry. I had to ask."

"It's okay."

"The person behind you must have had chloroform on the cloth. And it sounds like they used just enough to put you out for a brief moment and set you up for the death of your campaign manager. That would mean the person behind you had a lot of practice with chloroform."

Cassandra bit her lower lip for a moment, then asked, "Are you suggesting the person was a doctor?"

"Or some other medical professional. Does that ring any bells with you? Is there anyone who would want to hurt you, to set you up for murder?"

Cassandra shook her head, "No. No one I can think of." Then her eyes widened, "Do you think it was some pervert? He did something to Larrise...and then something to me...?"

"No, there wasn't enough time for that. At least for you. And everything points more to a setup than a sex crime."

A quiet exhale came from Cassandra.

Rory gently broached another subject, "You said you were mad when you headed up to her room. Is that something that happened often? Especially between you two?"

Cassandra didn't take offense and her eyes misted, "Larrise Abbatiello was not only my campaign manager, she was my best friend. She has - had - a Latin temper and I have an Irish one and we clashed like two sisters at times. But we loved each other. She was the one rock in my life after my family died."

Rory nodded in sympathy, "Okay. So why didn't she go and tell you about losing the nomination right away?"

"It was the timing of the whole thing. I was still doing the CBC interview and she was off doing her thing when she found out." Tears filled her eyes, "She didn't get the chance to tell me."

They walked on in silence for half a block and then Rory asked about something else that puzzled him, "You said you won the riding nomination fair and square–"

"I did."

"I'm not disputing that. The question is...how can they run this other person in the election in your place?"

Cassandra took a deep breath and began to explain, "It's one of the things about our politics in Canada that a lot of people don't understand. Or even know about for that matter. Even if you win the democratic nomination in your riding, the Prime Minister or the leader of the party has to approve your running for election before you can actually run under the party banner. He can overrule the local riding and run whoever he wants. It's happened with other parties like the Liberals and the Conservatives in the past."

"That sounds more like a communist regime." Rory glanced back over his shoulder, "That's how they do it. They put up the candidates to run. They choose who the people vote for and the voters have no choice."

"Well, you can run as an independent here in our country. But without the party machinery behind you, it's almost impossible to win. And even if you do win, you have no clout at all when you get to parliament in Ottawa."

Rory mulled over the information and wondered if it had anything to do with the situation. He glanced back again and then asked, "You said they chose Demario Gomez, the hockey player, instead?"

Cassandra nodded.

Rory considered the man's reputation, "He was always an aggressive player. Playing on the edge of the rules. And he was noted for being ambitious - and ruthless - once he moved into management."

Cassandra shrugged, "I guess they needed - or wanted - his star power to put more focus on the party. It's happened before, especially in Canada where hockey players can have a high public profile. I wouldn't really care but... I really wanted to run for office and push all the causes my husband cared so much about. After his death... and with my children gone...it was all I had left...."

Rory's heart went out to her, "I'm sorry."

Cassandra hung her head as she flicked tears off her long eyelashes, "None of that really matters now. Screw politics. None of that explains why Larrise Abbatiello was killed or by who. Or even why my family was killed deliberately."

Rory had no answers for her.

They were now entering an area filled with pubs and clubs on both sides of the street and loud music reached their ears. Within minutes, they were weaving through crowds of people who were talking and laughing and having a good time. Rory glanced back several times to see if their two friends were still following, but they were nowhere in sight.

Reaching a spot between two nightclubs, where the sound wasn't quite as loud, Rory stopped with Cassandra against a building and took a look back up the street.

Cassandra squeezed herself against the building, "Do you see something?"

Rory shook his head, "No. Just checking. But we can't keep doing this forever. I think I should head back to the convention center. I have to try and figure out why Larrise Abbatiello was killed. And why someone wants to frame you for it. Any idea why someone would have killed her? Did she have any enemies? Any problems that you know about?"

Cassandra shook her head, "No, not really. Larrise was well liked. She was easy to work with. She was one of those people who basically got along with everyone. She had a temper at times - like I said - but she really wasn't confrontational."

"Okay. Those two guys following you were at the convention center when she died, are they involved with the party or the convention in some way?"

Shaking her head, Cassandra said, "No. Like I said before, I didn't recognize them. And I don't remember seeing them at the convention center or anywhere else for that matter. Why do you keep asking that?"

"Because that's what I do. Come on." They began walking down the street again.

Cassandra's nerves flared up as they walked. Her eyes darting back and forth, concerned now that someone in the crowd might recognize her - or want to harm her.

They crossed a busy intersection and Rory noted the men in the crowd checking out Cassandra Glynn front and back. She was definitely a tall, stunning woman.

Despite her watching for danger, Cassandra was totally oblivious to the stares and ogling. Her mind was elsewhere.

Rory glanced back – he spotted the two men who had been trailing them before.

They were on the other side of the street and still quite a ways away, but they were moving fast.

How in the world did they find them again?

Chapter 13

RORY TRIED TO MOVE Cassandra faster without alarming her. He looked for a way out of the situation while trying to keep an eye on the men closing in on the other side of the street.

After a few moments, the two men suddenly turned left and braved the traffic to move across the busy street. Once on this side of the street, the two men began to weave faster through the crowd, heading directly for Rory and Cassandra.

To Rory, it appeared as if the two men had some way to track them. But how? He desperately looked ahead, trying to find a place to hide. Just up ahead was the entrance to a noisy pub. Rory glanced back to make sure the men weren't looking at them at that moment - then he took Cassandra's elbow and quickly turned her into the pub.

"Why are we going in here?" Cassandra asked as Rory guided her through a boisterous crowd.

"I just spotted our two friends again."

Cassandra's eyes filled with fear, "*How* do they know where we're going if we don't know?"

Rory spoke louder over the noise as he looked back at the entrance, "I don't know how they're tracking us but we have to figure out some way to get away from them." He moved with her through the crowd, trying to spot some back way out. There had to be one but he couldn't see it.

Discarded peanut shells crunched under their feet and Cassandra looked down in disgust.

There were a number of tables where people could stand and drink and Rory pulled Cassandra to one, trying to blend in with the crowd. He picked up a handful of peanuts and cracked several as he looked around, popped the peanuts in his mouth, and tossed the shells to the floor.

Cassandra looked horrified, "*What* are you doing? You can't just throw the shells on the floor."

Rory shrugged, "Yes, I can. It's a tradition in many of the bars and clubs. You discard the bar peanut shells onto the floor. I'm trying to blend in."

"You're an idiot," she said as she looked around nervously, "and I have no idea why we're in here."

Rory broke a few more peanuts and he kept an eye on the entranceway, hoping the two men would simply pass by outside.

After a moment of glancing around, Cassandra asked, "Why don't we just go outside and take a cab? If they don't see us sneaking out of here, maybe we can get away from them that way?"

"Possible," Rory admitted as he gave it some thought. "Then again, cabs report back to their dispatch when they pick someone up to let them know where they're taking the fare. No, we have to find some way that eliminates every method of them tracking us."

Cassandra thought for a minute, "Then why don't we take a car?"

Rory gave her an amused smile, "Hot-wire one like in the movies? You're suddenly a bad-ass."

"No, we could use the keys. Those young women over there came in just ahead of us. I saw them park a red convertible outside just as we came down the street."

"They found a parking space in downtown Toronto? I'm impressed."

"Very funny, smart-ass," Cassandra replied. She looked over at the women for a few more moments and then turned back to Rory, "I need you to distract them. The driver has her key ring on the table front of her."

"You want me to try and pick them up while you steal their keys?"

"No. I doubt you could handle that," Cassandra replied.

"Very funny," Rory said.

"I said, I needed you to distract them." She pointed ahead through the crowd.

Rory looked at where she was pointing. He saw a large stage, where he presumed the house band was going to play, but nothing else that made sense. He looked back at Cassandra.

Cassandra pointed ahead again in emphasis.

Rory looked at the crowd, at the stage and then back to Cassandra, "What are you talking about?"

Flashing a devious smile, Cassandra said, "I guess you missed it when we walked in here. This is amateur male stripper night."

Rory looked at Cassandra for a moment and then his head swiveled as he took in the entire room. It was filled with young women. He noticed a few young men dressed in leather, but for the most part, it was filled with young women, drinking, laughing and having a great time. Then he noticed the signs around the club advertising the weekly event. He looked back at Cassandra, "You have to be kidding, right?"

Cassandra shrugged, "We need a distraction and you're it. Unless you have a better plan right now?"

Rory blinked his eyes several times as he looked at her. "The woman has a point," he finally said.

"You saw mine, now I get to see yours," Cassandra stated with amusement.

"Very funny," Rory said. He looked at the stage again and took a deep breath, making a decision. "Okay. Just hurry up and grab those keys when I get up there." He headed for the stage at the back of the bar.

Cassandra wore a mischievous smile as she watched Rory walk away. It was still evident as she worked her way through the crowd to where the three young women stood around the table where the keys sat.

Chapter 14

RORY JUMPED ON STAGE and grabbed onto a stripper pole towards the back of the stage. He held on with one hand, walking around it several times, trying to grab the attention of the ladies in the room over top of the loud conversation. To Rory's chagrin, someone in the club started up some stripper music over the PA system.

Spotlights at the foot of the stage lit up.

That did it.

Rory heard some whistles and catcalls and he suddenly realized he *did* have everyone's attention.

Every single woman in the room was looking at him.

Rory looked out at the eager eyes, waiting for his act, and he mumbled under his breath, "Oh great." He tried to act like a sexy male stripper as he walked around the chrome pole. Peering through the stage lights, he tried to pick out Cassandra.

The young women in the audience yelled out for him to start stripping. Yells of 'take it off' and catcalls sounded from every corner of the bar.

Rory tried to waste time by moving around the pole a few more times. He desperately searched for a sign of Cassandra in the crowd.

More catcalls and more whistles.

Rory had no choice at this point. He let go of the pole and danced awkwardly to the front of the stage. His hands went to the top button on his shirt and the room went crazy.

Young women yelled, clapped and stamped their feet to the beat of the stripper music.

Undoing his shirt buttons slowly, Rory found the table where the young women with the keys were. They were looking up at him, which was good. Rory saw Cassandra standing behind the girls. He wondered what she was waiting for. *That* was not good. Rory got down to the last button and he had no choice but to pull open his shirt.

The muscles and six-pack sent the ladies in the room into a loud group cheer.

Rory looked at Cassandra and then down at the now neglected set of keys. Why wasn't Cassandra moving?

Cassandra simply continued to stand there with an amused grin on her face.

Dropping the shirt to the floor, Rory did his best to gyrated on the stage. He used his eyes to try and get Cassandra to snag the keys.

But she just stood there.

Rory kicked off his shoes and reached down to his pants and undid the belt buckle.

Women whistled.

He undid the snap.

A cheer went up. Now the ladies were up and clapping to the music. Dozens of ladies in the audience moved up to the front of the stage to get a better view.

Rory continued his awkward dancing, trying to get Cassandra's attention. He had no choice and slid his zipper slowly down, trying to buy time. Now the dancing made it difficult to hold his pants in place. Finally, his pants had a mind of their own and slid down to the floor. He nearly tripped over them and he had no choice now. He finally pushed his pants over his feet and dropped them to the stage floor. Rory was left dancing on the stage in black boxer shorts and black socks.

A young woman jumped onstage and stuffed something in his boxer shorts.

A laughing stagehand quickly moved in and pulled her off the stage.

Rory moved back to the silver stripper pole where he felt safer. But he wondered if the shorts were going to have to go in a few more minutes.

Another young woman jumped onto the stage and ran for Rory.

She was intercepted just in time by the stagehand. As she was pulled away, her fingers caught in the waistband of Rory's boxers at the back.

Rory caught them just as they were halfway down his butt and he pulled them back up to safety.

The crowd of young women exploded into cheers and fist pumps at the near miss.

Rory grabbed the stripper pole and made another strut around the stage, desperately looking for Cassandra. After another strut around the chrome pole, he spotted her between the waving hands and jumping bodies.

She was holding up the keys, smiling at him. Then she turned and disappeared through the raucous crowd of young women.

Rory quickly stopped his awkward strip tease and ran to the front of the stage. He gathered up his shoes and clothes in a bundle and hustled off the stage.

Women grabbed at him as he passed, imploring him not to be so shy and to finish the act.

Panic struck his heart as he reached the front entrance way. He had expected Cassandra to be there waiting for him. But she wasn't. Had the men caught her?

Rory ran through the doorway and into the street, dressed only in his boxer shorts and socks, clothes in hand, looking up and down the street in concern.

Surprised laughter - quickly mixed with whistles and catcalls - exploded from the crowds of people on the sidewalk.

Rory spotted Cassandra dead ahead through the crowds.

She was already in the red convertible and had the car running.

Rory threaded his way through the crowd and jumped over the closed door and into the passenger seat.

Cassandra looked over at Rory, a self-satisfied smile on her face.

"You did that on purpose," Rory complained as he dumped his bundle at his feet on the car floor.

"How much did you make?" Cassandra asked as she eyed his black boxers.

Rory thought for a moment and then reached down into his boxer shorts. He pulled out a folded piece of paper. He unfolded it. It had a phone number scrawled across it.

"Don't quit your day job," Cassandra said, "you'll starve to death."

"Ha, ha, very funny," Rory said as he reached down to sort out his shoes, shirt, and pants.

"So, you're a boxer man," Cassandra said with amusement.

"I need a lot of material to hold it in," Rory replied as he separated his pants from his shirt.

"Your act - which needs work by the way, - didn't get far enough for me to verify that."

"Very funny," Rory said as he put one foot in a pant leg.

"Oh, crap."

Rory looked up quickly to see Cassandra staring ahead of the car. That's when he saw the two men in black leather jackets running through the crowd towards them. "Go, go go," Rory yelled.

Cassandra cranked the steering wheel hard left and stomped down on the gas pedal.

Rory was thrown back in his seat as he watched one of the men reaching into his jacket for something.

The convertible shot out of the parking space, narrowly missing cars as Cassandra tore through a u-turn in the street. The convertible swish-tailed and then shot off down the street.

Chapter 15

CASSANDRA KEPT HER FOOT DOWN as the convertible flew through a red light. Car brakes screeched and horns complained loudly as other drivers fought to avoid a collision.

Rory yelled as he tried to pull his pants on, "Slow down."

"But the men!" Cassandra yelled as she accelerated around another car, narrowly missing another vehicle in the oncoming lane before she got back on her own side of the road.

"I know, I know," Rory said as he put a hand on her arm. "But they're long behind us right now and we don't need to get stopped by the police."

Cassandra grimaced and let off on the gas, "You're right. I never thought about that. I just wanted to get away from those guys back there as fast as possible."

"I understand," Rory said as he returned to pulling his pants on.

Cassandra swerved in and out of traffic to pass another car.

Rory was thrown left and then right on his seat. "Just take your time," he urged Cassandra.

"But what if they steal a car too and–?"

"If we crash into another car, they'll catch us for sure," Rory reasoned. He lifted his butt off the seat and pulled his pants up, zipping and snapping.

Cassandra nodded as she took a break deep breath and let it out, trying to calm herself.

Rory picked up his shirt and slipped it on. As he was buttoning the shirt, his thoughts went back to the two men. And particularly to the one who had been trying to pull something from his jacket. From the long bulge evident under the leather, he was sure the man was trying to pull a weapon with a silencer on it. He was sure the men would have simply shot them dead and slipped away into the crowd. That was brazen and open. What in the world was going on here? What had this woman stepped into?

Rory slipped his shoes on and sat back, thinking. Just then the iPhone in his left pants pocket rang. He pulled out the cell phone and answered it, "Hello?"

A very authoritative voice sounded on the other end of the call. "Is this Rory Mack Steele?"

Rory thought for a moment, trying to place the voice, "Who is this?"

"Mr. Steele, this is Detective Camron MacKinnon of the Toronto Police Services. I need you to listen to me very carefully. Make a note of this phone number. Then dispose of your cell phone immediately. And dispose of any cell phones anyone else with you may have as well. Go to a store and buy a new cell phone and call me back. Immediately. Do you understand me?"

"What's this all about?"

The caller hung up.

Cassandra glanced at Rory."Who was that?"

Rory looked at his phone for several moments. Then he checked for the last number that called him.

Glancing back and forth between the road ahead and Rory's face beside her, Cassandra's voice was strained, "Rory? You're scaring me."

Rory looked at Cassandra. He looked back at his phone. Rory made a decision. He held his iPhone out over the side of the convertible and threw it down onto the pavement. It hit hard, breaking into pieces that bounced in different directions as they left it far behind.

Cassandra's eyes opened wide, "Did you just throw your phone to the pavement Why–?"

"The caller said he was Detective Camron MacKinnon of Toronto Police Services."

"The police? Why are they calling you? Do they know where we are?"

"I don't know. All I can tell you is he sounded pretty serious. He told me to get rid of my cell phone." He shook his head softly, as confused as she was. A moment, he looked quickly at Cassandra, "Do you have a cell phone on you?"

Cassandra shook her head, "No. Why?"

"Nothing stuffed in your underwear?"

"You've seen my underwear, big boy," Cassandra retorted. "You know there's nothing stuffed in there."

"Same goes for me," Rory said. Rory looked ahead, pondering the situation.

"That I can verify, nothing stuffed in your shorts either," Cassandra said. "At least not a package UPS would have trouble delivering."

"Very funny," Rory said as he sat up straighter in his seat. "Turn right at the next corner."

Cassandra complied. They headed westbound until Rory told her to pull over.

Cassandra parked the convertible at the curb, leaving it running.

Rory got out of the vehicle, slamming the door shut.

Cassandra turned off the engine, jumped out carrying the car keys, and ran around to Rory as he headed into a convenience store. "What are we doing?"

"Doing as I was instructed," Rory said. He led her into the store where he picked up two small Samsung prepaid cell phones from a rack. He paid the cashier in cash and exited the convenience store without a word.

On the sidewalk, Cassandra watched him take the cell phones from the plastic bag, tossing the bag into a receptacle.

"Do you have a small side pocket in that dress?"

Cassandra nodded, "Yeah, I do. Why–?"

Rory handed her one of the cell phones as he headed for the car, "Okay, hold onto this one. We may need it later."

Cassandra took it and placed it in a small pocket, still not sure what was happening.

Heading back to the car, Rory checked the sidewalk in both directions before he got back into the convertible.

Running around the front of the convertible, Cassandra got back into the driver side, questions still evident on her face.

Rory simply sat there, thinking, looking at the other cell phone in his hand.

Cassandra stayed silent but she nervously glanced back and forth between Rory and the sidewalk. Then she glanced into the rearview mirror, half expecting to see the two men who had been trailing them appear again.

Finally, Rory started punching numbers into the cell phone.

The same authoritative voice answered, "Detective MacKinnon."

Rory paused for just a moment, "Detective, this is–"

"Mr. Steele, glad you could call me back. I trust you got rid of all cell phones?"

"Yes. Can you tell me with this all about?"

MacKinnon paused for a moment, then asked, "Is Mrs. Glynn still with you?"

"Who?"

There was another pause on the other end of the line. "Mr. Steele, my partner and I found Sebastyen Pipes shot this evening at the forensic center."

Chapter 16

RORY SHOT UP STRAIGHTER in his seat, "Shot? Is he all right?"

The voice was somber, "I'm sorry, he's in surgery as we speak. They tell me he may not make it. But before the paramedics took him away, he told us about your visit with Mrs. Glynn. And about what he had found regarding her husband's accident."

Rory felt sick. Was it his fault? He dreaded the answer, "Do you know who shot him?"

"Apparently, after you left, two men flashing CSIS credentials demanded entrance to the building."

He wasn't quite expecting that, "CSIS agents?"

"That's how it looks right now. Pipes told us about their first visit when he put the information on Mr. Glynn into the computer system. On this visit, they asked the security guard if he had seen a woman in a red dress with a dark-haired man. The guard told them about you and Mrs. Glynn being there earlier."

Rory dreaded another answer, "And Ernie...?"

"I'm sorry, they shot him as well and he's also in surgery. The two men were shooting to kill, but I think they were in such a hurry, they were a little off target."

Rory grimaced at the news.

"The guard was in bad shape but he wouldn't let the paramedics take him away until he filled us in."

"Yeah, that's Ernie."

Cassandra reached across to Rory, her face a mask of worry, "What's happening?"

Rory put his hand over the cell phone, "Two men shot Sebastyen Pipes and Ernie after we left."

Cassandra put her hands prayer-like to her mouth in shock, "Oh, no."

Taking his hand off the cell phone, Rory asked the Detective, "Did you get a description of the two men?" Despite the supposed CSIS angle, he had a suspicion who the two shooters might be.

"According to the security guard, both were about 6 foot tall, dark complexion, black leather jackets–"

"Your description fits two men who were trailing us from the convention center."

That surprised MacKinnon, "The shooters were trailing you and Mrs. Glynn from the convention center? Why?"

"The two men trailing us talked about throwing Cassandra Glynn off the roof of the convention center. It looks to me like they were trying to make it look like a remorseful suicide over the murder of Larrise Abbatiello."

MacKinnon's voice went quiet, "I see."

Rory looked down the street, pondering the conversation, "This doesn't make any sense. Why would two CSIS men want to kill Cassandra Glynn? And then shoot Sebastian Pipes and a security guard? And take evidence from a completely unrelated case?"

Cassandra pulled back at the mention of her name and the word kill.

Rory looked across at her, feeling bad about the open but one-sided conversation on her situation.

MacKinnon spoke quietly, "These men may not be CSIS. At least, that's what I'm told by my contact over there. But according to the security guard, their credentials were real. CSIS has visited there before so I think he would know. Besides, Pipes and the security guard said the men had Spanish accents. Unless they were disguising their voices, CSIS says they don't have anyone like that on staff."

"I pegged them as Colombians when I heard them talking."

"Colombians?" repeated a surprised MacKinnon.

"Yeah. None of this is making any sense."

"Tell me about it."

Rory hesitated for a moment, then revealed something else, not sure how the detective would take it, "There is one other thing. One of the men trying to kill Mrs. Glynn had a detective's shield around his neck."

There was a period of silence before MacKinnon spoke again, "So we may have bogus credentials all over this thing. Or maybe not. Which is even more disturbing. But even if they have bogus credentials, they may have access to someone on the inside - like at CSIS. That's why I had you get rid of your cell phone. Once they knew your identity from the security guard, they could find your cell phone number, use the CSIS surveillance capabilities and track you. That's the only thing that makes sense. Unless you're driving a vehicle with a GPS service they could track?"

Rory looked over at Cassandra at the wheel of the stolen vehicle, "No, there's no way they'd be able to do that right now. The cell phone is the only thing that makes sense to me as well."

Detective MacKinnon went quiet for a few more minutes, obviously thinking, before he spoke again, "Can you answer me one question Mr. Steele?"

"If I can," Rory answered cautiously.

"Can you tell me how the murder weapon, the scissors, ended up in Mrs. Glynn's hand?"

Rory looked at Cassandra. She was definitely uneasy at the one-sided conversation.

Cassandra mouthed 'what?'

"She told me when she went into the room and saw Larrise Abbatiello on the floor, covered in blood, someone came up behind her and put a cloth over her mouth. She passed out briefly. When she came around, she had the scissors in her hands and she had some blood on her. That's when the people entering the room saw her."

MacKinnon went silent for a moment. Then there was the sound of rustling and muted voices. Then MacKinnon came back on again, "Mr. Steele, I'll be upfront with you. My partner and I have concluded that the evidence definitely shows Cassandra Glynn *was* set up for the murder of Larrise Abbatiello."

Rory let that news sink in before asking, "Do you know why?"

"No. And that is bugging the hell out of us too."

"I see."

"And now you tell me someone tried to make it look like she committed suicide over the murder? Trying to hide your crime by framing someone else is one thing. But trying to throw her off the roof? And then - if it's the same people - they take evidence in a separate case and shoot up a forensic center? That adds a whole layer of complexity to the matter. Nothing - absolutely nothing - is adding up here."

"I hear you," Rory said as he looked at Cassandra.

Cassandra was chewing on a thumbnail and she mouthed What? again at him.

"Do you want us to come in?" Rory asked after a moment.

Cassandra shook her head emphatically no.

There was a moment of silence. "No," MacKinnon said finally. "Until we can figure out what exactly is happening here, I don't know who we can trust. At this point, I don't want CSIS, the Mounties, the O.P.P., the Toronto police, the county police, the local mall cop or the friggin Boy Scouts involved. Call me back later. My partner is Detective Jeanette Sepulveda. One of us will answer this cell phone. If anyone else answers, hang up."

Rory pressed a button on the phone and ended the call.

Leaning over, Cassandra hit him on the arm, "What did he say? What did he tell you? Why wouldn't you tell me?"

"According to Detective MacKinnon, the evidence shows you were definitely set up by someone to take the fall for Larrise Abbatiello's murder."

Cassandra immediately looked relieved.

"The problem is they have no idea why you were set up. And get this. Those two guys who showed up at the lab and shot Ernie and Sebastyen? They flashed CSIS credentials."

"CSIS?"

"But according to CSIS, they don't know who those guys are."

Cassandra shook her head, "None of this makes any sense."

"I agree," Rory said. He sat back, looking down the street, thinking.

"What did they say about me coming in?"

Rory just stared down the street, shaking his head no.

"I...I wasn't for it before. But if they know I'm innocent...maybe I turn myself in for protection?"

Rory turned his head and looked at her, "MacKinnon had the same feeling I did. That the detective shield or the CSIS credentials are bogus. The problem is...you never know. To be honest...MacKinnon and his partner are not really sure who they can trust on their side right now."

Cassandra threw her hands up, "Oh, isn't that great. *Now* what do we do?"

Rory looked back down the dark street again. Then he said, "We're not far from the back of the convention center You can stay here while I make a visit over there. Maybe if I nose around, I can add some more pieces to the puzzle."

Cassandra shook her head emphatically. "No way, I'm not staying here alone. I'm going with you."

"And what if someone recognizes you back to the convention center? It's filled with party members, reporters and–"

"They could recognize me sitting here too. And what if those men come along while you're gone? How am I going to hide in an open convertible? And if the police come along, looking for the stolen car...?"

Rory opened his mouth and closed it.

"Besides, Larrise Abbatiello was my friend. I want to help find her killer."

Looked at her for a moment, Rory took in a deep breath and nodded, "Okay, let's go. He opened the car door.

Cassandra looked immensely relieved as she exited the driver's side.

Rory waited on the sidewalk for her to run around the front of the convertible. He glanced up and down the street, looking for the two Colombians.

Cassandra stepped onto the sidewalk beside Rory. "Just don't make me climb anything so you can try to look up my dress again. Okay?"

"As long as you don't turn me into a male stripper again," Rory complained.

Cassandra looked at Rory, thinking for a minute. Then she patted him on the cheek, "Just make sure you don't have me climb anything too high this time to get your look, sweetie."

Chapter 17

AS A PRECAUTION, Rory dumped the cell phone he has just used in a public trash bin. Then he and Cassandra walked west-bound towards the back of the convention center. The street here was fairly quiet and they only passed a few people. As he was about to cross the last intersection before the back of the convention center, Rory realized Cassandra wasn't beside him. He looked back in panic and saw her standing in front of a large store window. He ran back to her quickly, "What's wrong?"

"Nothing," she said. She pointed into the window.

Rory looked at where she was pointing. He saw a number of mannequins in a window display dressed in sexy lingerie, bustiers, corsets, sexy bras, panties, nylons and garter belts. "What about it?" he asked.

Cassandra looked at him like he was a dodo bird. "I could wear *that* so no one would recognize me when we go back to the convention center."

Rory looked at the mannequins and then back at Cassandra, "*Under* your dress," he asked, "or instead of? Cause I'm okay with either one."

"Isn't that just like a man," she complained, her hands on her hips. She stabbed a finger at the mannequins in the window again, "I'm talking about the *wigs* on their head!"

"Oh," said an obviously disappointed Rory.

She growled at him as she pointed at one of the mannequins, "Go in there and buy me that black wig."

Rory headed for the shop door.

"And if you buy any other thing on those mannequins for me," she warned, "I'll strangle you with it!"

Rory disappeared into the lingerie shop.

Cassandra stepped away from the window when she saw the sales lady inside head over to the window display. The sales lady removed the black wig from a mannequin. A few minutes later, Rory walked back out of the lingerie shop. He carried a large red and black plastic bag. Rory pulled the black wig out of the bag and handed it to Cassandra.

Cassandra walked to the next building and stepped into the doorway where she used the glass as a mirror. Looking at her reflection, Cassandra pushed her long red hair up under the black, bob style wig.

When she turned back around, Rory handed her another small plastic bag.

Cassandra gave him a sharp look, "What did I tell you?"

"It's not what you think," Rory replied.

Cassandra grabbed the plastic bag, "With you, I'm not sure what to think." She looked inside and raised her eyebrows.

"I thought it might help to disguise your face a little more," Rory explained.

Cassandra pulled out a pair of long black, self-adhesive eyelashes, black eyeliner and a tube of black lipstick. She looked at him for a brief moment. Then she gave him the empty plastic bag back, turned back around and went to work on her makeup as she looked at her reflection in the glass.

Rory looked up and down the street as he waited for her to apply the full disguise.

When she was finished, Cassandra turned around and looked at Rory with her arms crossed over her chest. She had applied the long eyelashes, black mascara, and black lipstick. "I look like a *hooker*!" she said with some emphasis.

"I think you look hot," Rory said.

Cassandra tapped her foot several times, "Yeah, well you have the taste of an amateur male stripper. And not a very good one from what I saw."

"Hey," Rory complained, "that hurts. I tried. The sales lady said it would work together with the wig. At least no one will recognize you now."

"Getting caught and tried for murder would be better than letting someone I know see me looking like this," she complained.

Rory shrugged, "I still think you look great."

Cassandra shook her head and then stepped down onto the sidewalk, "Let's go before I strangle you."

Chapter 18

RORY AND CASSANDRA crossed the intersection and walked to the entrance of the large parking lot at the back of the convention center. Rory held his arm out, "Hold on to me like we're a couple going for a stroll."

"Why?"

"Because we don't want to get separated. And if something happens, I want close contact so we move as a unit."

Cassandra took his arm, "Okay, fine, I get it." She held a finger up in front of his nose, "But no getting fresh with this close contact stuff."

"Duly noted. Just try and relax."

"Yeah, right."

"Okay, try to *look* relaxed."

Cassandra grumbled but closed her eyes, opened them after a moment and said, "Okay. Let's go."

Rory led across the parking lot for the back door. As they neared the back door, a large number of men, including several uniformed policemen, leered at Cassandra and smiled at Rory.

Cassandra complained to Rory under her breath, "I told you. They probably think I'm a hooker you picked up."

Rory pulled the back door open for her, "Hey, I'm into role-playing. Whatever it takes to get the job done."

She glared at him and gave him a light shot in the ribs with her elbow as she passed through the doorway.

Once inside, Rory and Cassandra continued their stroll down a long curved hallway, following the signs until they finally approached the front lobby. There was a large crowd milling around and an immense buzz of activity. No doubt the sensational murder was going to keep everyone up all night, waiting for the latest breaking news.

As they stood in the hallway, just on the edge of the lobby, Rory looked around, wondering where they should begin.

Cassandra stood nervously beside him, still holding onto his arm like they were a couple, "I know this place is fully booked but this is ridiculous."

"Probably a lot of reporters and lookie-lous."

"Lookie-lous?"

"Yeah. You know? The people who show up at fires and scenes of an accident."

"They're idiots."

"True. Okay. Let's start at the beginning. What room was Larrise Abbatiello in?"

Leaning slightly forward, Cassandra looked around the lobby, "She was on this floor in the blue section of rooms. Room number 29. That's the hallway over there. But I'm not sure if it's a good idea to go there. Maybe the police are still there."

"Yeah, I agree. It's a crime scene and I imagine they'll have at least one or two officers still there. But I want to see where everything happened - the original crime scene is where you start an investigation."

"But if you can't get inside...?"

"I just want to look in a general sense. Maybe it tells us something, maybe it doesn't. Are you game?"

Cassandra nodded reluctantly.

Taking a deep breath, Rory let it out slowly, "Okay, we're just part of the crowd. We're just inquisitive like everyone else. Right?"

"Oh for sure. I look like a hooker on your arm and I'm just part of the crowd." Cassandra waved her hand, "Forget it. Let's just go."

Rory took her across the lobby and they did their best to fit into the crowd and not attract attention.

For her part though - Cassandra received a lot of looks from the men in the crowd as she walked by them - and she complained under her breath, "I know *exactly* what they're thinking, the pigs."

Bending his head sideways, Rory said, "I think you're reading too much into their looks."

"Yeah, right. In your mind, I'm probably bent over a chair somewhere."

Rory opened his mouth–

"Shut up."

Rory could only smile. Despite the seriousness of the situation she was in, Cassandra Glynn remained a feisty woman.

As they reached the wide cross-hallway leading to room #29, Cassandra slowed her pace.

"It's okay," Rory whispered as he tapped her hand on his elbow to reassure her.

Cassandra bit her lip as she nodded and they turned the corner into the crowded hallway.

Everyone here was still talking in hushed tones about the sensational murder. Some people were concentrating on their cell phones, reading texts or texting their friends to keep them updated on the excitement. Others were talking into their phones and explaining what they were doing and seeing at that very moment.

Rory slowly led Cassandra through the crowd, watching for the possibility that someone recognized her. But the men who did look her way were more interested in her legs and bottom after a quick look at her face. And many of the women dismissed her quickly as a dark-haired bimbo.

Rory could feel her grip tightened on his arm as they moved closer to the scene of the crime. He could understand her reluctance but he hoped to get a look at where the crime happened. And maybe they would run across someone who was an actual witness to the events. A risky move, but he needed as much information as he could get.

But as they neared the yellow crime scene tape stretched across the hallway, Cassandra stopped. She refused to budge any further. Large tears welled up in her eyes as she looked at Rory and whispered, "I can't really go too much closer, Rory. When I think about poor Larrise lying there...."

Rory nodded. He couldn't push her any farther. Putting an arm around her shoulder to comfort her, he moved her away from the crime scene.

Cassandra kept her head down, wiping away tears as they walked back down the hallway through the crowd.

Once back in the lobby, Rory looked for a place where she could sit and compose herself while he did some thinking. But every chair and love seat placed around the space was occupied.

That's when he noticed a small coffee shop on the far side, separated from the lobby by a low railing. It looked out into the street and the front area of the convention center, so he would be able to watch the lobby as well as the street from in there. He guided a quiet Cassandra through the crowd. A sign told them to 'seat yourself' so he took her to a table at the back that was secluded from the other customers.

Rory sat with his back to the wall so he could keep watch.

Cassandra pulled several napkins from the holder on the table and lightly dabbed at her eyes.

A server appeared and Rory ordered coffees.

Lifting the napkin holder, Cassandra tried to use it as a mirror, "I'm going to look a mess if I keep crying."

Rory shook his head, "No. You look okay. The clerk where I got the mascara said it was waterproof."

Cassandra set the holder back in place with a thud, "Great. I can look like a hooker underwater too."

Chapter 19

AFTER A FEW SIPS OF COFFEE, Rory asked Cassandra if she was up to going through the sequence of events again. There had to be something he had missed. Or maybe something she had forgotten to mention the first time around.

Cassandra nodded. She rubbed the back of her neck for a few moments before she began to go through everything that had happened to her.

Rory could see her go through a whole gamut of emotions as she talked. She recounted her meeting with Clarke Navarro and it was obvious she still felt hurt about the Prime Minister not signing off on her candidacy. He could see her eyes flash with anger when she talked about the retired hockey player being chosen instead. Then there was the pain in her eyes when she recounted how she was told Larrise Abbatiello already knew and hadn't told her.

When she finished recounting the events, Cassandra wiped tears from her eyes again with a napkin and tried to compose herself.

"Okay," Rory said after a moment, "one of the things we don't know is, what did Larrise Abbatiello do after she found out you weren't going to be allowed to run in the election. Any ideas?"

Cassandra looked down at the table and shook her head no.

"What was she supposed to be doing that day?"

Cassandra gave him a little shrug, "I'm not really sure. Like I said, it was her thing. I left most of the daily details of the campaign and everything else up to her. She was really good at it. I didn't even see her that day. She had set up the interview with the CBC for me, but she wasn't there, her assistant was. The interview took just over two hours."

"You never talked to her?"

"Oh, I did talk to Larrise on the phone from my room. But that was well before the interview started though."

"How long before?" Rory asked, trying to pin down the timeline.

Cassandra did some thinking, "I guess...I talked to her about...four hours or so before I headed down to the all candidates meeting."

"What did you talk about?"

Shrugging, Cassandra said, "Nothing really important. She was checking on me, making sure I was getting ready - that I hadn't forgotten about the interview.. We talked a bit about the excitement of what was happening and she told me she was working on some other interviews. That's about it."

Rory drummed his fingers on the table."Okay, so two hours before the interview then."

Cassandra nodded, "That sounds right."

"We need to know what happened to her in those hours from when you talked to her to the end of the interview."

Cassandra took a sip of coffee, then removed another tear from one of the long black eyelashes with a finger.

"Somewhere in those four hours," Rory said, "she learned about you not being the candidate. Who exactly would tell her that?"

Cassandra thought about it for a few minutes. "That would be Clarke Navarro's job. He could have farmed it out to someone but I doubt it."

"Why would you say that?"

Raising an eyebrow, Cassandra said, "People in his position as well known for having tough hides and a willingness to do the dirty work. It's the part of politics - dirty ticks and all that stuff - that I hate. My husband hated it as well, but it's part of the business if you can call it that."

"So, nothing out of the usual with this guy, then?"

"Not really."

"Okay. So *where* would they talk? In his room or...?"

Cassandra considered the question, "I would say it probably was down in the York Room where the meeting was going to take place. Knowing Clarke, he would've spent all day there."

Rory nodded, "Okay, so Larrise Abbatiello is told you wouldn't be able to run in the election - probably inside or outside the York Room. She would be upset. She would head up to your room to tell you–"

"Probably not. More than likely, I was still being interviewed. And Larrise wouldn't want to embarrass me in front of other people. She was very considerate about others that way. She would have waited until I was alone and told me in private." More tears formed in Cassandra's eyes and she flicked a tear from her cheek, "That was Larrise. I feel bad about being mad at her now."

Rory took a couple sips of coffee as he mulled over the information to revise his theory, "Okay. So Larrise is told. Maybe she heads back to her room first and–"

Cassandra shook her head no as she rubbed the back of her neck.

"Why not?"

Cassandra looked up, "Why not what?"

"I said - maybe she headed back to her room - and you shook your head no. Why wouldn't she do that?"

Cassandra smiled and fondly remembered her friend, "Because she would have been wandering all over the convention center."

Rory was puzzled, "That doesn't make any sense. Why would she do that?"

"Because Larrise Abbatiello was dyslexic. Beyond her family, I was only one who ever knew. No one ever realized it, but when she got upset, it would kick in."

Rory narrowed his eyes as he considered what she was saying.

Cassandra reminisced as she smiled, "I can remember one time before I was married, Larrise and I were going to a funeral for a school friend and we got on the wrong streetcar. She was leading the way as she usually did and we got on streetcar 42 instead of 24. She *didn't* want to admit her problem and she *wouldn't* ask anybody for help. She finally explained it all to me later." Cassandra shook her head in fondness at the memory, "But that day we got so lost...."

"So she mixed her numbers up," Rory said as he contemplated this new fact.

Cassandra nodded yes.

"Whenever she was under stress?"

Cassandra nodded yes. Suddenly, Cassandra's eyes widened, "So...if she was upset after talking to Clarke...."

"And *if* she was headed back to her room...."

Cassandra straightened up in her chair, "So instead of going to room 29, she went to...."

Rory looked her in the eyes, "Room 92. And what or who is in room 92 is the next question."

Cassandra got up from her chair, a look of determination in her eyes, "It's far-fetched, but it's worth a look, right?"

Chapter 20

RORY HAD TO HUSTLE to keep up with Cassandra as she headed into the crowded lobby. She was a woman on a mission to determine what had happened to a friend.

Cassandra threaded her way through people and across the lobby. Reaching the far side, she pointed up at the signs on the wall and said loudly back over her shoulder, "We want room 92 in the blue section."

"I know, I know," Rory said as he finally caught her arm. "Just go slow. We don't want to attract attention, do we?"

Cassandra realized she had just barreled her way across the lobby and had gotten plenty of unneeded attention. She lowered her head and licked her lips. "Sorry," she said in a quieter voice. "I just wanted to...you know...."

"I know. Let's just take our time and try to blend in. You know, just a man and his hooker friend going for a walk."

Cassandra gave him an irritated look as she took his elbow again, "Very funny."

The hallway they were in had a lot fewer people than the one leading to the crime scene. Rory took his time leading her down the long curved hallway, keeping an eye ahead for any problems.

Cassandra glanced back several times, her voice low, "There aren't a lot of people in this section. It's pretty quiet."

"You're right," Rory agreed. He gestured to the room service trays filled with dirty dishes on the floor. They were sitting in haphazard fashion outside dozens of the rooms along the hallway.

"Why are there so many?"

"I imagine the hotel staff is busy with all the police and reporters coming and going. Clearing the hallways will probably come a little later."

Rory and Cassandra reached an area where a hallway led off to the right. Slowing their pace a bit, Rory took a cautious look around the corner and down the long, curving hallway. He didn't spot anyone, but he could see more trays with dirty dishes outside a large number of the rooms. Continuing on, they were soon approaching the area for room 92 - and something struck Rory as odd.

Cassandra must have noticed a change in his demeanor. "What's wrong?" she asked in a whisper.

Rory didn't reply. He just glanced back over his shoulder.

"Rory?" she whispered again.

Rory realized what was bothering him. Not only hadn't they seen anyone on this end of the hallway, there wasn't any *evidence* of people either. There were no dirty dishes or room service trays like the ones they had passed. He thought for a moment and then asked her, "I thought you said the rooms were fully booked."

Cassandra raised her eyebrows, "They are. I know a supporter who wanted to get a room and couldn't. She actually had her name on the waiting list from two months ago. Why?"

"Because, starting from room 80, I haven't seen any sign of hotel guests. That includes trays with dirty dishes outside the rooms."

Cassandra looked around and thought about it for a moment, "You're right. What do you think it means?"

Rory rubbed the stubble on his cheek, "I'm not sure. Maybe nothing. Let's keep going."

Cassandra nodded and gripped Rory's arm a little tighter as they continued on down the hallway. She nervously glanced over her shoulder every so often.

Moved with her over to the left side of the hallway, Rory tried to get a better look down around the gentle curve. After a moment, he stopped dead in his tracks. He turned to his right, took Cassandra's arms by the elbows and moved her back across the hallway.

Cassandra's gasped, taking quick little steps in her high heels as she was moved backward.

Rory pinned Cassandra up against the wall with her hands at her sides.

"Wha–?

Rory planted his mouth firmly against hers!

Cassandra's eyes were wide open in amazement as Rory held her against the wall and kissed her. She tried to move but Rory kept her pinned against the wall, lips firmly planted against hers. Over Rory's shoulder, Cassandra caught sight of two men walking by in the hallway. One of them was on a cell phone. Both leered as they leaned over to get a better view of Cassandra's body and legs. One of the men said something and the other laughed as they watched the two lovers in the hallway.

Once the muffled footsteps of the men disappeared down the hallway, Rory broke off the long kiss. He took a step away from Cassandra and leaned back, trying to see around the curve.

Cassandra cleared her throat and straightened her black wig. Her face was bright red as she spoke in a low voice, "I know you love the hooker look, Mr. Steele, but could you please control yourself a little–"

"I'm positive those were our two friends."

"What?"

Rory took a few steps down the hallway, trying to see where they had gone.

A suddenly sober Cassandra began shaking, "H-how did they find us? How-how did they know that we would come back here? Or where exactly we would be in the convention center.?"

Rory shook his head, "I don't think they did." He stepped back and looked straight into Cassandra Glynn's green eyes, "But here's the thing...they just came out of room 92."

Chapter 21

10 DIVISION POLICE STATION, Toronto

DETECTIVE CAMRON MACKINNON and his partner Detective Jeanette Sepulveda had the investigation records of Bryson Glynn's accident rushed over to them. They added it to the overflowing pile of paperwork already on their two desks. But nothing seemed to fit together despite the long hours of work the two had put in. The scent of stale coffee and donuts tangled with the aroma of fresh coffee as they tried to keep their energies up.

Sepulveda was typing away at her computer while MacKinnon was reading another report and drinking another Tim Horton's large, double-double coffee. "Timmy's entire profit for the year is based on your coffee drinking habits, you know that?" Sepulveda teased.

"Yeah. And Victoria Secret has made all their profits off you," MacKinnon shot back.

"Hey," Sepulveda complained, "you been rifling through my undies drawer again?"

"Undies? I thought those were parachutes."

"Oh," Sepulveda said as she shook her head and smiled, "you'll pay for that one, MacKinnon."

MacKinnon laughed and then grew serious. The joking helped break the tension but the frustration was beginning to mount.

Sepulveda stood up and rolled her shoulders, trying to get the kinks out of her neck, "None of this seems to fit together. Not a single thing."

"I agree. Maybe it doesn't fit together. But something sure *is* going on here. Why would those two guys be trying to kill Cassandra Glynn? Does she know something? Did she see something? And how does her husband's accident fit in?" MacKinnon took a deep breath and tossed the report he was reading down on the desk, shaking his head as he pondered his own questions.

Sepulveda shook her head as well and walked over to get a drink from the water cooler. "And why was her campaign manager killed?" she said over her shoulder. "I could see them setting up Cassandra Glynn for the murder *if* she stepped into the scene while it was happening. But why wait around for an hour? And *then* set her up?"

MacKinnon didn't have any answers for his partner's questions either. "Any red flags pop up in your computer search?" he asked after a moment.

"Not a thing," Sepulveda said as she filled a polystyrene foam cup. "Nothing on the husband, nothing on the wife, nothing on the campaign manager. Nothing, nothing, nothing. I checked every database possible. Those people led squeaky clean lives. Not even a parking ticket."

MacKinnon rubbed his five o'clock shadow, thinking.

Just then another detective stopped by the water cooler. Detective John Pelfrey was a 25 year veteran of the force. He was noted for wearing a crumpled hounds-tooth jacket with mismatched pants and shoes. "How's the case going?" he asked Sepulveda as she drank her cup of water.

"It's not," Sepulveda said as she tossed her cup forcefully into the wastebasket. "To tell you the truth, none of it makes any sense."

Pelfrey filled a cup for himself and wandered over to MacKinnon's desk. He flipped one of the folders around on the desk to read the label, "Bryson Glynn? Isn't that the politician who drowned with his kids? Why are you looking at Bryson Glynn's old accident report?"

"Just wanted to aggravate ourselves more," MacKinnon grumbled.

Pelfrey shook his head sympathetically. "Too bad about the guy. He actually seemed to be a decent guy." Then he added with a grin, "For a politician." Pelfrey drained his cup and tossed it in the wastebasket.

Sepulveda sat back down at her desk, "I heard he was a pretty good guy too. And they tell me his wife's the same. She might have done some good too if she had gotten elected."

"Yeah. Too bad she had to go and whack somebody."

MacKinnon and Sepulveda traded glances as they leaned back in their chairs.

Pelfrey started to wander away, "Well, there's one good thing about it."

"What's that?" Sepulveda asked.

"At least she won't kick the can like her husband and the others."

MacKinnon and Sepulveda stared at each other - then suddenly leaned forward in their chairs like the team they were.

A moment later, Sepulveda called out to the detective, "Hey John, what did you mean by that?"

Pelfrey turned around and walked back, "Mean by what?"

"You said she won't kick the can like her husband *and the others*. What did you mean by that?"

Detective John Pelfrey shrugged, "Apparently, there have been a number of accidental deaths of federal politicians over the last 6 or 7 years."

"Like who?" MacKinnon asked.

Pelfrey shrugged, "I'm not really sure off the top of my head. I'm not really the one up on this stuff."

Sepulveda shook her head in confusion, "Then how do you know?"

Holding his hands out - like they should know - Pelfrey said, "I got it from my father-in-law."

MacKinnon, repeated the statement, not sure he had heard right, "You got it from your father-in-law? Is he on the force?"

"Oh, I'm sorry. I thought you guys knew. He was a university professor, specializing in political science. He loves to kick around all that political stuff when the family gets together." Pelfrey pulled a pen from his shirt pocket and began to write on top of the Glynn folder. "My father-in-law is Professor Graham Conroy. That's his phone number. Give him a call if you want to know more. He's up at all hours and he *loves* to talk about this stuff. Just be prepared - he'll talk your ear off for hours."

MacKinnon spun the folder around, "Thanks, John."

"Yeah, thanks, John," Sepulveda said as Detective John Pelfrey headed down the hallway. Once he was out of ear-shot, she looked across at her partner, "You think this means anything?"

MacKinnon shrugged as he drummed his fingers on the folder.

"Think we should call him?" Sepulveda asked.

"Can't hurt," MacKinnon shrugged as he reached for a phone, "we've got squat so far."

Sepulveda nodded as she watched her partner dial the number.

"Professor Graham Conroy?" MacKinnon asked as someone answered at the other end of the line. "Professor Conroy, this is Detective Camron MacKinnon. I work with your son-in-law, Detective John Pelfrey. No, sir, he's fine. He suggested I give you a call about a case I'm working on. Is this a good time? Good. I'm investigating the accidental death of Bryson Glynn. That's right. John mentioned there were a number of federal politicians who died over the last half-dozen years or so that you were aware of. I was wondering–"

Sepulveda sat still in anticipation as she watched her partner listen.

MacKinnon motioned urgently for his partner to get a pen and paper.

Sepulveda picked up a pen and then reached to the other side of her desk to grab for a notebook She flipped open the notebook as her partner began dictating names.

Chapter 22

CASSANDRA WAS STILL SHAKING as they moved back down the hallway in the direction where the two men had disappeared. "What if we see them again?" she asked in a low whisper, afraid they might hear her.

"Then get ready for a big kiss again," Rory answered as he paused and tried to see around the curve of the long hallway.

Cassandra looked at him. She reached up and straightened her black wig, "Are you sure that isn't why you're following them? So you can?"

"Could be," Rory answered.

Cassandra reached out and ran a finger gently across his lower lip, "Well, black lipstick doesn't become you."

Rory lightly touched his lip where she had wiped as he kept an eye on the hallway ahead. A moment later, he began to walk cautiously down the hallway again.

Cassandra kept pace just behind and to his right, checking back over her shoulder from time to time. She licked her lips as they drew close to the end of the hallway–

Rory quickly put his arm out and moved himself and Cassandra back a few feet.

"What's wrong?" Cassandra whispered, her lips trembling.

Rory took a few cautious steps forward again and peered into the lobby.

Cassandra moved right behind Rory and looked over his shoulder.

The two men they had been trailing were slowly walking through the crowd of people still milling around the lobby.

"That's them, isn't it?" Cassandra whispered.

"I think so."

The two men walked did a slow walk around the large lobby, scanning the crowd as they moved around the knots of people still talking and sharing the latest gossip and theories regarding the sensational murder.

Cassandra's fingernails dug into Rory's shoulder with anxiety, "What are they doing?"

Rory grimaced and gently reached up to touch her hand.

Cassandra realized what she was doing, released her grip and whispered, "Sorry."

"I'm not sure," Rory admitted as he kept his eyes on the two men. "Maybe they're looking for us."

The two men worked their way down to the front doors of the convention center. One of the men said something as he pulled a package of cigarettes from one of the side pockets in his leather jacket. The other man nodded as he swept the lobby with his eyes again. The man with the cigarettes pushed his way through the front door and the other followed him outside.

Rory gave it a few moments and then turned to Cassandra, "Let's go into that coffee shop again. It gives us a nice view of the street and we can watch them from there. Just keep your eye on the front door as we pass, so they don't catch us by surprise coming back in."

Cassandra took Rory's arm and they slipped across the lobby and past the front doors. They made it into the small coffee shop without incident and took a table out of the way in the back again. A server appeared and they ordered two coffees, all while trying to keep an eye on the street outside as well the lobby and the front entrance. The server appeared with the coffees and left.

Cassandra whispered, "What now?"

Rory whispered back with some amusement, "Are you afraid the men will hear you?"

Irritation was quite evident in her voice as Cassandra said, "Can you blame me? They're trying to kill me."

"That's true. Do you still have that other cell phone?"

"Yeah," Cassandra said. She reached into the pocket of her red dress and passed it over. "Who are you calling?"

"I think it's time we called Detective MacKinnon again." Rory punched in the numbers from memory. He listened for someone to answer the phone as he looked across the table at Cassandra, "Do you want me to sit beside you in case they come back in?" He winked, "You know what I mean?"

A flush crept across Cassandra's cheeks and she turned her head slightly, rubbing the back of her neck with her left hand, "You're a jackass."

"But a good kisser, right?"

Cassandra raised her eyebrows and opened her mouth–

"Detective MacKinnon here."

"Hello Detective MacKinnon, this is Rory Mack Steele."

"Good to hear from you again," Detective MacKinnon said. "You've changed phones?"

"Yes," Rory answered, "I didn't want to take any chances."

"Good idea," MacKinnon said, "is Mrs. Glynn still with you?"

"Yes, she's fine," Rory answered, "In fact, she looks really good right now."

Cassandra stuck her tongue out at him.

"Where are you?"

"We're back at the convention center," Rory told him. "We're sitting in a small coffee shop next to the front lobby, and watching everything that's going on."

"You're kidding?"

"Nope. Hide in plain sight, I always say." He winked at Cassandra again.

Cassandra wrinkled her nose at him but the blush crept across her cheeks again.

Rory glanced toward the lobby area, "I called you because I needed to talk to you about something."

"Just a minute Mr. Steele," MacKinnon said, "if you don't mind, I'm going to go to a secure room with my partner and put you on speaker phone."

"Okay." After a few minutes, Rory heard MacKinnon grumbling about not knowing how to handle the complicated buttons on the cell phone.

"Mr. Steele, we now have you on speaker phone. Detective Janet Sepulveda, my partner is here with me."

"Hello, Mr. Steele."

"Hello, Detective Sepulveda."

"So, what's on your mind, Mr. Steele?" MacKinnon asked.

"I called you because I learned something very interesting about Larrise Abbatiello from Mrs. Glynn."

"What's that?" Sepulveda asked.

"She was dyslexic. She mixed up her numbers."

"And that helps us how?" MacKinnon asked after a moment.

"Larrise Abbatiello was booked into room number 29 in the convention center. Mrs. Glynn said that whenever Larrise Abbatiello got upset, her dyslexia would kick in. She mixed her numbers up. When she found out that her good friend Cassandra Glynn was not going to be allowed to run for election in the riding, that would have put her under a lot of stress. If she headed back to her room, she would have gotten the room number mixed up. At least, that's what we assumed due to her condition. Instead of going to room number 29, she would have mixed up the numbers and ended up going to room number 92 instead."

"Okay, I follow. But what's so special the room 92?"

"That's what we wondered about as well," Rory said. "We wandered down there...and you will never guess who we saw coming out of room number 92?"

"I'll bite. Who?"

"Our Spanish speaking friends. I'm pretty sure they were the two who were following us from the beginning. And probably the same pair who shot Sebastyen Pipes and the security guard."

MacKinnon and his partner talked quietly for a moment and then MacKinnon said, "I'm going to have Detective John Pelfrey go down there to the convention center. I'll have him wait in the lobby. If you see those two Spanish guys again, you tell him. John will try to figure out who they are. We'll keep this in a small, tight circle. Don't talk to anyone else but him. Okay? I don't want too many people involved in this until we can figure out what the hell is going on here."

"Okay. But there are still a lot of people in the lobby, as well in the street out front. The murder has still got everyone milling around. How will I know which one is your detective?"

There was a discussion again and it was Sepulveda who spoke, "We'll go a little James Bond on this. I have a red handkerchief. We'll have him wear it his top pocket."

Rory nodded, "Okay, That sounds like a good plan to me. Can you folks find out who was in room 92 while you're at it? Maybe it helps us to figure out what's going on."

"That's the same thing I was thinking," MacKinnon said. "We'll have Detective Pelfrey look into that as well. He can talk to the convention center manager and get us as much information as possible."

Rory looked at Cassandra before he asked his next question, "Were you able to find anything more on Bryson Glynn's accident?"

Cassandra sat up a little straighter at the mention of her husband's name.

"Not anything solid, I'm afraid. Detective Pelfrey gave us some interesting information that we followed up on, but we're really not sure what we have."

"Can I ask what the information was?"

"We talked to Detective Pelfrey's father-in-law, Professor Graham Conroy. He was a professor on political stuff in a couple of universities around Toronto. According to him, Bryson Glynn was number 12 in a list of federal members of Parliament who died under accidental circumstances over the last seven years."

Rory narrowed his eyes as he considered the information, "But people die all the time, in or out of politics."

"I would have said the same thing," MacKinnon admitted. "There have been a number of others who have died of heart attacks, cancer or what-not. But 12 people dying *accidentally* over the last 7 years was kind of an unusual anomaly that piqued Professor Conroy's curiosity. These deaths were spread right across the country, so I think only a political junkie like him would have noticed it."

Rory was still skeptical, "Okay. I'll go with his expertise on it. Do you have the names of those twelve people?"

"I've got a list of the people right in front of me," Sepulveda said, "Cam doesn't write anything down. He makes me do all that work."

MacKinnon complained defensively, "Your penmanship is better, that's all."

Sepulveda's voice was teasing, "Of course, Camron, you keep telling yourself that."

"Can you give me the list of names?" Rory asked as he looked at Cassandra and motioned he needed something to write with.

Cassandra Glynn got up and approached one of the waitresses.

"Yes. But even with the list of names," MacKinnon said, "it doesn't seem to add up to much of anything."

Cassandra returned with a pen and a piece of paper.

"I'm going to give the phone over to Cassandra Glynn," Rory said, "she is obviously more up-to-date on this political stuff than we are. Maybe she can see something we don't."

"Worth a try," Sepulveda said.

Cassandra Glynn took the cell phone, exchanged pleasantries, and began writing down the list of names.

Rory took a sip of coffee and glanced out into the street. Everything was still hustle and bustle out there as the police and the media spearheaded the search for a murderer. He looked over at the lobby. People inside the convention center were still buzzing about the sensational events that had taken place as well.

And in the middle of all this frenzy, two men were still looking to kill Cassandra Glynn. Rory wondered why. Everything seemed to point to reasons beyond a simple frame-up for murder. But *what* were those reasons? He wondered if a list of dead politicians could supply a clue.

Chapter 23

CASSANDRA GLYNN LOOKED at the list of names she had written down. Twelve names of dead politicians that had all served in Parliament at one time or another. She lifted the pen, and after some hesitation, she wrote the name of Bryson Glynn at the bottom of the list. Now it was thirteen men and women in all...thirteen men and women who had all died in accidents.

Rory noted her writing down the name of her husband. His heart went out to her, "Does any of that make any sense to you?"

Cassandra shook her head as she looked over the names. "No, not really. I mean, I recognize some of these names. But...."

Rory took a deep breath, pondering what to do next.

"Can you find us a computer?" Cassandra asked him. "We need a computer with Internet access."

"Hotels and convention centers usually have in-room access to plug in your laptop. But many of them also have a small business room with computers and Internet access for guests without their own computers." He stood up, "Let's go to the front desk and see what they have here. Just keep one eye on the front entrance as we head back, just so we don't get any surprises."

Cassandra stood up, looking at him with mock indignation, "Maybe you're going out there in the hopes they do so you can have an excuse to kiss me again."

"And maybe you're going with me in the hopes I *do* have to kiss you again."

Blowing a light raspberry, Cassandra took his arm, "Fat chance of that, big boy."

Rory smiled but stayed on alert as he led her out of the coffee shop. They walked back through the lobby and over toward the front desk, keeping an eye out for the return of the two men.

As they watched for the two men, the rest of the males in the lobby turned their heads and watched Cassandra's legs and bottom as she passed.

"I still know what those pigs are thinking!" Cassandra complained to Rory.

Rory patted her arm, "And if they didn't look, you'd feel like you were getting old."

Cassandra grumbled under her breath.

Reaching the front desk, Rory asked the clerk if they had a computer room.

"Yes, sir, we do. I can add it to your room bill or we can use a credit card."

"Credit card." Rory pulled his slim wallet and passed over a credit card, "You can charge me for eight hours. I'll come back if we need more."

During the transaction, Cassandra held onto his arm but tried to keep her face turned away in case they recognized her despite all the heavy makeup.

Rory was given directions to the public computer room and he and Cassandra headed back across the lobby for the entrance to another long, curved hallway. Within moments, they found the computer room. On the other side of an open doorway sat a number of tables outfitted with computers, chairs, and several scanners and printers.

Cassandra went inside, "Looks like we have it all to ourselves."

Rory nodded but he was bothered by the fact the wall to the hallway was all glass. They would be totally exposed to anyone passing by, like those two men if they came up this hallway for some reason. But what choice did they have?

Cassandra sat down at one of the computers. She turned it on, used the password given to Rory, and she had Internet access within seconds. Cassandra began keyboarding in the names on the list immediately.

Rory pulled a chair to the open doorway and sat down, keeping watch as Cassandra worked. He suddenly wished he hadn't been in such a rush to get down here after Sebastyen had called - he should have taken the time to get his handgun. Just another error in a line of them - one that might just get them shot like Sebastyen and Ernie.

Chapter 24

TIME PASSED SLOWLY. Rory occasionally stood up and walked up and down the hallway, stretching his legs, trying to remain limber in case–

"Son of a bitch!" Cassandra exclaimed under her breath.

Rory rushed back into the room, "What is it?"

Cassandra shook her head as she looked around the room, "Just find me another piece of paper."

On the far side of the room, Rory saw some paper stacked up for the printers. He hustled over and picked up a wad of blank sheets. He placed them on the table beside Cassandra, pulled another chair over and sat beside her, "What did you find?"

Taking several pieces of paper, Cassandra began writing, her voice angry, "I'm not totally sure. Just give me a bit more time."

"Okay, okay. No problem."

Cassandra would check out something on the computer and then write something down. Back and forth she worked. Cassandra crossed her legs as she typed on the keyboard.

When she did that, Rory's gaze was drawn to her legs. He admired them for a few moments and then caught himself. He pushed the chair back, got up and went back over to the chair near the door to resume watching the hallway.

Cassandra looked over at him and smiled briefly. She continued keyboarding and writing down information. After another hour, Cassandra pushed her chair back and stood up.

Rory quickly got up and went to her side, "What did you find?"

Cassandra looked around at the computer room, "To be honest, I'm still not totally sure. But can you phone your police friends again? We'll have to go to the front desk and fax them something."

"Why not email them?"

"Just in case. I'm assuming CSIS could be monitoring the cell phone towers near the entire convention center. And I'm assuming a fax has a better chance of going through without anyone noticing."

"Okay, that makes sense."

"It does?"

"Yeah." Rory pulled the cell phone out and called MacKinnon. As he led Cassandra out into the hallway and back towards the lobby, it was Sepulveda who answered. Rory got a fax number from her and gave it to Cassandra. Not seeing the two men, he led Cassandra across the lobby to the front desk. He took the pieces of paper Cassandra had written on and handed them to the front desk clerk along with the fax number. Rory paid with cash for the fax service and then drummed his fingers on the front desk while they waited.

Cassandra kept her face turned away from the front desk staff again. But it was getting harder, trying to look nonchalant without arousing suspicion.

Rory continued drumming his fingers.

Turning to face the desk but looking over her shoulder, Cassandra whispered urgently, "Rory?"

Rory followed her gaze and realized their two Spanish friends were coming back in the front door of the convention center, "Oh, crap."

Cassandra took Rory's arm as she watched, "Yeah. No kiss this time?"

"I've reformed."

Cassandra raised an eyebrow as she watched the men, "Too bad, I'm feeling a little naked right now–" She held a hand up, "Sorry, poor choice of words"

Rory opened his mouth but the front desk clerk returned with the sheets of paper along with a fax receipt. Rory took them in hand and then led Cassandra a few feet to the side of the front desk and behind three people talking.

As they watched, the two men walked over to the left of the lobby, intently looking over the milling crowd.

The best escape route was the hallway back to the computer so Rory took it. Once they reached the hallway, Rory quickly took out his cell phone. He dialed Detective MacKinnon as he instructed Cassandra, "Keep an eye on the lobby for our two friends. If they come this way, let me know."

Cassandra nodded okay as she crossed her arms tightly over her chest. Her fingers tapped her arms in anxiety as she kept watch.

"MacKinnon," came the answer on the other end of the call.

"It's Rory Mack Steele again, Detective MacKinnon. Is that detective you were sending anywhere close? Those two guys are back in the convention center."

MacKinnon cursed under his breath, "Traffic is crazy down there. He should be there soon. My partner is going to call and speed him up. Just stay out of sight."

"Okay. I'm going to put this phone on speaker so Cassandra Glynn can explain the fax we just sent you."

"Give me a moment," MacKinnon said, "My partner is just on the cell with our detective"

"Okay." Rory set the cell phone on speaker and watched with Cassandra.

A few minutes passed before MacKinnon came on, "Okay, you're on speaker phone, Mr. Steele. My partner is listening in as well."

Rory nodded at Cassandra and she moved closer to the phone.

"You have the fax I sent you?" Cassandra asked.

"Yes," Sepulveda said.

"Okay, good. I'm not sure if any of this makes sense but...."

Rory simply nodded at her, encouraging her to continue on.

Cassandra took a deep breath and started to explain what she'd found. "What I sent to you is the same list of names you gave us. I used a computer to access a few government databases that are open to the public to gather some information. First. Beside each name, I listed the name of the electoral riding each person ran in."

"These are for federal elections?" asked Sepulveda.

"Correct," Cassandra confirmed, "each person was elected to the federal government in those ridings. And next to each person and the riding is the name of the person who replaced them *after* they died."

"Okay, we follow," MacKinnon said.

Cassandra cleared her throat and now sounded very shaky, "Can you check out the accident report of each person who died? And check out everything you can on each person who replaced them? Besides the regular political stuff, I mean?"

"Of course," MacKinnon said, "but why?"

Cassandra Glynn licked her lips.

"What's wrong Cassandra," Rory asked, suddenly very nervous himself.

Cassandra spoke in a shaky voice, "I'm not sure if what I found means much but...."

Sepulveda encouraged her, "Go ahead, Mrs. Glynn, Just say what you have to say. So far we don't have much to work on so the smallest thing may just be the break we need."

"Okay. It's just that...I found something that connects these people. At least...I *think* it does...."

"Go ahead, Mrs. Glynn," MacKinnon said gently.

Cassandra cleared her throat and stumbled nervously through her reasoning, "Okay. It's just...as you know the Canadian Federal Party is in power right now....and they hold 207 seats. The...the strange thing is...out of *all* those members to choose from, *each* and *every* one of the men who replaced a person who died - is a member of Prime Minister Martin Estrada's inner Federal Cabinet."

"They are?"

"Yes. Out of all the elected members for the party, these men effectively form the Government of Canada. No matter how many elected members there are - and it's become apparent over the last few decades that for all intents and purposes the sitting Prime Minister ignores the will of the majority - Estrada and these twelve men alone control the entire country."

Chapter 25

WITH CASSANDRA holding his arm, Rory led the way cautiously down the hallway toward the front lobby. As they neared the end of the hall, Rory glanced out into the lobby. He quickly stepped back with her.

"Our two friends again?" Cassandra asked him.

Rory nodded as he took her hand off his arm and stepped forward, leaning to look into the lobby.

"You look like something is wrong. And more wrong than before. What is it?"

"It looks like our two friends have found more friends," Rory said ominously.

Cassandra's voice squeaked, "They what? No."

"The men who were following us are standing and talking with four other men over near the front desk. From that vantage point, they're watching everything."

"You're right. That doesn't sound good. Not good at all."

"Not by a long shot."

Cassandra's foot tapped nervously, "So what are we going to do now?"

Rory ran a hand through his black hair, "Well...there's a man in a beat up, hounds-tooth jacket sitting in one of the chairs on the far side the lobby. He has a red handkerchief in his pocket. That *must* be the other detective MacKinnon sent down here to help us. The problem is...if I go out there to talk to him and I'm wrong...and the men see me...."

"So you need a diversion," Cassandra said quietly.

"Something like that," Rory said as he gave the dilemma some thought.

Taking a few steps forward, Cassandra leaned and looked into the lobby area.

Rory reached out to touch her arm, "Careful. They'll see you."

Cassandra nodded and took a step back, She took a deep breath as she adjusted her black wig, "Meet me back in the coffee shop."

"Pardon?"

Patting his cheek, Cassandra repeated slowly, "Meet me back in the coffee shop."

"What are you talking about–"

In a flash, Cassandra left the hallway for the lobby.

"Cassandra–" Rory cut himself off as he watched her in horror.

She was out in the open in the lobby now.

Rory moved forward as much as possible, looking at the six men. Then he glanced back to Cassandra, who was now strutting her way through the crowd. What in the world was she doing?

Cassandra was putting extra force into each step as she strutted purposely through the crowd. The clicking of her red high heels sounded louder on the hard lobby floor and echoed off the walls.

Rory clenched his fists and his body went on high alert, ready to rush out and fight if the men saw her.

Cassandra Glynn strode confidently across the large lobby area toward the front desk, making powerful clicking sounds with her high heels.

Everyone in the lobby turned to see what the noise was. That included the two Spanish men and their four friends. They turned and watched the black-haired beauty in the red dress and long, shapely legs strutting her stuff.

Cassandra went over to a low rack that held a number of different newspapers just beside the front desk. She stood in front of the rack for a moment.

Rory swore he saw her hold the sides of her red dress and work to lift the hem upwards.

Cassandra indeed rolled the dress up several times...and then she bent over from the waist as far as she could, examining each newspaper closely.

Almost every man in the room watched as her red dress lifted skyward, exposing a *lot* of her shapely thighs from the back.

Rory was positive he was about to see the crotch of her white panties again. Another inch higher and – he realized what she was doing. Rory shook his head. It was dangerous but effective. Taking advantage of the situation, Rory moved fast across the lobby while all eyes were still on Cassandra's exposed legs and the potential show that might come at any moment. Several of the men in the lobby bent sideways, hoping....

The man with the red handkerchief in his pocket was also watching Cassandra's legs intently.

Rory took the seat in a large plush chair next to him, asking in a low voice. "Detective John Pelfrey?"

The man continued to stare as Cassandra exposed her long, shapely legs.

"Detective Pelfrey?" Rory asked louder.

The man was broken out of his intense stare and turned to look at Rory. He cleared his throat and his face went red, obviously embarrassed at being caught staring at Cassandra's raised dress, "Uh, yes...?"

"I'm Rory Mack Steele. And that lady bending over so nicely in that red dress is Cassandra Glynn."

"Oh."

The high heels were clicking across the lobby again.

Pelfrey turned to look back in Cassandra's direction.

Cassandra was now striding confidently across the lobby towards the coffee shop, a newspaper in hand. All eyes in the lobby were on her legs and bottom as she strutted across the floor. She put a little extra swing in her hips.

"Uh...MacKinnon and Sepulveda filled me in on everything," Pelfrey said as he watched her shapely hips sway.

Rory gestured discreetly, "Do you see those six men in the black leather jackets, also watching Mrs. Glynn's body and legs?"

Pelfrey reluctantly took his eyes off Cassandra's long legs and looked at the six men standing near the front desk.

They were smiling and joking with one another as they watched the black haired beauty strutting towards the coffee shop.

"The two on the right are the two men who were following us from the convention center. I thought they may have been the two who shot up the forensic center as well. But now that I see all six together, we may have lost the first two like I thought. And two others picked up our trail when they went to the forensic center to deal with the information Pipes put into the computer system. That would make a lot more sense. They're all dressed the same and have similar dark hair and complexion."

Pelfrey straightened up and his eyes narrowed as he looked at the group of men more closely, "Anything else that could help us?"

"When I first heard them talking about throwing Mrs. Glynn off the roof, it seemed to me their accent was Columbian."

Simply nodding, Pelfrey said, "Okay, that will help us to narrow a search."

"I didn't have a cell phone that was capable of taking pictures. But if you have one, maybe we could snap a few pics and your tech people could use some kind of facial recognition software to identify them."

Pelfrey played with his faded tie as he shook his head, "No. I have a better idea. I noticed your two friends and the other four were all drinking from Tim Horton's coffee cups earlier. They threw them in that fancy trash container against the wall."

Rory understood what he was proposing, "As long as they don't see you digging in the trash."

"That's true." Pelfrey rubbed his chin, thinking, "I'll have someone from the front desk clean the trash container out and give everything inside to me. Then I'll have a cruiser hustle everything, including those cups, up to MacKinnon and Sepulveda."

"That should work."

Pelfrey looked at Rory, "I understand every single person at the Center of Forensic Sciences has shelved everything they were working on to concentrate on the shooting of Sebastyen Pipes and the security guard. They'll work at the speed of light to get us a real good start on figuring out who these bozos are."

"Good. We could use a break."

Pelfrey stood up and buttoned the middle button of his jacket, "Give my regards to Mrs. Glynn. And tell her we're going to do everything we can to figure this out."

Rory stood up, "Thank you, Detective."

Keeping one eye on the men, Pelfrey headed toward the front desk personnel.

Rory turned and headed over to the coffee shop.

Cassandra was at a table in the back again. She had discarded the newspaper on another table and ordered them both coffees.

"You took a real chance back there," Rory said firmly as he sat down.

Cassandra tilted her head and fluttered the long, black eyelashes, "The hooker look is really going over well."

"That - was- dangerous."

Putting an elbow on the table, Cassandra placed her chin in her hand. She looked directly into Rory's silver-blue eyes, "Thank you for your concern. Now answer me one question, Mr. Steele."

"What's that?"

"How long did *you* look?"

Chapter 26

IT WASN'T LONG before Detective John Pelfrey joined Rory and Cassandra in the coffee shop. "Those men have disappeared from the lobby," he said to Rory as he sat down.

"Any idea where they went?" Rory asked him.

Pelfrey shook his head, "No. I found a fingerprint team still on the premises and I passed the cups off to them. They're going to send images up to the lab. By the time I got back to the lobby, I didn't see those guys anywhere."

Rory clenched his jaw. It was better knowing where they were but there was little they could do about it at this point. He turned to Cassandra, "This is Detective John Pelfrey, the man sent to help us. Detective Pelfrey, meet Cassandra Glynn."

Pelfrey reached out and shook her hand, "I didn't recognize you earlier, Mrs. Glynn."

"Yeah, well, I don't normally look like a hooker. *And* it's hard to look at my face when you're so busy looking at my legs. *Especially* when I was bent over, Detective Pelfrey."

Pelfrey actually blushed a deep red as he pulled out a cell phone and began punching in numbers.

Rory smiled at the effect Cassandra had on him.

Clearing his throat, Pelfrey said, "While we're waiting for the lab to identify those gentlemen following you, I'll call MacKinnon and Sepulveda. They were diligently following up on your husband's case, Mrs. Glynn." He waited for someone to answer.

Cassandra looked at Rory with hope in her eyes.

"Hi, Cam. I'm with Mr. Steele and Mrs. Glynn now. Hold on." Pelfrey set the cell to speaker phone and placed it on the table between them all, "You're on speaker. We're all ears, Cam."

"We have set up a conference call with Professor Graham Conroy," MacKinnon explained over the phone. "He was a professor of political science at a couple of universities in the area before he retired."

A cultured, baritone voice sounded through the speaker, "Semi-retired. But I still lecture from time to time, Detectives."

"Correction. Semi-retired," MacKinnon said.

Pelfrey smiled and shook his head.

"Professor Conroy," MacKinnon continued, "we sent you that list of people who ran as replacement candidates for the Canadian Federal Party. In *every* case, they ran for election in a riding after someone died in an accident. And the strange thing is...they are *all* presently members of the Prime Minister's cabinet. Doesn't that seem to be the least bit unusual to you?"

"I guess you could say that when you first look at it," Professor Conroy answered, "but each one of these thirteen people was also chosen specifically by the Prime Minister to run for the party in the first place. As we talked about before, that's not unusual for any political party. The party could easily explain it away by saying these are the people the Prime Minister specifically, and very obviously. wanted in his government."

Rory spoke up, "I'm not naive but...isn't that a bit...un-democratic?"

"Well," Professor Conroy said slowly, "I understand what you mean. But that's part and parcel of the parliamentary system we work with. We inherited it from the British Empire. I guess you could say it's also part and parcel of the party system we inherited. Although everything is usually done in a democratic manner through the ridings across the country, the party leaders can pick and choose who will run under the party banner."

"Can you explain that again, Professor?" Sepulveda asked. "Like Mr. Steele, I find it contrary to a democracy."

"Yes, well...quite often they're simply trying to take advantage of someone with a very high profile. It could be a somebody famous or someone very popular like a hockey or football star. That's been done before. They can put them in a riding to try and attract votes because people know them or like them. And if you put a star in a riding where they're almost a hero - like a hockey star in his hometown - it's almost a slam dunk win for the party. And if the prime minister chooses them to run in a riding to raise the profile of the party, he could also do the same thing in Parliament by naming them to his cabinet."

"So nothing is being done illegally here?" Sepulveda asked.

"No, nothing illegal at all, Although the press would have a field day with the appearance of this whole thing. It may not be illegal, but to some, it could be considered highly immoral in a democratic system. Especially when it looks like they've done it so often like the cases you have here. But most people would never even notice unless a spurned candidate raises a public stink about it."

"Okay. Is there anything unusual about the specific ridings they were chosen to run in then?" MacKinnon asked. "Is there *anything* that would tell you why they chose these electoral ridings?"

The professor was silent for a few minutes. "Nothing unusual per se, no," he said finally. "But *each* of these ridings pretty well *guarantees* a win for the Canadian Federal Party candidate who runs there. The fact that they're scattered across the country tells me they didn't want someone to catch on to what they were doing over the years. Only a political junkie like me would probably see the pattern."

"So any political party can do this?" Rory asked. "They can run a handpicked, preferred candidates in place of candidates chosen at the riding level?"

"Oh yes. This is just one of the idiosyncrasies of the system we inherited from the British Empire."

"I see. And they can also have all those handpicked guys be part of the cabinet?" Rory asked.

"Oh yes. Under the party system, each party is dominated by their national leader. And the national leader of the party winning the election is allowed to choose any sitting member to be a part of his cabinet. Even candidates he hand picks to run for election. In this case, the present Prime Minister has chosen these sitting members to form his cabinet. All within the rules. The only unusual thing is the number of members - thirteen in this case - it is usually two or three times that."

"Why do you think there are only thirteen?"

The professor sounded hesitant, "I'm not sure. But...the last one added...was the replacement for Mr. Glynn."

Cassandra did her best to maintain her composure.

After a moment of awkward silence, MacKinnon said, "Okay, Professor Conroy, thank you very much for your time, we appreciate it. Please remember this is all confidential for now and part of an ongoing investigation"

"Yes, yes, of course. But - if I may - there is one other thing I noticed about this whole affair. When we talk about people who are chosen by a party to run for election, I mean."

"Go on," MacKinnon said.

"You do realize that's how the *present* Prime Minister got his job?"

Chapter 27

THE STUNNED SILENCE was broken by Rory, "Prime Minister Martin Estrada? Are you serious?"

"Yes."

Cassandra nodded and spoke under her breath, "I forgot about that. I remember Bryson talking about it. He didn't like the way it came down."

"Can you tell us how it happened exactly, Professor?" Rory asked.

"Yes. Every political party has what are called Rainmakers. These are the people who raise large sums of money for any candidate who wants to run for office. I guess you could also call many of them king-makers because the more successful ones have a lot of clout in a party. In this particular case, a number of very successful fund raisers banded together and worked behind the scenes with a rainmaker by the name of Jeremy Hanover to force a leadership review of then sitting Prime Minister Patric Malette."

"Hanover is a close friend of Party Whip Clarke Navarro," Cassandra said.

"I would say it's more a friendship of convenience," Conroy said. "But I take your point. Anyway, these successful fund raisers, using Hanover, backed Estrada - a successful businessman who had *never* run for political office before - in a run-off against Malette."

MacKinnon spoke up, "Estrada's business was importing and exporting machinery, if I remember correctly."

"I believe so," Conroy replied. "But the main point is that Estrada was successful in his challenge - he was elected leader of the Canadian Federal Party. And since he replaced Malette in that capacity, Estrada was now the leader of the government in power and the de facto Prime Minister."

Sepulveda sounded disgusted, "And he becomes the leader of the country, as simple as that?"

"Yes and no. Estrada still needed to win an election. All his backers then had to do was simply look for a riding where they had the staunchest support, where they could pretty well *guarantee* their man a win. They had Cleo Erikson - the Member of Parliament in Black Creek West - step aside and they parachuted Estrada into that riding for a by-election."

"They can do that?" Rory asked.

"Oh yes. It's been done by other parties over the years. And by Estrada simply winning that one by-election, he was suddenly the leader of the country. He and his small cabinet pretty well run everything now."

Rory nodded, his brow a furrow of puzzlement, "And this is all perfectly legal?"

"Of course, that's just part of our parliamentary political system. It's been done before. For example, Brian Mulroney did it in 1983. He was elected leader of the Progressive Conservative party despite never having run in a single election ever. Elmer MacKay stepped down in a Nova Scotia riding that was considered a safe bet for a win. Mulroney ran as the candidate in a by-election and won. This was *after* he was chosen leader of his party. All done within the rules of the game."

Everybody around the table shook their head in bewilderment.

"Then we have the case of Donn Berckhahn. He became the leader of his party and was actually the Prime Minister because they were in power at the time of his leadership win. *But* he didn't hold a seat and he couldn't even appear on the floor of Parliament to lead his party. He had to win a parliamentary seat in an election before he could really perform his duties as Prime Minister - he did that in the Belmont North riding. The same happened with Estrada. He became the leader of the party, was actually the Prime Minister but could not appear on the floor in Parliament until he was finally elected as a Member of Parliament in a by-election that was considered a lock for him to win."

"That's nuts," Rory said

Everyone went silent.

MacKinnon spoke up, "Anybody have any other questions of Professor Conroy at this point?" After a moment, he said, "Thank you again, Professor, we appreciate your help."

"You're very welcome, Detective MacKinnon." Everyone could hear him hang up.

Pelfrey was rubbing the top of his head. "So, no real reason to remove a sitting Member of Parliament by violent means. You can easily do it under our present political system."

"Maybe somebody simply got impatient?" Cassandra said.

"That's a likely possibility," Rory said, "but it would be hard to prove."

Shaking his head, Pelfrey said, "No, I doubt someone would be that impatient. They would have to be psychos to do that. No, none of this makes any sense to me—"

Sepulveda's voice came over the phone, "Things just took a turn for the worse, John."

Pelfrey stopped rubbing his head, "Why? What happened?"

"We just got our identification results back from the lab on those prints the team sent from the coffee cups."

"Already?"

"Yeah, they popped as soon as the prints were entered in the system. The two you say were trying to kill Cassandra Glynn are Cesar Santana and Teo Luna. They're both Colombian nationals as you thought, Mr. Steele. Their Interpol photos were in the system and we'll send them to you to confirm. We are also sending photographs of their known associates. Unless I miss my guess - their friends at the convention center are Damian Delatorre, Jacinto Ruvalcaba, Esquevelle Villasenor and Orlin Delacruz. They're all Colombian nationals as well."

Cassandra voice was filled with dread, "I'm not really sure if I want to know the answer to this. But why would Interpol have records on the men who were following us?"

Sepulveda's voice was solemn, "They have records on them because all six men are connected to Neron Blanco Soto."

Cocking her head, Cassandra said, "Where have I heard that name before?"

"Probably on the late-night news. Neron Blanco Soto is the biggest *drug lord* in Columbia."

Chapter 28

"**OH MAN!**" Detective Pelfrey exclaimed, "talk about psychos and one pops up."

"Why are Soto's men here in Canada? And why are they trying to kill Cassandra Glynn?" Rory asked.

"I'm not sure why they're here," MacKinnon said. "And I'm not even sure *how* they got here. People like those characters should have been flagged as soon as they tried to get into the country."

"Along with the photos," Sepulveda added, "Interpol sent over all the information they have on these guys. But get this," she added ominously, "the Colombian police and Interpol lost track of Neron Blanco Soto three years ago. He simply disappeared off the radar. They heard rumors he had slipped out of Columbia but they dismissed it. His organization is still going strong in Columbia and they figure some rival gang would have moved in on his operation if he had left. So they figure he *has* to be there."

Cassandra leaned forward, her eyebrows pushed together, "So...I'm being chased by men who are connected to a Colombian drug lord? Why?"

Rory and Pelfrey just looked at each other. They had no answer. And there was no answer from the other end of the phone either.

After a few moments of silence, Pelfrey discreetly pulled out his gun and checked it before he spoke, "Cam?"

"Yeah, John?"

"We have two people here who said they saw two dangerous Colombian nationals coming out of room 92 in the convention center. Two dangerous individuals who slipped through our border check somehow. That sounds like exigent circumstances to me. No warrant needed, right?"

"Right. It's under Criminal Code: 487.11, no warrant needed."

"It's also permissible under the common law doctrine of hot pursuit," Sepulveda said.

"Oh, I like that one. I'm in hot pursuit," Pelfrey said. "If it's okay with you, Cam, I saw constables Flynn and Esposito working the street just outside. I'd like to use them. I worked with them before I made detective and I can trust them."

"Sounds good to me. Just make sure they keep everything to themselves. Not even a word to their Sergeant. We'll put a Bolo out on all these guys. In the meantime, be careful."

Pelfrey terminated the call and pocketed the cell phone. He slipped the gun back into the holster under his jacket and stood up, "Wait here."

Rory stood up."I don't have a weapon but maybe I can help."

Cassandra stood up as well, "Yes, I'm in, too."

Pelfrey shook his head, "I can't allow it. It's too dangerous." He headed for the lobby in a hurry.

Rory and Cassandra were right behind him.

When the detective looked back, Rory said, "Right now, we're probably safer going with you."

Cassandra was taking small, fast steps on her high heels to catch up, "He's right."

Pelfrey stopped, holding a hand up, "I'm sorry, Mrs. Glynn. I can see Mr. Steele coming with me but I'm afraid you have to stay in the coffee shop. It's too risky."

Raising her eyebrows, Cassandra said, "I've already shown I have weapons Mr. Steele doesn't have. You are going after men. Maybe you'll need *me* to bend over and distract someone again? You can even look a little longer this time - if that helps."

Pelfrey blushed a deep red as he hesitated for a moment. Then he nodded his okay.

Making sure there was still no sign of the six men, Pelfrey, Rory, and Cassandra headed over to the front desk in a hurry. After talking to Mr. Kaluza - the convention center manager - Pelfrey was given a room key card for number 92 in the blue section. He Rory instructed and Cassandra to stay put and keep an eye open for the suspects while he hurried out the front door.

Cassandra became aware of the men in the lobby checking her out again. She lowered her head whispering to Rory."Do they have to all stare?"

"Well, you did use those weapons before - putting on quite a show and attracting their attention - so what did you expect?"

Cassandra turned her face towards the wall and grumbled.

"At least they're not looking at your face now."

Cassandra raised an eyebrow at him, "Is that supposed to make me feel better?"

Detective Pelfrey returned a few minutes later with two uniformed constables. "Okay," he said to Rory and Cassandra, "Just stay behind us in the hallway in case shooting starts as we approach the room."

As Pelfrey and the constables moved past them, Rory held his arm out.

Cassandra looked at him, "Seriously?"

"Like I said, inside the convention center, if something happens I want close contact so we act as a team."

"You said as a unit. But fine." She grabbed his arm, digging in with her fingernails.

Rory grimaced but led them off after the others. It wasn't long they were all cautiously moving down the hallway not far from room 92 in the blue section.

Pelfrey held a hand up to stop everyone behind him. He watched around the curve for a moment and then looked back over his shoulder, "The hotel manager mentioned something strange to me. It seems that no other rooms are occupied from 80 to 100 except for number 92. And yet all of those rooms are paid for."

Rory nodded, "That would explain why we never saw anyone in this area of the hallway when we first came this way."

Cassandra said what they were all thinking, "Twenty-two rooms paid for and only one occupied? Someone wanted to be private and secluded."

"Or protected," Pelfrey said. He drew his gun.

The two constables did the same.

Rory glanced back at Cassandra.

Cassandra licked her lips and whispered, "Somehow my weapons seem a little useless right now."

He patted her arm.

Pelfrey moved ahead, leading the way to room 92.

A television could be heard playing loudly inside the room.

Holding his weapon up in the air at the ready position, he signaled for the two constables to take up positions on either side of the door.

As they did that, Pelfrey handed the key card to Rory. "If you could do the honors? Sounds like someone is inside, so we need to keep our hands free."

Rory nodded in agreement, taking the card in hand and stepping away from Cassandra.

"I want you to stand by the side of the door, out of the line of fire. Then as quietly as possible insert the key card. Once you open the door, I want you to move out of the way down the hallway, okay?"

Rory nodded in understanding. He stood beside the door with the key card in his hand.

Detective Pelfrey and the two police constables got into position opposite the door.

Pelfrey gave Rory a nod.

Rory nodded back in confirmation and deftly slipped the key card into the door lock. The small light above the lock immediately turned green. He gestured for Cassandra to move a few more feet back down the hallway. She complied and he slowly pushed the door handle down and opened the door slightly. There was no chain across the door like you would normally expect.

Pelfrey immediately hit the door with his shoulder, yelling 'police' loudly as he moved swiftly into the room.

The two constables immediately followed Pelfrey into the room, guns at the ready.

Inside, Pelfrey checked quickly in the open bathroom door on his right as one of the constables slid further into the small entranceway to the room.

Rory and Cassandra waited outside the room in the hallway, holding their breath. They could hear the officers inside as they opened doors and shouted 'police' loudly. Then everything went quiet.

A voice - Pelfrey - called out loudly after a few moments of silence, "Steele?"

Rory immediately darted into the room, followed quickly by Cassandra.

Pelfrey was coming out a bedroom, "The place is clear," he said as he holstered his gun. The two uniformed constables were coming out of other rooms and they were putting their guns back into their holsters as well.

In the center of the large, luxurious room were two aluminum chairs facing the loud television. The channel was playing cartoons. Tied to the chairs were two men in black leather jackets. Their heads were tilted back and each had a bullet hole in the center of his forehead.

Pelfrey began to pat down the bodies, looking to see if they were carrying anything. He looked at Rory, "Do you recognize those guys?"

Rory nodded as he angled his head to look at the men's faces, "I pretty sure they were the ones outside the convention center, the ones who wanted to throw Cassandra Glynn off the roof. They also followed us to the forensics lab."

Beside him, Cassandra turned white as she looked down at the two men who had been so close to killing her.

Rory saw her discomfort and he put an arm around her shoulders to comfort her.

Pelfrey pushed down the zipper on the black jacket of the first man. He reached inside and pulled out a handgun complete with silencer. He whistled as he handed it to one of the constables.

Rory now had proof of his suspicions back outside that pub. He and Cassandra *would* have been shot to death in the street if they hadn't escaped.

Checking inside the jacket of the second man, Pelfrey pulled out another handgun. "Both are 9 mm pistols," he said as passed it over to the other Constable. He went through their jacket pockets, shirt pockets and patted their pants pockets as well. He shook his head, "That's all they have on them. No identification at all."

"What happened here?" Cassandra asked in a quiet voice.

Pelfrey shook his head again.

Rory offered a suggestion, "Maybe they were shot because they didn't take care of Cassandra?"

This time Pelfrey shrugged.

One of the young constables spoke up, "That bullet hole looks like it was done with a .22 caliber weapon. That makes it more like a professional hit instead of a whack job by drug runners."

Pelfrey nodded in agreement as he took out his cell phone, "He's right. That's not typically what we see with these kind of guys." He began punching in a phone number.

"Who would want to do a professional hit on these guys? And why?" Rory asked.

"I have no idea," Pelfrey added as he waited for someone to answer his call. "But this just added a whole new level of strange to an already strange case."

Chapter 29

CASSANDRA AND RORY headed back to the coffee shop at the front of the convention center. Detective John Pelfrey and the two constables had stayed behind in room 92 waiting for a team of Forensic Identification Officers. They had just finished processing the rest of the Larrise Abbatiello crime scene and were still in the convention center. Cassandra and Rory sipped coffee as they watched the continuing buzz and rumors in the lobby. No one was leaving and no one was going to bed. If anything, the lobby and the streets out front were becoming more and more crowded. News reporters had definitely grown in numbers.

TIME PASSED SLOWLY but before long Pelfrey came hustling into the coffee shop. He held up his cell phone as he approached them, "I've got the guys on the phone again," he said. He sat with Rory and Cassandra and placed his phone in the middle of the table, setting it to speaker, "So, what have we got now guys?"

Sepulveda's voice came across, "A lot. We finally processed all the rooms for the original crime scene. Despite someone trying to clean up, we found traces blood evidence that someone had tracked into the bathroom. The blood evidence in there had already started to coagulate. Which means someone stepped into the blood of the original crime scene and tracked it about an hour later into the bathroom."

"That would be the time that I entered the room!" Cassandra said.

"Correct. Once you headed to Larrise Abbatiello's room, they had the perfect opportunity to cover their tracks and frame you for the murder. After the put you to sleep temporarily, they probably hid in the bathroom when the crowd of witnesses came in and saw you on the floor. Then they probably slipped out and blended into the crowd once you ran."

Cassandra moaned, "You're telling me I helped to cover their escape?"

Rory put a hand on her arm. "Don't beat yourself up over it. You had no choice."

MacKinnon's voice came over the speaker, "The forensics guys are still working in room 92, but they tell me they found traces of blood on the bottom of the right boot of Cesar Santana. They've already sent it over to the lab and they're working to verify it now. But I'm pretty sure he's the one who killed Larrise Abbatiello. They also found a small bottle of chloroform on his partner, Teo Luna."

"That's probably what they used to knock me out," Cassandra said.

"It looks like it," MacKinnon said. "Interpol has suspected these two were involved in a number of kidnappings and murders for years. They have probably had a lot of practice with this stuff and knew exactly how much to use on you to keep you out for just a brief moment."

Cassandra shook her head softly, "But why would they kill Larrise? Even if she accidentally wandered into room 92, thinking it was her room and saw them, I doubt she knew they were men in a drug gang from Columbia, It doesn't make any sense."

"We think we know the motive," Sepulveda said. "One of the first pieces of forensic evidence sent back in a rush to the lab from room 92 were fingerprints from several coffee cups they found in the wastebasket. Interpol has told us they will work at light speed on the DNA to confirm who we believe was in that hotel room."

"Cut through the suspense," Rory said. "Who was it?"

MacKinnon spoke very slowly like the words were burning his tongue, "Neron Blanco Soto."

Cassandra's eyes grew wide, "The drug lord? *He* was in room 92?"

"That's what the evidence points to. If she accidentally walked into the room 92 and saw Neron Blanco Soto, he would never have hesitated to have her killed. Over the years, his picture has been in the news all over the world and he couldn't take a chance."

Rory rubbed the stubble on his chin, "At least some part of this is starting to make sense. When I first encountered the two men tracking Cassandra, they were talking about throwing her off the roof. Soto probably ordered a hit on her to cover their tracks on Larrise Abbatiello. It would look like Cassandra was overtaken with grief and committed suicide by jumping from the roof of the convention center."

"That's how we see it too," Sepulveda said. "The case would've been closed with the apparent murderer committing suicide."

Cassandra asked a pertinent question, "I can understand all that. But *why* were his two men shot dead in that room? Wouldn't "

There was silence all around and the question hung in the air.

MacKinnon offered a theory after a moment, "Maybe they were shot because they failed to kill you after all? Neron Blanco Soto is known to be very ruthless. He wouldn't hesitate to kill anyone, including his own men who failed to carry out his orders."

Cassandra shook her head, "But that doesn't make any sense. At least not to me. Why shoot them and leave them in his own room? Don't these types of guys usually dumped them in the alley or something like that?"

There was a period of silence again.

Sepulveda spoke up quietly after another moment," Actually, that's a very good question, Mrs. Glynn. It's one me and Cam wondered about."

Rory looked at Pelfrey, "Didn't you and the constables conclude it looks like a professional hit, rather than the brutal murders these guys usually perform?"

After a few moments of thinking, Pelfrey said, "He's right, Cam. Both Flynn and Esposito agree it doesn't look like a normal whack job. They were done with a 22 caliber weapon. That's a tool for a quiet hit man. In my experience, drug runners usually do their hits in a violent and bloody way to send a message. A professional hit like this just isn't Soto's style."

Rory spread his hands apart, "So why were there two dead bodies - hitman style - in Soto's room?"

There was silence for a moment and then MacKinnon spoke up again, "Maybe somebody else is trying to send a message to Soto."

"Maybe one of his own crew did it. Maybe someone is trying to take over," Sepulveda offered.

"That's a possibility," admitted Pelfrey.

"And here's another question for you," Rory said. "How did Neron Blanco Soto get into this country in the first place? And why is he here at all?"

"That I can't answer yet," MacKinnon said, "but we also received some information that links Soto and his crew to another part of our puzzle."

"Which part is that?" Rory asked.

"One of the Forensic Identification Officers called me on my cell just before we started talking. He is very observant and noticed something strange that he wanted to explain to me since it was going to be in his report."

Pelfrey smiled, "That has to be Tiny. What did have to say, Cam?"

"He said he noticed Teo Luna had an area of skin disease on his right hand. Tiny saw the same thing in a couple of previous cases of people who had used a certain staining compound in a biological laboratory."

"What was the compound?"

"Picric acid," MacKinnon stated.

Rory straightened up in his seat, "That's the compound Sebastyen Pipes said he found on Bryson Glynn's car." When he suddenly realized what he had said, he looked at Cassandra.

Tears were welling up in Cassandra's eyes as she said, "I can understand Soto killing Larrise - if she saw him. And I can understand why Soto and his men would try to frame me and then try to kill me. But why would this Neron Blanco Soto character have my husband and my children killed? They had nothing to do with him. And why would it happen six months before Larrise accidentally stumbled into his room? That doesn't make any sense."

"No, it doesn't," Sepulveda agreed.

"I have another question," Rory said after a moment, "why would Cesar Santana and Teo Luna wait around in the room for one hour after they killed Larrise Abbatiello - just to frame Cassandra?"

"He's right guys," Pelfrey said after a moment. "That doesn't make any sense at all."

"I agree. These guys were seasoned, professional killers," Sepulveda said. "Since they were simply going to kill a witness, they wouldn't have to search the room. So they wouldn't have any reason to stay around. And since no one knew about Larrise Abbatiello's death until Mrs. Glynn arrived an hour later, they had probably already made a clean getaway."

Rory tapped the table with a finger, "So who was it that told them that Cassandra Glynn was headed to Larrise Abbatiello's room? Who told them that she was in a foul mood and could easily be framed for the murder?"

Cassandra grimaced at the 'foul mood' comment but asked another question, "And why me in the first place? I didn't know about *any* of this. And there is no reason to ever believe I did."

Chapter 30

AFTER THE CALL ENDED, Pelfrey got up from the table, his jaw set with determination, "I'm going back up to see Tiny in room 92. Maybe he's coming up with more answers that might help us to fit this friggin' jigsaw puzzle together."

Rory watched him disappear into the lobby crowd. Then he looked over at Cassandra. She was dabbing a napkin against her long black eyelashes. "Are you okay?" he asked her.

Cassandra nodded as she collected herself.

"I saw a washroom down past the computer room we were in. Are you okay if I go use it?"

Cassandra nodded, "Yes. Go. I'll be okay."

"I'll be fast," Rory said as he left the table. He crossed the lobby through the crowd and headed down the hallway towards the computer room. Passing the glass wall that housed the computers, Rory pushed open the public washroom door and went inside. The smell of disinfectant soap mixed with urinal cakes. Walking over to one of the sinks, he turned the cold water on. Rory was weary as he bent over and splashed water on his face several times. His mind went back over everything that had happened, trying to figure out what exactly was going on–

A gun was pressed against his neck on the right side.

A man with a heavy Spanish - Colombian? - accent spoke, "You are the one who killed Cesar and Teo?"

Cold water dripped from his face as Rory stayed bent over the white, porcelain sink. The tap was still running, echoing lightly off the walls. Rory kept his voice quiet and calm, "I'm sorry, but I think you have the wrong man."

The man pressed the gun harder into his neck, "No. I just see you, another man and a woman come out of the room. We want to know who killed our friend. Ahora!"

Rory tried to see some way out of this. But it didn't look good. The man knew how to stand and protect himself. If Rory moved a single muscle, he was as good as dead. His mind raced as he tried to think of a way out.

"Who - killed - them? You?" The man cocked the gun hammer in emphasis.

Rory heard the click echo off the washroom walls. He had to think of something fast–

A woman's shrill scream pierced the deadly silence in the washroom.

Out of the corner of his right eye, Rory saw a flash of red streaking for the gunman.

The gunman brought the gun around but it was knocked out of his hand as a mass of red landed on his back, still screaming.

The gun bounced along the floor, the metallic sound echoing loudly of the tile walls.

Rory immediately rose up from his bent over position, ready to fight but he was stunned by what he saw.

Cassandra was on the gunman's back. Her arms were wrapped around his neck and her long legs were around his waist.

The gunman spun wildly in a hard circle, trying to dislodge the body on his back.

Losing her grip, Cassandra was thrown off, her bare legs flashing as she flew through the air into one of the washroom stalls.

Rory heard her land hard and the toilet flushed.

The door to the stall slowly closed.

Lowering his head, Rory tackled the gunman, driving him into another one of the washroom stalls.

Both of them landed hard against the toilet.

Rory's momentum spun him to the left and he landed hard onto the floor between the toilet and the wall of the stall.

The man whirled around and jumped on Rory.

Rory had expected it and had his foot up. He caught the gunman in the stomach and pushed him away. But the washroom door was closed.

The man smashed up against it, giving him the opportunity to drive himself back down on Rory. He connected with a fist to Rory's jaw.

Rory sagged, stunned by the blow.

The man was up in a flash and opened the stall door.

Rory fought to get back on his feet, knowing the man was heading for his gun. Finally pulling the stall door open, Rory realized he was too late.

The man found his gun on the washroom floor, picked it up and spun around to aim it at Rory's midsection.

Another flash of red smashed into the gunman, driving him back over the row of sinks. The gun flew out of his hand again, clinking off a faucet and then the porcelain sink before landing on the washroom floor tiles. The man swung a backhanded blow at Cassandra.

Cassandra was knocked back, regained her balance and rushed at the man again, her red dress swishing hard with the movement.

The man had turned, leaned back against the porcelain sink and lifted both his feet. He caught Cassandra in the stomach and pushed hard.

Cassandra was thrown right back into the washroom stall she had come out of.

Rory pounced on the man in an instant.

But the man was quick and a veteran of barroom brawls. He used Rory's momentum against him and Rory found himself sliding across the cold tiles of the washroom floor on his back.

The gunman turned and went for the gun. He bent down and came up with the gun in a flash, turning and pointing it at Rory.

Rory waited to feel the bullet penetrate his heart.

Crack!

Chapter 31

A LARGE PIECE of porcelain came down on the gunman's head from his left side. The man seemed to freeze in a painful grimace for a moment and then he dropped straight to the floor.

Cassandra Glynn was standing outside the washroom stall, the rectangular porcelain top from the toilet tank in her two hands.

Rory scrambled around on the washroom floor to the man and checked for a pulse. "He's dead. You probably fractured his skull."

"Well," Cassandra said between heavy breaths, "I did catch him flush."

Rory couldn't help but smile and he relaxed. He stood up and put a hand on her arm, "Are you okay?"

Cassandra looked at him and nodded.

"You just killed a man," Rory said gently. "That can be traumatic–"

"I know I should feel something," Cassandra said, "and maybe I will later. But right now, I just feel angry at losing my family and my friend and....."

Rory nodded, "Okay. It's probably the adrenalin rush as well. But if this does start to hit you, you talk to me. All right?"

"Yeah." Cassandra looked at the porcelain tank top, looked left and right as if she was looking for someplace to put it - then she turned and went back into the stall.

Kneeling beside the body, Rory began to pat the pockets as he heard the clinking of the porcelain top being set back in place - a wire at the man's shoulder caught his attention. He took the wire in his fingers. It disappeared under the man's collar and Rory immediately knew what it was. Cassandra's legs appeared beside him.

The red dress moved as she straightened it out, then Cassandra bent over, "What's that?"

Rory turned and put a finger to his lips.

"What?"

"Shhh."

Cassandra raised her eyebrows.

Rory held the wire tightly in his fingers and yanked. The wire popped out from under the man's collar and Rory tossed it to the side.

"What–?" Cassandra whispered, "What was that?"

"It's okay now. That was a radio earpiece."

"You mean like secret service stuff?"

"Yeah. This looks like one of the men we saw in the lobby. I don't remember any of them wearing an earpiece."

Cassandra shook her head, "No, I never noticed anything like that either. Course, I was petrified most of the time."

"I think you've done well. Let's see what else he has on him." Rory began to check through the pockets of the dead man.

"Maybe he is CSIS. You know - with the earpiece thing and all?"

"Maybe. But the way, thanks for coming to the rescue. How did you know?"

Cassandra shrugged, "Just lucky, I guess. I realized it was dumb not using the washroom while you were and I hurried to catch up to you. I caught a glimpse of a man in a black leather jacket going into the men's washroom. I just *knew* it was one of them."

"You took a real chance, but thanks."

"I was so mad for Larrise, I didn't think. I just attacked," Cassandra said.

Rory didn't find a thing in the man's pockets. He ran his hands down the front of the man's leather jacket and felt something. He pulled the zipper down on the leather jacket and felt on the inside. He found a zippered pocket. He undid the zipper and pulled out a booklet with a maroon colored cover.

Cassandra leaned over, "Is that a passport?"

Rory nodded. "A Canadian passport."

Cassandra shook her head, "No. It can't be. Canadian passports are navy colored."

"The gold lettering says this one is a diplomatic passport," Rory said. He underlined the lettering beneath the center crest with his finger.

"Why would a Colombian citizen have a Canadian *diplomatic* passport? Especially with his known background? He was in the Interpol database."

"He must've stolen it from someone," Rory replied.

"Impossible," Cassandra insisted. "Since 2009, diplomatic passports in Canada are what they call electronic passports. The biometric data would be nearly impossible to change. I could him see him doing it with a regular passport, but a diplomatic one would be extremely difficult."

Rory opened up the passport. He tapped the picture and looked at the face of the dead man, "Okay, but this *is* his picture. The name reads Alonzo Pizarro. That doesn't sound like any of the names from the Interpol report MacKinnon mentioned, does it?"

"No, you're right. That doesn't sound like any of the names. Maybe he's another member of the gang?"

That's a possibility." Rory flipped through the pages, "According to the stamps, this guy's gone back and forth between Canada and South America a number of times. He's even been to the United States and England. That would explain how these guys were able to get in and out of the country without being flagged."

Cassandra crossed her arms, "That's hard to believe."

"I agree," Rory said, "but it's all here in black-and-white...and maroon." Rory closed the passport and tapped it against his chin as he looked down at the body. "Why would someone need a diplomatic passport in the first place?"

"If they're a diplomat."

"I know. Who else? CSIS?"

Cassandra pondered that, "It's possible if he was the head of the Service. More than likely they would have a special green passport. That's also used by people in the Privy Council, Premiers of Provinces–"

"Stick to the diplomatic one. Who else?"

"Consular officials. Canadian officials going to diplomatic international conferences–"

That last one struck home with Rory, "How about a diplomatic courier?"

"Yes, diplomatic couriers have them," Cassandra said. "Why?"

"What do diplomatic couriers do?" he asked as he looked up at Cassandra.

Cassandra thought for a minute, "They usually carry diplomatic letters or correspondence. Usually in a diplomatic pouch or diplomatic bag. Why?"

"Take a look at his left wrist," Rory said.

Cassandra bent over and looked at the man's wrist, "It looks to be chafed. Like something like a bracelet was around it and rubbing."

"If a diplomatic courier were carrying something particularly sensitive - you know - guard with your life stuff - what would they do?"

Cassandra thought for a minute and then stood up, putting a hand to her mouth, "They would chain it to their wrist!"

Rory nodded. He pulled out his cell phone and called Detective MacKinnon.

"MacKinnon."

"It's Rory Mack Steele," he said quickly. "I'm with Mrs. Glynn. There's been a bit of a development here."

"What's that?"

"We just had a run-in with someone who I think it another one of Soto's men," Rory explained.

MacKinnon sounded concerned, "What happened?"

"He tried to kill us," Rory said, "we got him first."

"I'm sorry that had to happen. Is Mrs. Glynn okay?"

"Yes, she is," Rory said, "but our problems still keep mounting. This dead Colombian in front of me had a Canadian diplomatic passport on him."

"A *diplomatic* passport! Are you sure?"

"It's the right color and that's what it says on the front of the passport," Rory answered. "And this is definitely one of the Colombians I saw in the lobby earlier. The picture in the passport is his face. The name on it says he is Alonzo Pizarro. But I don't think that was one of the names you mentioned earlier."

"No. It doesn't sound familiar," MacKinnon said, "it may be an alias. I'll have pictures sent down to Detective Pelfrey. He can figure out who you have there."

"Okay," Rory said, "I'll let him know what happened here."

"He must have stolen someone's diplomatic passport," MacKinnon said.

"Cassandra says it's nearly impossible to change these new electronic passports," Rory replied.

"Nearly, but not totally impossible," MacKinnon said. "If this guy *was* part of Soto's organization, they would have the money and resources to buy equipment to manipulate the data. Or simply bribe someone, so it's not out of the question. But the other question is...why in the world would he have a *diplomatic* passport and not just a regular one? A regular one would be much easier to get or forge."

Rory looked down at the dead man's wrist again, "I have a theory. We noticed he has red chafing on his wrist. It would suggest to me that this guy was carrying something he chained or handcuffed to his wrist. And his passport stamps show he's been flying in and out of the country...just like a diplomatic courier."

MacKinnon's voice thundered across the call, "Someone involved with drugs, traveling as a diplomatic courier. That's all we need!"

Chapter 32

IT WASN'T LONG before Detective Pelfrey rushed into the washroom. He was followed closely by Constables Flynn and Esposito. Rory was leaning back with his butt against one of the white sinks. Cassandra's body was leaning right against Rory's as she dabbed a damp paper towel tenderly against a cut on his lip.

"Am I interrupting anything?" Pelfrey asked as he came to an abrupt stop. Flynn and Esposito bumped into him from behind.

Cassandra straightened up, turned to look at Pelfrey and raised an eyebrow, "No. Why?"

Pelfrey held his arms up in mock surrender, "Oh, nothing."

Cassandra crossed her arms over her chest, her green eyes throwing darts at Pelfrey, "Uh, huh. Men jump to conclusions easily, don't they?"

Pulling a face, Pelfrey walked over to the body lying on the floor.

Flynn moved in with the detective, squatted down and checked the pulse in the neck.

Rory pulled the dead man's passport from his back pocket, walked over and passed it over to Pelfrey, "This is what he had on him."

Pelfrey opened the passport and looked at the picture, then looked down at the body to compare. He flipped through the pages quickly before closing it and putting it in the side pocket of his crumpled jacket, "I didn't want to believe it when Cam told me."

"What now?" Rory asked.

"Let's all go outside into the hallway."

Rory, Cassandra, and the two constables left the washroom behind Pelfrey. Outside, the detective turned to Constable Esposito, "You and Flynn secure the washroom, make sure no one goes in. I'll get a forensics team sent down here."

"Yes, sir."

Pelfrey gestured to Rory and Cassandra as he started walking, "You two can come with me."

Rory held his arm out, giving her a smile.

Cassandra wrinkled her nose at him and held on, allowing herself to be escorted down the hallway.

As they walked, Pelfrey turned and passed a room key card back to each of them, "Here you go."

Rory looked at the key card before slipping it into a pocket, "What are these for?"

"You'll see. Just have patience."

Cassandra slipped hers into the small pocket on her dress.

Up ahead, three men in suits were walking toward them. One of the men was reading a text out loud from a cell phone he held. One other man was listening and nodding from time to time while the third trailed slightly behind.

Pelfrey moved his hand up to his suit jacket, obviously ready to pull his weapon.

Rory and Cassandra all went on alert as well, moving to the right in the wide hallway. As the three men drew closer, it became apparent another person - a Latino woman with short black hair and dark, hard eyes - was just behind them.

The Latino woman put a hand up near her ear, lowered it, slowed her pace, and narrowed her gaze.

Cassandra let go of Rory's arm and stepped behind him. She lifted a hand to her eye and pretended to rub it as she shielded her face from scrutiny.

Rory was sure the woman was staring at Cassandra. He moved just a bit to his left to block her line of sight.

The woman smoothly turned around and walked back down the hallway.

As the men drew alongside them, the man doing the listening looked down the hallway. Noting the two police officers, he asked Pelfrey, "What's going on up there?"

"Aw, just a couple of drunks getting into an argument," Pelfrey said offhandedly. His hand was still ready to pull his weapon.

The man just shook his head and returned to talking with the other man as the three continued on.

Pelfrey kept walking, looking back over his shoulder. When nothing transpired, he lowered his hand, relaxing, "I'll have to make sure the forensic team keeps a low profile as they come up here. No need to attract more attention than necessary while we get this all figured out."

Rory looked back, still wanting to make sure the men continued on past the officers. They did.

Cassandra moved back up beside Rory. As they walked past the computer room, she glanced through the glass wall.

The young Latino woman was just standing in the room, staring intently at Cassandra as she passed.

Turning her face away, Cassandra muttered, "Crap."

Rory noticed the woman from the corner of his eye as well and grimaced, "Do you think she recognized you?"

"I don't think so."

"I know the men didn't. They weren't looking at your face."

"Very funny," Cassandra complained.

"Just trying to help," Rory said.

Cassandra glanced back briefly over her shoulder, looking troubled, "At least...I don't think she recognized me. Now that I think about it...I think I saw that young woman with Demario Gomez earlier."

Rory glanced back, "The retired hockey player?"

Cassandra's voice was bitter, "Yeah. He's the one who was chosen to run in the riding over me. I think she's his girlfriend."

Rory shook is head, "No, I don't think so. More likely a body-guard."

"A bodyguard? You're kidding right?"

Rory shook his head again, "No. She was on full alert as she was walking our way, like someone heavily trained in martial arts. A lot of royalty and celebrities prefer to use a woman these days. They blend in much better, especially if they have young children. And the last thing you want to do in a fancy restaurant is have some big lug attracting attention."

Cassandra glanced back over her shoulder again.

The young woman was in the doorway now, still staring at Cassandra. She turned and headed in the direction of the con-stables.

Watching her for a moment, Cassandra then faced ahead and latched onto Rory's arm again.

Chapter 33

PELFREY LED THEM back across the lobby and up the hallway towards room 92. The door to 92 was open and flanked by two uniformed police constables. The sounds of hustle and bustle from forensic techs filtered through the doorway.

"Give me a minute," Pelfrey said. He passed between the two uniformed police constables and entered the room.

Cassandra crossed her arms and turned away from the gaze of the two officers.

A few minutes later, Pelfrey came out of room 92 and walked over to room 91 across the hall. He slid a key card into the lock, opening the door. "The key cards I gave you are for this room." He gestured for Rory and Cassandra to go on inside. Once they did, he followed them into room 91, closing the door behind him.

The room was large with a bathroom just inside the entrance, a small kitchen area and 2 doors leading off to bedrooms. On the other side of the room were a number of whiteboard stands filled with pictures and notes. In the center of the room was a long coffee table flanked by sofas on either side. On the table were two large coffee pots, surrounded by white ceramic mugs, several plates of sandwiches and donuts.

"How long have you had this set up?" Rory asked as he looked around the room.

"We just did it," Pelfrey. "When you told MacKinnon the Colombian who attacked you in the washroom had a diplomatic passport, he figured it was time we had a place to serve as a command post down here. It's away from prying eyes in case these guys have inside sources. But it also gives you two a safe place to stay."

"Thank you," Rory said, "this is a lot better than the coffee shop. Right?" He looked at Cassandra.

"Yes, it is," Cassandra said, "thank you, Detective Pelfrey."

"You're welcome, Mrs. Glynn. MacKinnon and Sepulveda emailed all their notes, along with pictures of the Colombians we got from Interpol and I got them printed out. I got these whiteboards from the convention center to hold everything as you can see."

Rory walked over to the whiteboards and looked at the series of pictures.

Pelfrey pulled out the dead man's passport and opened it. He walked over for a closer look at the pictures on the whiteboards as well. He tapped the passport on one of the pictures, "Orlin Delacruz. This is definitely him."

Cassandra walked up behind them, looking at the pictures.

Pelfrey turned and looked at her, "Do you recognize anybody else on these boards?"

Taking a step closer, Cassandra looked over the photographs, examining each one carefully. After a few moments, she shook her head, "No, I'm sorry. I don't recognize anybody, except the three dead guys. And I don't remember ever seeing those three guys before in my life either."

"Was your husband ever involved with any government initiatives involving drug running or drug dealing? Maybe these guys didn't like their business being targeted and they took revenge. We see that happening all the time in the drug trade."

Cassandra thought for a few minutes and then slowly shook her head again, "No. The government does have some anti-drug initiatives but I don't recall Bryson ever being involved directly with any of it. If he didn't discuss what he was doing with me directly, it was usually in the newspapers. Unless it was all done in secret, he was never involved with anything like that, as far as I know."

"The only other explanation would be an accidental meeting, maybe something like road rage or...."

Cassandra and Rory just looked at him.

Pelfrey realized they were staring at him. He just shrugged, "Don't mind me, I'm just throwing stupid ideas out there and seeing what sticks. Nothing else makes any sense in this whole thing."

Cassandra looked over at the table, "Could I have a sandwich?" I just realized I haven't eaten in ages."

"Oh, of course, Mrs. Glynn. I'm sorry. That's also why we got this room. Detective MacKinnon and Detective Sepulveda will be joining us to use this as a command center. Help yourself, please."

Cassandra and Rory each took a sandwich and a cup, sat down and began to eat. Pelfrey joined them on the other sofa, placing his cell phone on the coffee table. Rory poured them all some coffee. Each took turns using the bathroom. As they were sipping coffee and donuts, Pelfrey's cell phone rang. He simply pressed the speaker-phone button, "Pelfrey. You're on speaker."

"It's Cam, John," MacKinnon said.

Police sirens could be heard wailing in the background through the speaker.

Cassandra, Rory, and Pelfrey exchanged glances of alarm.

Sliding forward on the sofa, Pelfrey's voice was filled with concern, "What's happening, Cam? What's up with the sirens?"

"We're not going to be able to meet you down there right now. We're headed up to the airport. The Bolo we put out on those guys turned up a sighting. Airport security spotted Damian Delatorre getting out of a limo up there."

Pelfrey shot up out of his seat, "I'll be there as soon as I can!"

Rory and Cassandra stood up, ready to go as well.

"No, no, you sit tight," MacKinnon said, "we'll be okay, but thanks for the offer. Did you identify who attacked Mr. Steele and Mrs. Glynn?"

"It was one of the Colombian nationals we saw in the lobby when I first came down here. It was Orlin Delacruz."

"Okay, good," MacKinnon said, "I was afraid we might have some extra players we didn't know about. That leaves Jacinto Ruvalcaba, Esquevelle Villasenor and Neron Blanco Soto himself still unaccounted for. The last time they were seen was there at the convention center. That's why I want you to stay there, John."

"You sure? I can be up there in a flash to help."

"I know, but we need someone there I can trust. One other thing, John. Did we ever check to see if the convention center has any videotape of the hallways or of the entrances?"

Pelfrey thought for a minute, "If I remember correctly, Tiny said they checked into that for the original crime scene. And then for room 92. But somebody had erased all the relevant tapes."

"Figures. Can't catch a break in this case at all. Check and see what else they have at the front desk. Maybe you can spot these characters somewhere else in the convention center. We need to be proactive and stop them before they can try and strike again."

"You got it," Pelfrey said, "anything else?"

"No. I gotta go. If Sepulveda doesn't crash this thing we should be there in a minute." They could hear Sepulveda complaining in the background.

Pelfrey ended the call. Then he picked up the cell phone and headed for the door, "I'm going down to see the convention manager. You folks make yourself comfortable. I'll be back when I can."

As the door closed, Rory looked at Cassandra, "You want to freshen up? Maybe take a shower while we're waiting?"

Cassandra crossed her arms and raised an eyebrow, "Yeah. And I'm sure you're going to want to maintain the *close contact* theme you've been insisting on."

Rory pushed his eyebrows together, "I wasn't suggesting anything remotely like that." His face lit up, "But you definitely have a great idea there."

"You come anywhere that bathroom and UPS will be delivering your package in bits and pieces."

Chapter 34

TORONTO INTERNATIONAL Airport

DETECTIVE SEPULVEDA BROUGHT the police cruiser to a skidding stop in front of the airport terminal. She jumped from the driver side door and headed around to the other side, sprinting for the terminal door. The crowd immediately split apart for the short, athletic Hispanic woman with the piercing eyes. Detective MacKinnon jumped out from the passenger side and barreled through the crowd after his partner with a far less athletic gait.

They were met inside by several members of the airport security team. A tall, tough-looking security officer stepped forward, "MacKinnon and Sepulveda?"

"That's us," Sepulveda said.

MacKinnon just nodded when he caught up, his mouth open, out of breath.

"I'm Chad Hobbs, head of security. The suspect has passed through customs and is headed for one of the departure gates. We have not approached him as you asked. I have a single officer keeping an eye on him to minimize the chance of him getting suspicious."

"Good, good," MacKinnon said between breaths. "I want this son of a bitch taken alive, if at all possible. But keep in mind he is extremely dangerous. I don't want anybody taking any unnecessary risks, understand?"

Hobbs nodded, "I hear you. But we have a problem, Detective. This man had a diplomatic passport as well as paperwork that shows he is headed for a plane that *also* has diplomatic clearance and about to depart for the United States. Technically, I'm unable to touch him."

MacKinnon pulled a photograph and a folded piece of paper from the inside pocket of his sports coat. He thrust the picture at Hobbs, "Does this look like the person you have your officer watching?"

Hobbs took the picture, looked at it for a moment and then nodded yes.

MacKinnon unfolded the paper and thrust it at the officer's eyes, "This is an e-mail printout from Interpol identifying him as Damian Delatorre, a Colombian gunman working for Neron Blanco Soto, the Colombian drug lord."

Taking the note in hand, Hobbs read it. Then he thrust the note and the picture back to MacKinnon. He pointed at the escalator behind him and to the left, "This way." Hobbs then took off at a run.

MacKinnon and Sepulveda sprinted for the escalator behind him.

Ten other security officers followed behind them. The entire group ran hard up the escalator and turned to the left into the hallway at the top. Turning right, they went down another long open hallway until Hobbs turned them left and escorted the two detectives through customs. From there, they all turned right and hurried down a terminal wing with a series of exit gates on both sides.

Sepulveda looked around at all the people walking or sitting in the various lounge areas of the gates, "Cam, we have to see if we can get these people out of the way first."

MacKinnon nodded. But before they could act they saw Damian Delatorre up ahead.

Delatorre was looking back over his shoulder, now aware of all the uniformed officers moving down the corridor towards him. The Colombian was carrying a briefcase chained to his left wrist. There was a woman just walking past him and Delatorre moved without hesitation. He lifted the briefcase and placed his left arm around the woman's chest, pulling her up against him as a shield. His right hand came up holding a handgun that he pressed firmly against her temple.

Hobbs gestured to his men and the security officers immediately spread out to the left and right, seeking cover and preparing for a hostage situation.

MacKinnon and Sepulveda drew their weapons and also moved to the left and right respectively and about fifty feet away from the Colombian gunman.

A woman screamed somewhere and all the passengers began to scatter away from the man with the gun.

"I have diplomatic immunity," Delatorre yelled in a heavy Spanish accent in the middle of the chaos. "You cannot touch me."

"Yeah, well I have measles immunity," MacKinnon yelled back, "and it's worth about as much. Put the gun down. Now."

"Back away or I shoot this woman," Delatorre threatened. He began to slowly pull the woman towards the exit gate on his left.

MacKinnon and Sepulveda slowly advanced forward, moving at the same speed as the Colombian backing towards the gate with the woman.

"Drop the gun," MacKinnon yelled again.

Sepulveda noticed a large Lear jet was sitting at the end of the jet bridge for the gate Delatorre was heading for. She yelled at him. "Even if you get on that plane Delatorre, it won't be allowed to take off."

Delatorre looked at her sharply. For the first time, he realized they knew exactly who he was. He fired his weapon into the air.

MacKinnon, Sepulveda and all of the other officers nearby, instinctively ducked.

A man had been hiding behind one of the seats in the waiting area opposite Delatorre. He jumped up to run and the Colombian gunmen quickly turned his weapon towards the man and fired. The bullet hit the fleeing passenger in the back and he collapsed to the floor.

A woman hiding behind the row of seats to Delatorre's right screamed.

Delatorre swung the gun in her direction and fired.

She fell with a bullet hole in the middle of her forehead.

MacKinnon swore as he looked for a shot.

Delatorre moved backward quickly, still holding his hostage as a shield. He neared the jet bridge towards the waiting aircraft.

Sepulveda glanced at her partner, "I have a partial shot. Should I take it?"

Considering it, MacKinnon shook his head, "No. Too risky from this range. See if you can move over a bit more."

Nodding, Sepulveda slid more to her right.

Delatorre moved into the jet bridge against the left wall. One shot to the temple and Delatorre's hostage began to fall slowly towards the floor as the Colombian gunman disappeared down the jet bridge.

Sepulveda swore. As MacKinnon moved forward, she did the same. They took up positions on either side of the doorway to the jet bridge. They both peered around the edge, looking for Delatorre– the ducked back.

A gunshot rang out.

Hobbs was quickly beside MacKinnon and pulled the body of the hostage from the jet bridge entrance. He checked the pulse in her neck, looked up at MacKinnon and shook his head no.

MacKinnon cursed.

Hobbs got up and stood beside MacKinnon, gesturing with a thumb to the windows, "I could see into the parked aircraft. It looks to me like someone else on board has a gun to the pilot's head. I think they're going to try and take off. I've alerted the tower to cease all traffic in and out of the airport."

"Good. Too many deaths here already."

"What about the pilot?"

MacKinnon shook his head, "I doubt they'll shoot him. If they do, they can't take off and we storm the plane."

Sepulveda called over, "What now Cam?"

Blowing out a breath, MacKinnon looked back to Hobbs, "This is your airport. Any ideas?"

It was Hobbs' turn to shake his head, "I got nothing. Never been in anything like this."

The whining sound of plane's engines starting up echoed down the jet bridge

Sepulveda peered around the edge and then called across, "Hobbs? It's going to take them a couple of minutes to get this jet bridge unhooked from the plane. Can we get outside to another door on the plane? Take them from both sides?"

Hobbs shook his head, "Not really. We can give it a try, but once that plane is ready to move, they could just rip free of the jet bridge. By the time we get to the exit and outside, we'd be chasing them down the tarmac."

MacKinnon grimaced at the information. Then he looked at his partner on the other side. He made a gesture with his head to the jet bridge opening.

Sepulveda nodded in understanding, "You ready for the charge of the light brigade?"

"Ready when you are."

When Hobbs realized what they were talking about, he leaned out, "You guys are nuts."

Sepulveda smiled, "Tell my partner something he doesn't already know."

MacKinnon gave her a wink. Then - with a nod to each other - the two detectives were running in a low crouch down each side of the jet bridge. They came to the short left turn in the jet bridge and they stopped.

Sepulveda counted to three and they both leaped out and around the corner.

Delatorre was working frantically to disengage the jet bridge. He was having difficulty because he was holding the gun in one hand and the other was restricted by the chained briefcase around the wrist. Delatorre saw the two detectives, raised his gun and fired.

MacKinnon and Sepulveda fell to the floor of the jet bridge and returned fire.

Shot after shot rang out from both sides.

Delatorre was hit repeatedly and he stumbled backward as his handgun continued to fire into the air. He collapsed - body inside the Lear jet - legs splayed outside.

The two detectives were about to get up when another man appeared beside the fallen body in the doorway. Both detectives tried to fire but their guns just clicked, they were out of bullets.

The man on the plane took aim at Sepulveda–

Gunshots rang out.

Hit by dozens of bullets, the gunman suddenly danced like a marionette.

The gunshots stopped.

In slow motion, the gunman collapsed on top of the dead Damian Delatorre.

MacKinnon and Sepulveda rolled over onto their backs to look behind them.

Standing there with smoking weapons were a half-dozen security officers. Hobbs was in the middle of them.

Hobbs looked down at the two detectives, "I still think you guys are nuts."

Chapter 35

RORY AND CASSANDRA tried hard to relax in the room once Detective Pelfrey left. Rory turned the television on but he only half listened to the talking heads that were reporting on the day's extraordinary events at the convention center and the forensic lab. Cassandra ate a few more sandwiches and sipped some Dow and Egbert coffee but she was fidgety.

Cassandra's cup clinked on the saucer as she put it down, "We haven't sat on the sidelines since this started and I can't help but feel we should be doing something."

Rory switched off the television, "Yeah, I feel the same way."

"Why don't we go down to the front desk and see if Detective Pelfrey has found some surveillance video to look through. Maybe we can help. I'd feel better than just sitting here waiting and doing nothing."

Rory stood up, "Okay. Why don't we just do that."

"Thank you," Cassandra said, "we've been a good team so far."

Heading for the door, Rory nodded. "I agree with you, Red. We've been a good team."

"Red?"

"Okay. Blackie then. You fight more like a Blackie, anyway. Especially with that wig." He opened the door for her.

Cassandra shook her head no and wagged a finger in front of his face as she passed through the open doorway into the hall, "No, no, no. I don't do nicknames well."

Rory let the door close and held his arm out.

Grabbing his arm, Cassandra let out a sigh, "I think you're taking this a little too far, Steele. I think you're just getting a thrill walking around with a pretend hooker on your arm."

"The best-looking hooker on the premises."

Cassandra's cheeks flushed, "I'm not sure if that's a compliment or - forget it. Let's go."

The lobby was still filled with a milling crowd as the duo moved across to the front desk. Keeping his voice low, Rory asked if they knew where Detective Pelfrey was. When told he was in the security office in the back, Rory asked if someone could let him know they here and if they could join him. A female staff member disappeared through a doorway, returned a few minutes later and asked Rory and Cassandra to follow her. They were led behind the counter and through the door and over to a short hallway and the office for the security personnel. Inside, they found Detective Pelfrey in front of a bank of video monitors. He was running through footage of people moving up and down a hallway.

Pelfrey turned as they came in, "I thought you two would stay in the safety of the room."

"We decided it was better to help," Rory said. "Three pairs of eyes are always better than one."

Looking to Cassandra - who had moved to the side of the room - Pelfrey asked, "Are you sure."

Cassandra crossed her arms and nodded, "Yeah."

Pelfrey sat back in his chair, rubbing his eyes, "Okay. I actually could use some help. My eyes are getting a little blurry looking through all these tapes."

Rory moved beside him, "So what are you trying to do. And how far have you gotten?"

"I'm trying to see if I can find some trace of Neron Blanco Soto, the drug lord. And so far I've got nothing."

Cassandra moved to the other side of the detective, "If I remember correctly, you said there was *nothing* on room 92?"

"That's right. There are cameras that tape throughout the convention center, including down the hallways. But when the forensic team worked with the convention center security earlier, they found someone had wiped out all the tapes for the last couple of days dealing with room 92. So the first thing I did was look through all the outside cameras trained on all the exits to see if he left the convention center. It doesn't look like it. So now I'm looking through the other hallways to see if I can spot him. I've gone through almost all of it and nothing so far. Of course, I'm looking for someone who looks like the old pictures we got from Interpol. The problem is, he could be in disguise. I may have passed right over him."

Rory scratched the stubble on his chin, "You just looked on the main floor?"

"That's right."

Cassandra looked across at Rory, "What are you thinking?"

"This Soto guy had two dead bodies in the room we think he was using. If it was me, I'd be moving to another room."

Pelfrey looked up, "There were a lot of rooms paid for near 92. You think he might be in one of those?"

"Maybe but I doubt it. I'd use a room on a different floor. I'd probably do that right after Larrise walked in."

Cassandra shook her head, "No. But the whole place is booked."

"If he secured a whole block on the main floor, he could have secured rooms elsewhere as a backup." He looked at Pelfrey, "You didn't see him leaving, and you didn't see him in any of the main floor hallways. Right?"

Pelfrey nodded, "Right." He held a finger up, "Presuming I was looking for the right person."

"Have you looked at any video for the elevators?"

Looked down, Pelfrey scratched his forehead, "Actually...no." Pelfrey looked up looked over the console and pushed several buttons. A video popped up, showing one bank of the convention center elevators. Then he reached into an inner pocket of his jacket and pulled out a picture that he held back over his shoulder, "This is the picture they sent us of Neron Blanco Soto."

Cassandra took the picture and she and Rory examined it. Neron Blanco Soto was looking somberly into the camera. He had curly black hair, a pencil-thin mustache, and eyes that looked dark and angry.

Pelfrey put the video on fast-forward and they all watched intently, trying to see someone who resembled the Colombian drug lord. The bank of elevators was in constant use. When they didn't see anything, Pelfrey ran through the video for the second bank of elevators. Still nothing.

"Anything showing the inside of the elevators?" Rory asked.

Pelfrey looked over the console again, "Yeah. There's something on each one."

Cassandra frowned, "That'll take a month of Sundays."

Rory nodded, "Yeah. But it's all we got."

"Maybe I'll see if I can get some coffees."

"I'll do it," Rory said. "You watch with the detective."

When he came back with three coffees, Cassandra was sitting beside Pelfrey, both of them intent on the fast-forwarding view of the inside of an elevator. He set a coffee down in front of each person as he watched the Key-Stone cop movements of people moving in and out of the elevator doors.

After twenty minutes of sipping coffee, and four more videos, Cassandra shot forward in her chair, pointing, "There! Back it up just a bit."

Pelfrey brought the video back slowly–

"There."

He let the video run at normal speed. They all watched as the elevator doors opened and the crowd inside the elevator exited onto the ground floor. A number of people entered the elevator and one man stood out. He entered the elevator holding up a newspaper in a way that tried to hide his face. But as he turned and reached to press one of the floor buttons, the paper came away enough to see his face dead on. Pelfrey froze the frame.

"That man looks older than the picture we have," Rory said." But I swear *that* is Neron Blanco Soto."

"Or his evil twin," Cassandra said.

"He looks close enough for me at this point," Pelfrey said. He let the video run and they watched the man leave the elevator.

"Can you tell which floor he exited on?" Cassandra asked.

"No," Pelfrey said. "But we have the timestamp we can work with. I should be able to find the video for that floor." He worked the board again, punching buttons until he brought up the video for the hallway on the second floor. He fast forwarded to the same time frame and they watched as two people got out.

"Neither one of them is Soto," Rory said.

Pelfrey nodded in agreement and worked the board until he found the third-floor video. He fast forwarded to the same time frame and they saw a man exit the elevator.

"That's him, I'm sure," Cassandra said as she pointed at the screen.

Soto turned right and walked down the hallway. He walked five doors past the elevators. Then he turned right and inserted a key card into the room door. Pelfrey froze the frame. He jumped up and headed out to the front desk.

Rory and Cassandra looked at the man in the frozen video frame.

Cassandra crossed her arms, narrowing her eyes, "So that's the man who may have had my friend killed."

Rory stayed silent.

"And may have ordered to have *me* killed," Cassandra added. She reached out with one hand towards the image, "I wish I could just reach in there and strangle him."

Rory couldn't blame her. He wished he could do the same.

Pelfrey came back quickly with the convention center manager trailing him. He pointed, "That video shows floor three. That man is five doors down from the elevator. Can you tell me the room number?"

The convention center manager was obviously very nervous as he stepped forward and squinted at the video. After a few moments, he nodded, "That would be room 312."

"All right," Pelfrey said to the convention center manager, "unfortunately this is like room 91. I'm working under the same circumstances and I don't need a warrant. I need to know *who* is in that room. And I need a key card for that room, right now. Do you understand?"

The convention center manager held up his hands in compliance, "Of course, these people here are witnesses of what you're telling me, so that puts me in the clear, right?"

Rory and Cassandra both nodded yes as the man looked at them with pleading eyes.

The convention center manager felt satisfied he was in the clear and led them to the front desk area. There he instructed one of the front desk personnel to set up a key card for room 312. He then checked his computer system before turning to Detective Pelfrey.

The manager lowered his voice, speaking in a confidential voice, "That room is part of a block of rooms set aside for the All Candidates Meetings. It's being paid for...by the Canadian Federal Party."

Cassandra frowned, "Are you sure?"

The manager looked nervously at Cassandra. Then he looked back at Pelfrey, "Rooms 310, 312 and 314 were to be used as an after-hours meeting room. The inside connecting doors would be open, allowing people to go back and forth like one large room. Room 312, in the middle, is actually a very large meeting room itself. Key cards were made, but they were not assigned to any specific individual."

Pelfrey nodded in understanding.

The key card for room 312 was handed to the manager - who handed it over to Pelfrey.

Taking the card in hand, Pelfrey turned to Rory and Cassandra, "Probably best if you both wait here this time. This could get dangerous."

"True," Rory said, "but you don't have the two constables with you this time. You may need someone to pull your body out a danger if you get shot."

Pelfrey gave him a light grin and nodded okay.

Cassandra stepped forward, "And I could perform mouth to mouth."

The detective just blinked as he looked at her.

"Hey, don't scare the man," Rory said, "he needs to concentrate."

Cassandra folded her arms across her chest."Oh, really?"

Pelfrey opened his mouth and closed it. Then he said, "Can you two just stay out of the line of fire so I don't lose my pension?"

Chapter 36

THE THREE OF THEM rode the elevator to floor three in silence. The understanding that they may soon be face to face with a murderous drug lord weighed heavily on everyone.

When the elevator stopped, Detective Pelfrey pulled his gun out and prepared himself as the doors started to slide open

The floor outside the elevator was empty and Rory held his hand against the door to make sure it stayed open.

Pelfrey peeked out of the elevator and looked down towards room 312. The hallway was empty except for a yellow janitorial caution sign. The air smelled like the floor had been freshly mopped. Pelfrey glanced back, whispering, "The floor might be wet. Be cautious."

"Oh great," Cassandra grumbled under her breath.

Looking both ways again, Pelfrey then took a step into the hallway, gun held down in both hands.

Rory cautiously stepped out behind him, watching his step.

Cassandra was right behind Rory, her head already held low in anticipation of danger.

Pelfrey went into a combat stance, just a foot off the right wall as taught. Watching the floor for wet spots, he slowly advanced towards room 312. As they neared the room, he glanced back at Rory.

Rory held up the key card, indicating he was ready.

Cassandra's foot slipped - she let out a squeak - slamming her hand against the wall to stay upright.

Both men looked back.

Her eyes widened and Cassandra whispered, "Sorry–"

Rory raised a finger to his lips, "Shhh."

"I said I was sorry."

Pelfrey had the gun up near his shoulder, obviously listening. A moment later, he gave Rory the indication he was moving again. Reaching room 312, Pelfrey stayed on this side of the door, stretched his neck out and listened. Then he ducked down, so no one could see him through the peephole, and stepped across to the far side, holding his gun up at the ready. He nodded at Rory to insert the keycard.

Rory slid the key card into the lock, careful to make the least amount of noise.

The light in the door flashed green, indicating it was now unlocked.

Rory slowly pushed down on the door handle.

Pelfrey slid forward, putting his shoulder against the door. After a brief moment to prepare himself, the detective burst into the room yelling, "Police! Nobody move!"

There was no sound or movement inside the room.

A washroom door was on his right. Pelfrey used his foot to push it open and brought his weapon to bear, sweeping it back and forth as he stepped inside quickly.

It was empty.

Stepping back out, Pelfry then moved forward into the room, sweeping his weapon from side to side.

Rory followed behind while Cassandra held the door open, ready for a quick exit for all three of them.

Pelfrey indicated for Rory to stay put while he moved across the room and out of sight. After a few moments, Pelfrey came back to the entrance way and motioned for Rory and Cassandra to come right inside the room.

"Nobody here," Pelfrey said. "Although somebody was definitely staying here." He pointed to a small cart with a half-eaten dinner on a plate. There were also a number of coffee cups on the small table in front of the sofa.

Rory took in the room - and the cart - and nodded, "Yeah. I bet if we had looked further in the surveillance footage, we would have seen him leaving."

"You're probably right. I should have thought of that, but I wanted to get up here so fast." Pelfrey slipped his weapon back under his rumpled jacket. "I'll get a forensics team up here. Maybe somebody else besides Soto was in here."

Cassandra crept forward, leaning forward, her arms crossed, "Did you notice? The adjoining door between the two hotel rooms is not fully closed–"

Rory heard a sound, turned and flew across the room, knocking Cassandra from in front of the adjoining door–

Three shots rang out. Crack. Crack. Crack.

Slugs splintered through the door, shattering a mirror on the other side of the room.

Pelfrey dove for the floor to the side of the adjoining doorway.

Cassandra screamed as she landed on a long sofa and bounced, Rory on top of her.

Rory pulled her off the sofa and they landed hard on the floor, with Cassandra landing hard on top of him.

Another gunshot sounded and another bullet splintered through the door and buried itself in the wall next to the mirror.

Pelfrey had his gun out and stood up slowly against the wall just beside the doorway. He reached out cautiously to the door handle and pulled the door open, moving out the way and then holding it against the wall.

Another two gunshots sounded and bullets penetrated through the adjoining door and shattered more glass.

Rory slid himself out from underneath Cassandra and scrambled over to sit against the wall beside the doorway and opposite the detective.

Pelfrey yelled, "Police! Throw out your weapon. Now!"

There was no response and no additional gunshots.

Rory slid around to his knees and cautiously peered around the door jam. He could see the adjoining door was open about an inch. He reached his hand around and pushed on the door, then pulled back quickly expecting gunshots.

Nothing happened.

After a moment, Rory peered cautiously through the open doorway into the adjoining room. "It's a long meeting room in there, just like the manager said. I can see the pass-through door on the far side of the room. I think it's open a crack, just like this one was."

Pelfrey peered through the open doorway from his side, "Can you see anyone from your side?"

Rory took another careful look and shook his head, "No. No one. But I see some chairs on your side where someone could be hiding."

Scanning his side for movement, Pelfrey said, "I don't see anyone from this side either. What do you think?"

Rory sat with his back against the wall again and looked around the room. Then he turned crawled on his hands and knees back across the front of the sofa. He grabbed a lamp off the small table beside the sofa and then started crawling back. He spotted Cassandra. She was huddled on her knees just inside the washroom door, her face a mask of fear. Rory gave her a nod of assurance but it didn't do much for her. Placing his back to the wall, he said to Pelfrey, "Let's see what happens."

Pelfrey nodded as he got into a crouch, his weapon held in both hands at the ready.

Rory drew his arm back and heaved the lamp as far as he could through the open doorway.

It landed with a crash on the floor inside the next room.

There was no reaction. There was no gunshot.

Pelfrey bent his knees, getting ready to run, and took a deep breath. Then he was off, running low into the next room. He moved quickly to the right and dropped for cover behind a large beverage cart.

Rory hesitated for a moment and then ran in a low crouch through the open doorway and moved left. He dropped for cover behind a large easy chair.

There were a number of easy chairs, club chairs, folding chairs and long tables along both sides of the meeting room. The center of the long room was basically wide open.

Pelfrey began to push the beverage cart forward, using it as cover as he advanced across the room.

Rory peered over the easy chair, trying to spot any target for the detective.

A dark, hooded figure rose from behind a large easy chair at the far end of the room and fired a shot towards the beverage cart. A bullet shattered a number of beverage cans and sent spray into the air.

Pelfrey returned fire and then ducked.

Another bullet slammed into the side of the beverage cart.

Everything went quiet.

Rory peeked over the easy chair. He glanced at Pelfrey and said in a low voice, "I think someone just went through the adjoining door on the other side of the room."

Pelfrey looked over the top of the beverage cart.

An adjoining door was closing slowly on the far side of the room.

Pelfrey began to push the cart across the floor towards the other side of the room.

Rory saw another big easy chair, midway up the room on his side. He ran for it hard, diving to the floor for cover behind it.

The beverage cart stopped rolling when it hit an extension cord laying across the floor. Pelfrey tried to push it over the impediment, but it wouldn't budge. The detective decided to abandon his cover. He ran low to the right to take cover behind a club chair.

No more gunshots rang out. Everything was deathly quiet.

Pelfrey took a peek over the club chair and then looked over at Rory, "The next adjoining doors are open about one-quarter. It might be too dangerous to go any further. I'll call for some back-up."

Rory nodded as he watched the detective pull out a cell phone while trying to keep his weapon at the ready. Rory looked around the room they were in and spotted the door to the hall-way. It gave him an idea and he called to the detective in a low voice, "The Hotel manager said there were three adjoining rooms, right?"

Pelfrey nodded yes.

"So that's the last adjoining room. He would have to run into the hallway from there to get away. Let me look outside this room into the hallway. If he runs, we'll know it."

"Be careful," Pelfrey said as he pressed speed dial.

Just then they both heard a muffled sound inside the room ahead.

Rory and Pelfrey exchanged knowing glances.

"That sounded like a muffled gunshot," Rory said.

"You're right," Pelfrey agreed. "Suicide?"

Rory shrugged.

Pelfrey jumped up from behind the club chair and headed for a spot beside the adjoining door to the next room.

Leaving his safe spot behind the easy chair, Rory ran low for his side of the adjoining doors. Placing his back against the wall he looked across as Pelfrey. As the detective went into a crouch, Rory slowly reached out to the door handle and pulled hard, flat-tening himself back against the wall as the door swung open.

There was no response.

Detective Pelfrey edged out from the wall, lifted his left leg and push the far door open. He ducked back against the wall.

No response.

In a low crouch, Pelfrey moved quickly through the open doorway, his weapon ready to fire.

Rory waited.

There was no sound.

He peered around the open doorway into the next room.

"It's clear," Pelfrey yelled.

Rory moved inside the other room. It was a regular style hotel room, much like the first one they had first entered on the other side of the long meeting room. The only difference was...this one had a body on the floor.

Pelfrey opened a door on the left and stepped outside the room into the hallway.

Rory moved to the body. It was a man, lying on his back with his arms spread out. It looked like he was about to make an angel in the snow, or in this case, in the rug. In the middle of the man's forehead was a single bullet hole.

Pelfrey came back into the room, holstered his weapon, "I didn't see anyone fleeing down the hallway."

Rory was looking down at the body, "That sure looks like Neron Blanco Soto."

Pulled the picture from his pocket, Pelfrey had held it near the face, "An older version, but I think you're right."

Kneeling beside the body and looking closer, Rory said, "That looks like a close contact wound. And it looks like it's from a 22 caliber weapon, just like the other two down in room 92."

"You're right. And since he wasn't tied up, whoever did this was probably working for - or guarding - Soto. And they took him out before we could get in here. That's ballsy."

"And weird. If the shooter could get away - why not both of them?"

Pelfrey put his hands on his hips, shaking his head, "I have no idea."

Rory stood up, looking down at the body, "I think we have a real problem here."

"What do you mean?"

Whoever did this is a stone-cold killer - acting out of self-preservation - or working to eliminate people for some reason. And they're always one step ahead of us,"

"Like they have inside information."

"Yeah–." Rory looked at Pelfrey in alarm, "Talking about eliminating people - where is Cassandra?"

Chapter 37

TORONTO INTERNATIONAL Airport

LED BY HOBBS, the airport security officers quickly stormed the plane. MacKinnon and Sepulveda got up from the floor of the jet bridge and reloaded as they waited. One set of security officers penetrated the flight deck and found a pilot with his hands up, scared out of his wits. They handcuffed him until he could be checked out. The rest of the security officers turned right and stormed into the body of the Lear jet. They moved efficiently, sweeping the rest of the plane for additional gunmen.

When everything was secure, Hobbs went back to the plane's doorway where MacKinnon and Sepulveda were waiting, guns at the ready, "Okay. Everything is secure, Detectives."

MacKinnon slipped his weapon into his shoulder holster, "Good work, Hobbs."

"Thank you. How do you want to proceed from here?"

"Let's start with this guy and see what we've got here." MacKinnon knelt down and began to search the dead body lying on top of Damian Delatorre.

Sepulveda holstered her weapon and pulled pictures out of the side pocket of her jacket. Looking through them, she selected one, bent down and placed the picture next to the head so her partner could see for himself, "This one is Jacinto Ruvalcaba."

MacKinnon glanced at it. "You're right. And another one bites the dust. Here we go." He pulled a red diplomatic passport from the inside of the dead man's black leather jacket. Flipping it open, he said, "Passport says he's Senon Alberto Corrales. But that's Jacinto Ruvalcaba's picture."

Sepulveda shook her head, "How in the world did these guys get diplomatic passports like that?"

Hobbs wrinkled his brow, "Are you absolutely sure these guys *aren't* diplomats?"

MacKinnon grumbled, "If they are, we're all in trouble."

Smiling like he'd been through this before, Hobbs said, "Yeah, well, it wouldn't be the first time. It just seems to go with the job."

"Ain't that the truth," MacKinnon agreed. He flipped through the diplomatic passport, looking at the various customs stamps on the pages. Then he came across a folded piece of paper held between two of the pages. He unfolded the paper.

Sepulveda tilted her head to read it, "What is it?"

"It's an address down on the waterfront."

Hobbs hooked his thumbs in his belt, "The waterfront? Maybe he's got a yacht waiting or something?"

"It's gonna do a lot of waiting," MacKinnon said as he refolded the paper and slipped it back inside the diplomatic passport. He then slipped the passport into his pocket. "Nothing else on him. Help me roll the body off so I can check out the other guy."

Hobbs bent down to help roll the body over, "Crime scene guys are gonna get pissed at you."

Sepulveda grabbed the body around the knees to help roll Ruvalcaba off Delatorre, "My partner does have a tendency to do that."

As the body was rolled, MacKinnon for the briefcase shackled to the dead man's wrist, "It seemed to me a couple of bullets bounced off the briefcase and I thought...." He looked up at Hobbs, "Yep - just as I thought - a bullet broke the lock."

Hobbs realized what the detective was driving at, "Yeah. I guess that means we didn't break into a diplomatic pouch. At least we won't get in trouble for that."

A devious smile on his face, MacKinnon clicked open the snaps on the briefcase."You should be a lawyer, Hobbs."

"I was gonna be a lawyer but my wife didn't want that. You know - in case we ever got a divorce?"

"Women."

Sepulveda frowned, "Hey, watch herself. I'm a woman."

"Nah. You're one of the boys," MacKinnon said. He held one hand under the briefcase as he opened it, "There's something sliding inside - whoops." The briefcase tilted and a number of chunks of ice - the size of sugar cubes - poured out. They formed a small pile on the floor of the airplane.

Bending down, Sepulveda scooped a pile of the items with her hand and stood up, looking at them closely.

Hobbs leaned in to look, "What are they?"

Sepulveda took one of the chunks of ice and held it up against the light, "I worked on vice for a number years. I'm positive these are raw, uncut diamonds."

MacKinnon looked down at the pile on the floor and what was left in the briefcase, "How much do you think we have here, Jeanette?"

She pursed her lips as she rolled the ice around in her fingers, "I'm not totally positive but...unless I've forgotten my stuff...I'd say we could easily have $20-$30 million of uncut diamonds here."

Hobbs whistled.

Just then one of the other security officers appeared from back in the airplane, "Chad? I think we might have made a mistake back here. We found something that we opened...and then we realized it had those tamper-evident seals you see on diplomatic containers and–"

"Don't worry about it," Hobbs said. "Show us what you've got."

MacKinnon set the open, diamond filled briefcase on the floor of the plane and followed Hobbs - with Sepulveda right behind him - into the back of the plane.

The other security officers - looking worried - were gathered around an area where rows of seats had been removed and six large, black, metal boxes sat heavily on the floor. Each box had sturdy carrying handles on the sides. The lid of each box was open and each box was filled with a clear plastic bag. Each bag held a white powder.

Sepulveda slid past everyone to one of the boxes, took out the car keys, bent over and poked a hole in one of the plastic bags. She slipped a wet finger inside and tasted the white substance.

"Is that what I think it is?" MacKinnon asked.

Sepulveda nodded and stood up, "Pure heroin."

One of the security officers whistled in amazement, "Each box they carried on board is about 27 kilos." He pushed his hat back on his head, "When we did that bust last month on that bozo trying to smuggle a kilo in, the detective from narcotics told me it was worth about $175,000 per kilo on the street."

"Yeah, I remember that," Hobbs said.

MacKinnon's mouth moved silently as he did some quick math in his head, "That means we have $20-$30 million of uncut diamonds and...nearly $30 million worth of pure heroin onboard."

Sepulveda looked around at the security officers, Anyone know where this airplane was going?"

"Pilot said his destination was Chicago," answered one of the officers.

"Wow," Hobbs said. "All of this was being smuggled into the good ole U.S.A."

Sepulveda returned the car keys to her pocket, "Yeah. And it was being smuggled in under the guise of diplomatic pouches and containers That means customs on both sides of the border would never know."

Everybody shook their head in silent bewilderment at what they were seeing - and discussing.

MacKinnon reached into his side pocket and pulled out Jacinto Ruvalcaba's diplomatic passport again. He flipped through it until he found the folded piece of paper.

Sepulveda watched her partner unfold the paper."What are you thinking of, Cam?"

Thinking for a moment, MacKinnon took a deep breath and let it out slowly. "Damian Delatorre is the one we tracked here. He had the uncut diamonds in that diplomatic pouch he was carrying. More than likely, Ruvalcaba was responsible for getting the containers of heroin onboard."

"Maybe that address is the source of this heroin?"

"That's what I'm thinking," MacKinnon said. "But until we know who is involved or how high up this goes, I really don't want to use a swat team to check this address out."

"I hear you."

MacKinnon taped the passport against his hand for a moment, then pulled his cell phone, "I didn't want to get too many involved but...maybe we can get Pelfrey's partner to pick him up at the convention center. They could check it out while we finish up here."

Sepulveda raised her eyebrows, "Delroy Green?"

MacKinnon punched in the numbers."Yeah, you okay with that?"

"Oh yeah. He's solid. I worked with him in vice for a year before he insisted on going over to narcotics. His background is perfect for this. His father was a policeman in Jamaican and they came to this country because of drug dealers threatening the family down there. I just feel sorry for our friends at that address. Green is one bad Jamaican dude when it comes to drug dealers. He not only knows where a lot of the dead drug dealer bodies are buried - word is he put a lot of them there himself."

Chapter 38

RORY LED THE CHARGE back to the first room, Pelfrey doing his best to keep up. Rory found Cassandra still huddled on her knees inside the washroom, her body shaking. He got on his knees beside her, putting an arm around her shoulders, You're safe. The shooter is gone. Okay?"

Pelfrey watched from the doorway, "He's right, Mrs. Glynn." He pulled out his cell phone, "I'm calling for constables to secure these rooms and get a forensic team up here."

."That Soto is dead, too," Rory said. "You don't have to worry about him anymore."

"He is?"

"Yeah, he's lying in the far adjoining room. It looks like who-ever was with him shot him."

"Why?"

"Who knows with these drug dealers. But that's one less wor-ry like I said. Why don't we get you on your feet?"

Cassandra nodded woodenly again and rose to her feet with Rory's help, "Sorry, I'm such a mess...."

"Don't worry about it. Getting caught in a shooting can be traumatic."

"Yeah. And then you two come barreling in here like someone was coming after me. Why would you think that?"

Rory didn't answer.

Pelfrey closed his phone, "Everything is backed up but Flynn and Esposito are going to get a team down here for me. I need to go to the video room downstairs in the meantime. Are you two coming now or...?"

Rory looked at Cassandra, "Are you ready? Or do you need more time?"

"I'm fine. Let's just get out of here." Cassandra held onto his arm this time like it was a safety net. The three of them left the scene behind and re-entered the elevator on the third floor of the convention center.

Pelfrey pressed the button for the ground floor.

Rory moved to the back of the elevator with Cassandra. "Do you want to go back to that room they set up? They have officers posted in the hallway there."

Cassandra shrugged, "I don't know. What are you two going to do now?"

Pelfrey's voice was filled with determination, "*We* are going back to the video room. Whoever shot Soto had to leave that room by going into the hallway. There was no other way out. The windows are sealed shut. If we can get down there quickly, before anyone could erase the video feed for that hallway, we should be able to see who came out of that room."

Cassandra gave a soft nod of her head and looked pensive.

"Are you sure you're okay?" Rory asked Cassandra as the elevator descended.

"Yeah. Just a little shaken. Thanks for saving my life by the way...again." She then lightly touched the back of her hip, "Although I'm going to have a lot of bruises on my butt."

"I don't have any bruises," Rory said with some amusement, "you make a great cushion."

Cassandra let go of his arm and her feistiness reemerged as she crossed her arms, "Oh really? And why exactly would that be?"

Rory grimaced and looked to the front of the elevator, "Forget I said it."

"Oh no, sport. You don't get off that easy with that great cushion comment."

Leaning against the side of the elevator, Pelfrey shook his head and smiled as he looked at Rory.

Cassandra gave Pelfrey a stony glare, "And what are *you* shaking your head for over there?"

Pelfrey immediately looked up to the floor indicator, willing it to move faster. When the elevator stopped, Pelfrey squeezed his way out before the doors were fully open. Rory followed him with Cassandra close behind. As they crossed the lobby, Rory looked back, expecting her to take his arm again.

Cassandra merely flicked her fingers at him to keep going.

Pelfrey instructed the front desk to have someone stay outside the rooms on three until his team could get there. Then he led Rory and Cassandra back into the security room, where he headed immediately to the controls. Sitting down as the other two stood behind him, Pelfrey worked as fast as possible to call up the video feed for the hallway on floor three. Fast forwarding the feed, he finally reached the time frame where Soto was leaving the elevator and heading for room 310. He pressed the pause button, "Okay. Everyone keep an eye out for anyone else entering or exiting rooms 310, 312 or 314 after Soto goes in."

Rory and Cassandra moved up closer behind Pelfrey as the detective started the fast forward again.

The figures on the video moved rapidly up and down the hallway. Time passed. A few people came and went but no one entered or exited the three rooms. The elevator opened and three figures emerged.

Pelfrey hit the stop button.

"That's us," Cassandra said as she pointed at the screen.

Pelfry nodded, "We're just about to go into 310."

"I didn't see anyone enter any of those rooms before Soto did," Rory said.

"No," Pelfrey admitted. "Someone may have been in there *before* he went in. Let's run through the rest and see who comes out after the shootout." He let the video play at normal speed. The video showed the three of them moving into room 310. The minutes passed–

Suddenly, a white reflective glare lit up the screen.

Cassandra squinted, "What was that?".

"I don't know," Pelfrey said. He stopped the video and backed it up to the spot just before the white reflective glare. He searched for and found the speed control - set it to half-speed and they carefully watched.

Time moved like molasses now. Then the exit door at the far end of the hallway opened. The white reflective glare lit up the screen again. It lasted for a period of time and then cut out. A brief glimpse of the side of a dark, hooded figure was seen slipping into room 314.

The hallway was empty again.

"What just happened?" Cassandra asked.

"Green lasers," Rory answered.

Both Detective Pelfrey and Cassandra looked at him.

"How do you know that? And what does that even mean?" Pelfrey asked.

"I learned about green lasers at a counter-surveillance seminar a year ago. It's a little-known trick used by agents in the field under the right circumstances. If you don't want someone to recognize your face from a surveillance video, then you arrange a number of green lasers around your head or other parts of your body. You could wear a hat with green lasers strapped to it, for example. The lasers bounce around in the lens of the surveillance camera and create that flare we saw."

Pelfry looked back at the dark figure frozen on the screen, "So someone went in *after* we did? Like I said before, ballsy."

Rory looked at the figure, "I get the impression someone has been watching us somehow."

Nodding, Pelfrey then cursed, "And we led that someone right to Soto."

Cassandra shifted on her feet, "Maybe we can see the person coming out. If they don't put the lasers on the back of their head....? I don't know. I'm just reaching here."

"It's possible," Pelfrey said in agreement. He allowed the video to run through the period where the shootout was happening inside.

Everyone held their breath in anticipation. Before long, someone exited room 314.

They caught another brief glimpse of a figure wearing a black hoodie, black pants, and black shoes before the white reflective glare lit up the screen again. The flare disappeared just as the exit door at the far end of the hallway closed.

Rory clicked his tongue, "Green lasers front *and* back. Ingenious."

Pelfrey's voice was hard and bitter, "Great. An ingenious hit man who knows everything we do is all we need."

Chapter 39

PELFREY MOVED with purpose out of the video room and down the hallway to the front desk area. Rory and Cassandra were close behind. When they got there, Constables Flynn and Esposito were just entering the lobby, followed by a small team of forensic technicians.

Pelfrey turned to Rory as they exited from behind the front desk, "Why don't you two head back to room 91 now while I get these guys started up in rooms 310, 312 and 314. Maybe we get lucky and find some prints or DNA on the shooter."

"Okay. Can you let us know if you find anything?" Rory asked.

Pelfrey nodded and headed off to the elevators with his team following closely behind him.

Rory and Cassandra crossed the crowded lobby and headed down the hallway toward room 91. They were side by side but not on the close contact mode they had used to this point. It proved to be a mistake. The hallway was quiet and they only passed a couple of people. Their footsteps echoed lightly off the walls.

As they passed the cross hallway on the right, Rory made the mistake of not being alert.

A man in a black leather jacket had been hiding against the left wall. He jumped out behind Cassandra, placed his left hand around her mouth, and pulled her back and away from Rory.

Rory turned but his reaction time was too slow. He froze in his tracks as the gunman placed a 9 mm pistol against Cassandra's right temple. Rory could only watch helplessly as the gunman slowly pulled her back into the cross hallway and against the right wall.

Putting his hands out, Rory maintained a low, calm voice despite the turmoil he felt inside, "Please don't hurt her. She doesn't know anything–"

The gunmen motioned for Rory to raise his hands, "Up. Up." He complied.

The gunman's words came hard in a heavy Spanish accent, "Are you the one who shot my friends?"

Rory shook his head no. He kept his hands high where the gunman could see them.

Forcing the 9 mm pistol harder against Cassandra's right temple, the gunman bared his teeth, "Tell me the truth. Or did she shoot them?"

Cassandra emitted a little cry of pain as the barrel dug into her skin.

Rory shook his head again, harder this time, "No. No. I swear to you. I don't know who shot them. That's the truth. They were both dead when we found them inside the room."

The gunman's eyes were filled with pure hatred and rage. He snarled as he pressed the gun harder again Cassandra's temple, "I don't believe you. Tell me who shot Cesar and Teo or she is *dead*."

"I'm telling you we found them like that when we entered the room. Please don't hurt her. She had *nothing* to do with their deaths."

The gunman shook his head and began to pull Cassandra slowly back along the wall and down the hallway, "Sorry, but I just don't believe you. I guess you don't want this woman to live."

Rory slowly walked forward with his hands up, trying to follow the gunman. He hoped he could get close enough to do something.

The gunman smiled, flashing a front tooth inlaid with a gold star. He knew Rory was trying to get close and he enjoyed the deadly cat and mouse game. He pulled Cassandra across the hallway to the other side where he stopped, quickly removed the gun from her temple and jammed his elbow against the wall behind him.

Rory heard the ding of an elevator. He'd been concentrating so much on trying to find a way to attack the gunman that he hadn't noticed where the man was pulling Cassandra. He cursed under his breath. This couldn't be good–

"You should go outside my friend," the gunman said, "so you can watch the lady hit the ground."

Rory heard the elevator doors slide open. It was a single freight elevator. There was no chance to take another one to follow if the man got inside with Cassandra.

The gunman waited until the doors began to slide closed - he pulled Cassandra back quickly.

He knew what was about to happen and Rory lunged - the elevator doors were closing. He tried to jam his fingers into the closing gap but he was too late.

The gunman smiled out at him a second before the doors slammed shut against any rescue.

Rory looked up at the floor indicator. He could see the elevator was going up.

It *was* going up to the roof!

Rory banged the elevator down button over and over again. When the elevator obviously didn't respond, Rory ran over to the stairs. He ran up to the first landing and realized he would never make it in time. He *had* to wait for the elevator to come back down. Running back down the stairs and into the hallway, Rory began to bang the down button over and over again, trying to will it to return. He looked up at the floor indicator and saw it stop at the top floor. Then it slowly began to head back down to him. Rory stepped in front of the doors and waited in agony. He wanted to run to the stairs again but he knew he had to wait. He had no choice.

Chapter 40

WHEN THE ELEVATOR finally reached the main floor and opened up, Rory dashed inside. He jabbed the button for the top floor and then hit the close button. He considered stopping at the floor just before the top in case the gunman was waiting for him, but running up that last flight would definitely take too long. Every second counted. No, Rory had to take the chance the man was waiting for him. He squatted down on the left-hand side of the elevator, against the front wall, and waited for the doors to open. If someone *was* there, maybe he could catch them by surprise.

No one was there waiting.

Rory pressed the button to keep the doors open and stuck his head out.

There was an unpainted musty hallway running left and right. And dead ahead were stairs leading up to the roof.

Rory ran to the door and bounded up the stairs. He pulled the door open at the top of the stairs and burst into the cool night air.

He couldn't see anyone.

Rory took a few steps straight ahead, scanning the rooftop for any sign of Cassandra and the gunman. There were a number of sheet-metal ducts on this side of the roof that blocked his view.

He heard a scream to the right.

Rory pivoted and ran in the direction of the scream, skirting around the first square, sheet-metal duct. He ran across the rooftop as fast as he could, feeling the course surface under his feet. As he moved around a large brick chimney he saw two figures struggling against the parapet at the far edge of the building - it was the gunman and Cassandra.

Cassandra was twisting and turning, her red A-line dress swishing hard as she hit him with her fists and clawed at him in a fight for her life.

The gunman's head jerked violently when her nails raked across his face. A guttural sound erupted from his throat, he swung around hard with his gun hand and struck her on the shoulder.

Cassandra fell back and screamed as her red high heels came off the rough surface of the roof - her long legs flashed in the night and she disappeared over the parapet.

"No!" Rory yelled.

The gunmen wheeled around.

Rory ducked–

A shot rang out, followed by a metallic ricochet sound.

Scooting to his left, Rory got behind the chimney–

Another shot rang out.

The bullet glanced off the red brick, sending sharp, painful chips against Rory's jaw.

Rory slid to down sit with his back to the chimney, knowing full well he couldn't stay put. Once the Columbian gunman figured out Rory had no weapon, it would be over in a heartbeat.

He glanced around the chimney and saw the Columbian moving wide to get a killing viewpoint behind Rory's hiding spot.

With the gunman moving slow and cautious - Rory had a few seconds to act.

The path back to the doorway was too open and offered no escape route.

There was no other choice and Rory ran low and straight back, trying to keep the small chimney between him and the gunman as long as possible. He ducked under a large, square sheet metal duct–

A shot and a ping off the metal.

Moving low across the roof, Rory desperately looked for cover. Up ahead was a long row of lounge chairs. He hurdled over them and another shot rang out. One of the lounge chairs bucked and fell over, wounded in the battle.

Rory ran behind a small mini-bar. He grabbed several bottles of liquor and heaved them back over his head in the direction of the lounge chairs. They shattered like gunshots and Rory saw the Columbian jump to the side and throw himself flat. The diversion bought Rory some time and he sprinted away from the bar and the prone gunman on the other side. Rory nearly ran into the deep end of the rooftop pool. He skidded to a stop and veered to the right to skirt the pool. But as he neared the other side, he realized the only cover was a number of lounge chairs by the pool and another mini-bar bar just ahead. Rory skidded to a stop and looked back.

What now?

Chapter 41

RORY DESPERATELY LOOKED for an answer. He noted some pool work had been going on. A small gas pump sat about ten feet away from the mini-bar. The pump had a coil of blue lay flat hose attached to one of the motor outlets. Near the pump were a couple of aluminum ladders, a couple of saw horses and several coils of extension cord. He looked at the mini-bar and noted it had an electrical outlet for running the blenders to mix drinks.

He realized he had one chance...if everything worked.

Rory ran over and grabbed the gas pump and attached hose. Dragging it back to the side of the pool, he set the pump in place and unfurled the blue lay flat hose towards the pool. As the end of the hose flipped over the edge of the pool and entered the water, Rory tried to start the pump. It sputtered a couple of times, then caught and began chugging away.

Rory ran back across the roof to grab a coil of extension cord and then ran back behind the mini-bar.

The pump was doing its job and water was slowly sucked up into the blue lay flat hose from the pool. The lay flat hose began to swell and, after a moment, pool water was shot out through the open outlet of the pump. Pool water now began spreading slowly in a puddle across the rooftop.

Rory picked up an empty bottle of whiskey. He was about to smash it when he spotted something on a small shelf under the mini-bar. It was a small knife used to cut lemon wedges for drinks. Setting the bottle down, he picked up the knife and sliced a V-shaped cut into one end of the outer cover on the extension cord. Rory then worked feverishly to cut and strip away enough cover to expose an inch of the bare inner wires. It would work with less but he wanted to make sure - he only had one shot at this. Glancing around the mini-bar, he saw the gunman was now creeping slowly up to the lounge chairs on the other side of the pool. Time was up. Rory took loops of extension cord in hand, pulled his arm back and tossed the end with the exposed electrical wires into the spreading pool of water.

THE GUNMAN WAS MOVING quicker now, no doubt realizing his quarry was trapped somewhere beyond the rooftop pool. The Columbian moved low around the end of the pool, heading towards the mini-bar where Rory was hiding. The gunman began to skirt the water. He was playing it smart. By moving wide, the gunman was maintaining a distance advantage for himself as he tried to see behind the mini-bar.

Rory cursed under his breath - his plan wasn't going to work unless - he grabbed the bottle of whiskey and hurled it high over the mini-bar and to the gunman's right.

When the empty bottle hit the rooftop and smashed to pieces, the Columbian turned and stepped back into the water, firing a shot in the direction of the sound.

Rory plugged the extension cord in.

There was a sharp crack and the gunman's body seized and danced on a string.

Waiting for 5 seconds to make sure, Rory unplugged the extension cord.

The gunman fell on his back - body rigid - electrocuted.

Rory ran cautiously to the body and checked for vital signs.

Dead.

Picking the gun up, Rory wiped it against his jeans and took off at a dead run over to the parapet where he saw Cassandra go over. He was hoping there was a small drop to another rooftop level. He reached the parapet and looked over.

It was a sheer drop!

His heart sank.

He leaned out more, expecting to see a body far below. As he stretched out, he saw a flash of red hair and two hands holding onto a pipe that ran across the building about two feet below the upper edge. Rory stuck the gun in his waistband, braced himself against the low wall and reached down to grip Cassandra's arms firmly above the wrist.

Cassandra looked up, fear etched deep in her face.

"It's okay, it's me," Rory said.

Relief filled Cassandra's eyes, "Well at least you're not below me trying to look up my dress again, Mr. Steele."

Chapter 42

DETECTIVE PELFREY RUSHED into room 91 with Constables Flint and Esposito close behind him. He saw Rory pouring a coffee, "You called? What's wrong?"

Before Rory could answer, Cassandra walked out of the bathroom, drying her hands on a towel.

Pelfrey's eyes opened wide in surprise.

The two young constables stared from behind him.

The black wig was gone, revealing Cassandra Glynn's own long, red hair. The heavy black eyeliner was brought down to a more subtle shade that still made her green eyes pop. The large, black eyelashes were still glued on, but they only enhanced her beauty as she stood there in the red dress and red high-heeled shoes. She was back to the tall, stunning, redheaded Amazon her husband had loved to see.

Rory smiled at their reaction

For her part, Cassandra's eyebrows rose when she realized Pelfrey and the two young constables were simply standing there, staring, "What's wrong?"

Pelfrey managed to stop staring and found his voice, "Uh...w-what happened to your disguise, Mrs. Glynn?"

"I lost the wig. It's probably still floating somewhere over the city."

"I don't get it. What does that mean?"

Rory set the coffee down, "When we first left you to come back here, she was taken hostage by one of our friends who tried to throw her off the roof."

Pelfrey straightened up, reaching for his weapon, "Who was it? Where is he now?"

The two constables reacted by reaching for their weapons as well, ready to move.

"Rory electrocuted him on the roof," Cassandra said with finality.

Pelfrey's jaw dropped, "E-electrocuted? Seriously?"

Cassandra nodded, "And then Mr. Steele rescued me from the precipice. Without my wig, I've had to revert to my true self." She frowned, "And I'm tired of hiding anyway."

And I still think it's a bad idea," Rory told her.

She wrinkled her nose at him.

Changing the subject, Rory got up and handed Pelfrey another red passport, "I didn't want to say anything over the phone when I called you. But we have another one with a diplomatic passport. And a 9 mm pistol." He pulled the gun from his waistband and passed it to the detective.

Pelfrey took the gun and handed it back to one of the constables. Then he scanned through the pages of the passport. Pulling pictures from his inner pocket, he compared them to the picture in the passport. He finally found a match, "This one is Esquevelle Villasenor. At least we know where he is now."

"Have they found anything at the Soto crime scene yet?" Rory asked.

"Tiny says there are a ton of fingerprints up there." Pelfrey put the diplomatic passport and the pictures into a side pocket of his crumpled jacket. "It's going to take them some time to process and identify each individual. I'm going to have Flynn and Esposito here help me to look through surveillance footage of the stairways where we saw that figure with the green lasers come and go. If we can track the unsub from the stairways into other areas of the convention center - maybe even slipping outside - we might be able to catch the killer yet."

Cassandra glanced at the two young officers, a slight flush on her cheeks as she asked Pelfrey, "You're *all* going to be looking at the videos? Inside and outside views?"

"Yes. That's right. I thought it would work better with more eyes watching."

"Are...are there any cameras with a view looking *up* the outside of the building? You know, looking up to the roof?"

Pelfrey scratched his head, "Uh...no. Why?"

Cassandra visibly relaxed, "Oh, just wondering."

Rory couldn't help but smile. She was a classy but feisty lady who always seemed to worry about the strangest things in the face of danger and death.

Pelfrey simply shrugged his shoulders and turned to the constables as he pulled his phone, "I want you guys to get some constables and take them up to the roof to secure the crime scene. I'm going to call Tiny and get him to send a forensic team up there. Once you get the scene secured, come back down here and we'll work the videos like I said."

"The dead guy is over by the pool on the far side," Rory added.

The two constables nodded and left the room.

As he waited for Tiny to answer, Pelfrey sat on a sofa, reached for a cup on the table and then the coffee pot, "I need a caffeine shot. Bodies are starting to pile up around you two and I need to be able to keep up."

Cassandra raised her eyebrows at him.

Pelfrey didn't see it but Rory did. As Pelfrey began talking with Tiny, Rory lightly squeezed her shoulder, "He's just teasing. Why don't we sit and have a coffee as well?"

It took a moment but Cassandra agreed, taking a seat across from Pelfrey and watching Rory place a cup in front of her and pouring hot liquid. She doctored her coffee and sat with her feet flat on the floor.

Rory took his coffee straight black and took a seat beside her. "Try to relax," he whispered.

She just sipped at her coffee without a word.

Pelfrey ended his call, set the phone on the table and sat back on the sofa as he sipped the coffee. Ten minutes later, Pelfrey's cell phone rang. He leaned forward quickly and stabbed the speaker button. "Pelfrey here. You're on speaker phone."

It was MacKinnon, "It's me, John. You're on speaker here too. We just wanted you to know that Damian Delatorre and Jacinto Ruvalcaba were killed in a shootout at the airport."

Pelfrey's back straightened, "Is everybody okay?"

"Yeah, everybody's fine here. With those two gone, that means you only have one of his friends to watch out for, Esquevelle Villasenor."

Rubbing the top of his head, Pelfrey said, "Not really."

"What do you mean?"

Pelfrey looked across at Rory.

Rory sat forward, "It's Rory here, Detective MacKinnon. In a nutshell - Villasenor tried to throw Mrs. Glynn off the roof of the convention center. I took exception and electrocuted him."

"Really? Well, that only leaves Neron Blanco Soto. He might still be around the convention center."

"Not really," Pelfrey added as he rubbed the top of his head again.

Sepulveda broke into the conversation, "Why not? Was he spotted somewhere else in the city?"

"No," Pelfrey replied. "Using the surveillance videos, we tracked him up to room 310 here in the convention center. We ended up in a gunfight as he fled into room 312 and over to 314 through the adjoining doors. Before we could get to him in 314, somebody shot him in the forehead like the other guys. Whoever did it, used a silencer at close range."

There was the sound of surprise talk between MacKinnon and Sepulveda on the other end of the call.

Pelfrey continued, "We took a look at the video for the hallway, looking for the shooter, but someone used green lasers to cover their image–"

"Green lasers?" MacKinnon asked. "What does that mean?"

"I'll explain it more when we get together. This was all *before* Villasenor tried to throw Mrs. Glynn off the roof. Oh...and both Soto and Villasenor had diplomatic passports on them."

There was a long silence on both sides of the phone.

MacKinnon broke the silence, his voice low, "What do you think Jeanette?"

"I don't know what to think," Sepulveda said quietly. "Maybe Esquevelle Villaseno was trying to take over. Delacruz was killed by Mrs. Glynn and Delatorre and Ruvalcaba were shot dead by us at the airport. Santana, Luna, and Soto were shot by someone else. Since Villaseno was the last man alive, he must've assassinated those three before he was electrocuted on the rooftop."

"I don't think so," Rory said. "When Delacruz put his gun to my head in the washroom, he asked me who shot his friends, Cesar and Teo. I didn't think too much about it until Villaseno asked me the same question, *who shot Cesar and Teo?*"

Cassandra leaned forward in her seat, "That's true. I remember him saying that as he held the gun to my head. He wanted to know who shot Cesar and Teo."

"If he was trying to take over, why would he pretend for our benefit?" Rory asked. "That doesn't make any sense."

"No, it doesn't," MacKinnon admitted.

"One more thing Cam," Pelfrey said. "I checked with Tiny and he confirms that Cesar Santana, Teo Luna and Neron Blanco Soto were all shot with 22 caliber weapons. So far, every weapon we've collected from Soto and his men were 9 mm. Not one of them had a 22 on them."

"Same thing here at the airport," MacKinnon said. "Both men had 9 mm weapons as well." He swore.

Rory, Cassandra and Detective Pelfrey looked at each other, trying to figure out what was going on.

Sepulveda added a theory, "Maybe we have a major drug war on our hands? Considering what we found up here, someone may be trying to take over their turf."

"Why do you say that?" Pelfrey asked.

There was a moment of silence before MacKinnon spoke, "Because after we shot Delatorre and Ruvalcaba...we found out what kind of lucrative smuggling program Soto was running here."

Now Rory, Cassandra, and Pelfrey all moved up to the edge of their seats.

"Delatorre and Ruvalcaba were also carrying diplomatic passports. Delatorre was carrying $30 million worth of uncut diamonds in a diplomatic briefcase chained to his wrist."

Detective Pelfrey emitted a low whistle.

"And on the airplane he was boarding...we found several diplomatic boxes containing nearly $30 million worth of heroin. Everything was being smuggled into the United States under diplomatic papers."

Detective Pelfrey, Rory, and Cassandra were speechless.

"We have the Royal Canadian Mounted Police with us right now. And Ron Allbritton, Director of CSIS, the Canadian Security Intelligence Service has been called in as well because of the security implications for the country. Right now, this thing is quickly becoming above our pay grade. The RCMP has taken over at the airport and we'll head down to your location once we finish our report up here."

Pelfrey rubbed his head again, looking down, "So...Soto set this all up using diplomatic passports...just so he would have an easier way to run his drugs?"

Sepulveda spoke, "Running drugs that way would definitely make it nearly impossible for us to catch them. In fact, running drugs using diplomatic agreements is basically foolproof. Diplomatic agreements would make it impossible for any authority to check inside any diplomatic pouch. It's absolutely ingenious."

MacKinnon agreed with her, "Jeanette is right. But CSIS Director Allbritton also opened up a little more on Soto. They had undercover information to suggest Soto was using Canada as a safe haven. Apparently, the Colombian government was too close on his heels and he had to flee. They rejected the rumors because they couldn't see how he could've gotten into the country. But if all these guys came into the country under diplomatic passports, they would have been under our radar."

Cassandra spoke up, "But something still doesn't make sense."

"What's that, Mrs. Glynn?" Sepulveda asked.

"Well - according to your forensics - this Teo Luna had an area of skin disease on his right hand that tied him into the death of my husband. Right?"

"That's correct, Mrs. Glynn," Sepulveda said.

"So...why would they need to kill my husband? How exactly would that help them with their scheme?"

Everyone was silent on both sides of the phone for a few moments.

MacKinnon spoke in a soft voice. "These men don't have to have much reason to kill, Mrs. Glynn. But with nearly $60 million being smuggled on just this one airplane is a powerful incentive-"

"But they could have infiltrated the diplomatic courier service itself," Cassandra interjected with conviction. "With $60 million dollars on just *one* airplane, they could have *easily* bribed someone. And how does this connect to my husband and someone wanting his electoral seat? He never had *anything* to do with diplomatic couriers and there was *nothing* to indicate he ever would. Is there any indication my husband ever stumbled onto their scheme?"

"None," MacKinnon admitted after a moment.

"My husband *never* had anything to do with anti-drug initiatives either. There is nothing that I can see that would cause them to cross paths. My children were just in the wrong place at the wrong time. That I can accept. But *how* does killing my husband benefit them *in any way*? And the way Rory and Detective Pelfrey came back after they found this Soto shot, they looked like the person who did it was coming after me–"

"We were just worried," Rory said.

"Why? Like I said, I can see why some bastard killed my husband to get his seat - but why me? Especially since I'm out of the way and Demario Gomez has the nomination. Why not shoot that son of a bitch instead?"

No one had an answer.

Chapter 43

"**I WISH WE COULD ANSWER** your question, Mrs. Glynn," Detective Sepulveda said after a few quiet moments.

Cassandra crossed her arms and took a deep breath.

"There's one another thing, John," MacKinnon said. "We have an address on the waterfront that needs to be checked out right away. We've given the address to your partner and he's going to pick you up at the back of the convention center. It may just be where the drugs are being kept. But maybe there's more to it. If the shootings down there at the convention center are tied to someone trying to take over Soto's turf, maybe you can find something there to tell you who it is. We need to figure this out before a lot of innocent people get hurt in a turf war."

"Okay," Pelfrey said. "I'll take Flynn and Esposito with us if that's okay."

"Yeah," MacKinnon replied. "I wish you could take a larger force, including a SWAT team, but we need to keep this under wraps until we can figure out exactly what's going on and *who* is involved. Even if it's someone on our side in the force, just follow the evidence and smoke them out. Got me?"

"Understood," Pelfrey grabbed the cell phone, stood up, and held it flat as spoke into it, "I'm heading to the back door of the convention center now."

"Thanks, John," MacKinnon said.

Detective Pelfrey ended the call and thumbed the numbers as he headed for the door.

"I'll go with you," Rory said as he stood up.

"It's too dangerous," Pelfrey told him firmly.

"It's been pretty dangerous around here already. Besides, without being able to call for a SWAT team, it sounds like you'll need all the help you can get. You have no idea how many men are in that building, do you?"

Detective Pelfrey paused with the door open and looked at Rory for a moment.

"Ten years, Canadian Army. Seven years with the Canadian Special Operations Forces regiment."

Pelfrey raised an eyebrow and then finally nodded his assent, "I'm sure Green will have extra weapons." He spoke into the phone as he headed out, "Yeah, I need you two at the back entrance on the double."

Rory sprinted to the door and joined Pelfrey as he pocketed the phone. Ten steps down the hallway, they both turned when they heard high heels clicking just behind them. They turned around and looked at the woman in the red dress and red, high heeled shoes who stood in the hallway just outside the open door.

"What? I'm going with you," Cassandra said with certainty.

"No, you're not," Rory said firmly. "Someone might recognize you and we'll have a hoard of reporters following us–"

Cassandra crossed her arms, "I don't care. I'm going with you."

Rory felt his frustration mount and he gestured to Pelfrey said, "Like he said, it's too dangerous—"

"More dangerous than here? Do you know if *all* the men trying to kill me are dead?"

Both men exchanged glances in uncertain silence.

She looked at them sternly, "And - from what I understand - you two are taking *all* the police officers from here that *you* can trust. Who exactly do I trust *if I stay behind*?"

Rory looked at Pelfrey, who just shrugged his shoulders in defeat.

Cassandra Glynn shut the door behind her and hurried to them. All three hustled down the hallway to the back entrance of the convention center. A large, Chevrolet Suburban SUV came sliding to a stop just outside the doors as they exited.

Pelfrey headed to the front passenger door.

Cassandra and then Rory piled into the back seat.

Flynn and Esposito came running out of the back doors of the convention center.

The large black man in the driver's seat turned and looked back at Cassandra as she got in. His eyebrows pushed together, "Why—"

"Don't even ask, Green," Pelfrey said as he settled in at shotgun.

"You going to have to sit on my lap in the center seat," Rory said to Cassandra.

She looked at him like he had two heads.

Rory pointed at the two other police officers running for the vehicle.

Cassandra held a finger up in Rory's face, "No funny business," she warned. Then Cassandra grabbed the back of the front seat and lifted herself up to let Rory slide into the center seat. She sat back down on his lap as the two police officers took the seats on either side of her.

Detective Delroy Green looked at Rory, a grin splitting his face, his Jamaican accent heavy "How come dat one gets all the fun?" He looked down at Cassandra's long legs.

"Hey!" Cassandra said firmly.

Detective Delroy Green looked up into her eyes.

Cassandra stuck a warning finger in his face, "Be a gentleman and stop trying to look up my dress."

Green's eyebrows shot up, "I wasn't–" He grimaced and turned back around quickly. He glanced at Pelfrey, pulling a scared face.

"I told you not to say anything," Pelfrey said as he buckled up a seatbelt, "but do you listen? Nooooooo."

"Okay, everybody, you buckle 'em up," Green said as he put on his seatbelt, "no guarantees on how well I drive this big mutha."

Rory put his arms around Cassandra's waist.

"What are you doing?" Cassandra asked him.

"The man said buckle up. Since you can't–" Rory explained.

Cassandra raised a finger to her shoulder, "Your hands stray once - even by *accident* - and you're a dead man!"

Rory gave a wink to the officer on his right who was smiling.

"What are you smiling about?" Cassandra said to the young officer on her right.

The smile immediately left his face and he looked straight ahead.

Detective Delroy Green slammed the pedal to the floor and he was right - there were no guarantees on his driving. Everybody swayed left and right as he swung the big vehicle around, bounced left out of the convention center parking lot and then swung the big SUV to the right and down the busy street. Green had the lights flashing and he used the siren when they needed it to get an oblivious driver out of the way. Green wove his way back and forth through the traffic towards the harbor front address.

Chapter 44

AS THEY REACHED THE WATERFRONT, Green turned right and drove the SUV down a street that was vacant of people and cars. He pulled to a slow stop in front of an old brick, two-story industrial warehouse. Old green glass windows swept across the length of the upper story. The street side of the building was quiet and dark but there were lights on in the back half. At the back of the warehouse was a large wharf. A 200-foot freighter was docked at the wharf. There was no visible activity on board the freighter or in the area between the warehouse and the freighter.

Everyone poured from the vehicle. The hot, sweet scent from a nearby sugar processing factory carried across the night air. The men went to the back of the SUV where Detective Green opened the hatch and he passed out protective vests.

"What about me?" Cassandra asked as she watched the men donning the vests.

"I'm afraid this is as far as you can go, Mrs. Glynn," Pelfrey said, "you *have* to stay in the vehicle. No argument this time. Lock the doors."

Cassandra looked very worried as she climbed back into the backseat of the SUV.

Green handed out 9 mm Heckler & Koch MP5A3 submachine guns to each man.

"Did we get any schematics of this building?" Pelfrey asked him.

"They were supposed to send me something," Green answered. He pulled a computer tablet from a case and turned it on. With a few taps on the screen he was able to bring up the schematics. They all gathered around to look over the building layout on the tablet screen.

"Looks like we have front and back entrances. And an entrance on the far side," pointed out Constable Flynn.

"The front and side are probably locked," Constable Esposito said, "but there are lights on in the back. Maybe we find an unlocked door back there?"

Pelfrey shrugged his shoulders, "Since we don't have any equipment to break down a door, that probably makes the most sense."

"Sounds good to me," Green said."But then, I'm a little crazy. I like the direct approach."

Nods were exchanged all around as everyone agreed with the plan.

Rory looked in on Cassandra as they prepared to leave the SUV. She looked petrified.

Shutting down the computer tablet, Green set it back inside the case and closed the back hatch of the SUV.

Everybody had their weapons at the ready.

Green led the way as the group jogged down the left side of the building towards the back. Pelfrey followed right behind Green. He was followed by Constable Flynn, then Constable Esposito. Rory served as the rear guard. The assault group reached the back edge of the building.

Green knelt at the corner. He leaned forward and checked the rear of the building. A large gravel lot led to the wharf and the freighter one hundred yards away. A number of 40 foot containers sat on the far side of the lot - next to three black loading vans - but was otherwise empty. The only light came from open loading at the center of the building. There was no guard in sight.

Green signaled all clear and moved around the corner. The others followed closely behind in a tight line, cautiously watching all sides. Green crept low under the first window and stopped at the far side to keep watch.

Pelfrey stopped on this side of the window and raised his head to take a peek inside the building. Not seeing anyone, Pelfrey motioned for his partner to move ahead. Green moved low and quiet across the back of the building to the entrance way. The team crouched in a line behind him as Green checked the door.

It was locked.

Green then spotted something ahead and indicated for everyone to follow him. He moved low for 30 feet before he halted and knelt down this side of a wide loading ramp area. The large loading door was halfway up. Green cautiously peered around the corner of the half-open doorway. After a few moments, he looked back and indicated he was going inside.

Pelfrey used hand signals to alert the men behind him. They all silently acknowledged his signals and prepared for the move inside the building.

Green readied his weapon. He took a deep breath and slid around the corner and under the raised loading door. He was greeted by the smell of wooden crates and light, industrial oil.

The others moved efficiently and quietly under the door behind him.

They were now inside the buildings large receiving area. Wooden crates containing large electric motors were stacked up ten feet high just inside the loading doors. The five men spread out across the receiving area for safety. They watched high and low for any sign of danger. Up ahead was a long workbench lit up under rows of fluorescent lights. Behind the long workbench, they could see a large group of men working at various tasks.

"Cops!" someone yelled from above.

Green reacted quickly and moved to his left against a line of stacked wooden crates. He was followed immediately by Pelfrey, Esposito, and Flynn.

Someone opened fire from above with a submachine gun.

A woman screamed.

Rory was frozen on the spot. He realized the woman's scream had come from directly behind him. He turned to look.

Cassandra Glynn was right there, on her knees behind him with her hands over her head.

Something else caught his attention and he turned back and looked up.

A man was on the catwalk near the ceiling. He began firing down at Green, Pelfrey, Esposito, and Flynn who were exposed as they pressed themselves against the line of crates on the left.

Rory raised his H&G and fired a short burst.

The man's chest exploded as he was hit dead center and fell over the railing. As he tumbled over the railing, the man's submachine gun kept firing. He took out two of his own men back at the workbench with shots to the head before he landed on his back on the concrete floor.

Rory looked back.

Cassandra was gone!

Chapter 45

THE REST OF THE MEN inside the warehouse had reached for submachine guns of their own and a deadly firefight broke out.

Green, Pelfrey, Esposito, and Flynn moved back, looking for cover behind the wooden crates. Bullets splintered through the wood, ricocheting off the heavy motor casings inside.

Rory realized he was too much in the open on his side to stay alive for very long. He was beside a long line of closely stacked wooden crates with no place to hide. Moving low and fast, he ducked around the front of the crates to the other side. He took cover just as bullets sprayed the wooden crates. Bullets ripped through the wooden crates and bounced off the metal shelving just behind him. Rory heard screaming. He spun around.

It was Cassandra, crouching behind him with her hands on her head.

Rory's voice was filled with anger and fear for her at the same time, "What are *you* doing here? You were told to stay in the car."

Cassandra peeked between her raised arms."I was scared out there. So I decided I'd rather be with you."

"And how is that working for you now?"

Bullets sprayed through the stacked crates again, showering them with wooden splinters.

Cassandra screamed again. Then she looked at Rory, "I guess this wasn't my best idea."

"Not by a long shot," Rory said, "follow me." Rory took off running down the aisle formed by two long lines of metal shelves.

Cassandra followed him, running in small, fast steps in her high heels. Machine-gun bullets marked a trail, chipping the concrete floor just behind her shoes.

Rory veered left and ducked into the shelving behind a very large wooden crate. The sounds of automatic weapons bounced off the walls as Cassandra ducked in behind Rory, squatting with her hands over her head in the midst of a deadly firefight.

Leaning right, Rory glanced around the wooden crate and saw more men, running from the front of the building, joining the firefight against his team. He cursed. They all carried submachine guns. And from his vantage point - he could see the drug runners were well fortified behind large wooden crates and large, cast-iron motors - something his own team lacked.

Rory knew there would be a lot of bloodshed - mainly on his side - if he couldn't find some way to stop this war quickly. Leaning left, Rory glanced around the wooden crate towards his team. He caught a glimpse of Green running towards the far side of the building, firing his weapon. He was aggressively trying to outflank the drug runners. Rory surveyed the situation. The drug runners were preoccupied with the team in front of them and Green to their right. Rory had a brief opportunity to act. He slipped the machine gun sling over his shoulder and turned to Cassandra behind him. "Stay here, you'll be safe."

Cassandra had a very concerned look on her face, "Where are you going? You can't leave me here."

"*Stay here.*" Rory moved across on his hands and knees and eased his way out on the other side of the shelf. Crouching low, he went across the aisle to the next row of shelving. He ducked through that one and went across to the next row. He needed to be one more shelf over to be behind the fortified position of the drug runners. Rory took off and ran low across the aisle to the next role of shelving.

"What are we doing?"

Rory spun around.

Cassandra had come right behind him.

"I thought I told you to stay put?"

Her voice had some heat in it, "And I thought I told you I was too scared to stay by myself. Now *what* are we doing?"

Rory just shook his head in frustration, "I'm climbing up the shelves." Rory pointed upwards.

Cassandra looked up. The shelving rose up nearly two stories. She looked into his silver-blue eyes and said in a hard, low whisper, "You sure you're not doing this just to get me climbing in this dress again?"

Rory just rolled his eyes. He jerked his thumb upwards, "If we're staying together, get going."

"You're not going to look, right?"

"*That's* what you're worried about?"

Cassandra gave him a half-smile, half-shrug, "I was just making a joke to relieve the tension?"

Rory shook his head, letting out an exasperated sigh, "For gosh sakes woman- is that a statement or a question - never mind, just climb. I'll probably be too busy looking for someone trying to kill us."

"Probably? You go first."

Rory grumbled, "You're a pain in the–"

"Don't say something you'll regret."

"Believe me, I won't regret it." He began climbing the shelves.

Cassandra began climbing behind him.

Rory knew he was taking a chance. The shelves filled with boxes and motors concealed their movement to some extent. But if anyone came this way, they would be vulnerable and dead in a heartbeat. He moved as quickly as he could but this was not like climbing a ladder. The shelves were wider apart and he had to stop every so often to pull Cassandra up behind him. Rory finally reached the top shelf, turned and pulled Cassandra up beside him, "Stay here."

Cassandra knelt on the top shelf, her voice shaky and nervous, "This is high. I thought we agreed before you wouldn't make the climb anything too high–"

Rory put a hand to his lips and gave her a hard shhhhhhh, motioning for her to stay put. Crawling to the far edge of the shelf, he peered over, looking to see if anyone had spotted - or heard - them. There was no indication they had. But the smell of gunfire was getting heavier. Rory crouched low and began to move faster, heading for the end of the shelf that should put him over the drug runners. His heart skipped a beat when he heard a light clacking on the metal shelf - he spun around–

Cassandra was right there - crouched low in her red dress and high-heel shoes in the middle of a gun battle - following him. Her eyes widened, "What?"

"What do you mean what?" I told you to stay put."

"Yes, I know."

He ground his jaw and made a hard gesture for her to stay put. Turning on his heels, he continued on - and heard Cassandra moving right behind him. He gave up and continued to the end of the shelves. On one knee - he motioned for Cassandra to kneel behind him - he made sure his weapon was ready. Peering over the edge of the shelf, Rory could see the flashes of machine gun fire from both sides - but his team's flashes were more sporadic. They were definitely outgunned.

Rory slowly stood up. From this height, he had a great vantage point over the entire firefight. He aimed - and opened fire - taking out a line of drug runners on the left. He saw a number on the right turn to look up at him. He shifted his firing and took them out quickly.

When the rest realized what was happening, they quickly threw their weapons down.

Silence filled the building. "Down on your face," Rory yelled down to the drug runners, "hands on your head. Do it *now*."

Chapter 46

UNDER RORY'S WATCHFUL EYE from above, Pelfrey and Green moved in quickly, followed by Flynn and Esposito. First, they removed the weapons from the floor between the men. Then they began to secure the hands and feet of their prisoners with plastic tie handcuffs.

Detective Pelfrey looked up and gave Rory a thumbs up. He did a double take as Cassandra peeked over the edge of the shelf. He turned to look at Green who only shook his head.

Rory looked down at Cassandra on her hands and knees, "You are one strange woman. You tackle a drug dealer one minute–"

Cassandra wagged a finger at him, "You *never* call a woman strange if you want to live. I'm *complicated*."

"Complicated?"

"Yes." She peered over the edge, "Now how do we get down?"

"Same way we got up here," Rory answered.

"Oh." Cassandra sat back on her knees, "I didn't think about that part."

Rory shouldered his weapon, "I'll go down first and help you down."

Cassandra started getting up, "Okay–"

Rory just grinned.

Sinking back to her knees, she narrowed her eyes at him, "Not on your life." She looked back, trying to find another way.

Rory looked out over the warehouse, looking for something he knew should be here. Through the still lingering haze of gunfire, he could see Constables Flynn and Esposito heading toward the front of the building, weapons at the ready. Green and Pelfrey had the prisoners lying face down and were starting to search them. He spotted what he needed.

Rory called down, "Detective Pelfrey? Can you move that lift over here to get us down?" He pointed.

Pelfrey looked at where Rory was pointing. There was an eight-foot-long hydraulic scissor lift with an outrigger system sitting against the concrete block wall. It was used to move people up and down as they picked and placed boxes on the shelves.

Green was looking over as well and he gestured for Pelfrey to go do it. He stood up and watched over the prisoners as Pelfrey shouldered his own weapon, went over to the scissor lift and drove it to the spot below Rory.

Pelfrey activated the controls and divided his time watching over Green and the prisoners as the platform rose up to a spot level with the top shelf where he stopped it, "Welcome to Pelfrey limo service, folks."

Rory stepped across the one-foot gap to the platform, "Thanks." He looked back at Cassandra, "You coming?"

"Is that thing safe?"

"Yes, c'mon." He held a hand out.

Cassandra got up from her knees and approached the bucket. She looked down.

Green was looking up at her.

She yelled as she pointed down at Green."No looking. Back off."

Green put a hand up in mock surrender and turned away.

Reaching out and holding Rory's hand, a nervous Cassandra jumped across the gap to the platform, smiling, "I think that's called busting his balls, right?"

"If you say so. You put everyone's life in danger, you know."

"I know. I'm sorry. I just trust you to keep me safe." She held onto the side railing with an iron grip.

"If you say so, sweetheart."

"Who are you, Humphrey Bogart?"

Pelfrey lowered the bucket back down to floor level where they got off. The three of them walked over to where the prisoners remained lying face down in a long line, hands on their head, Green was back to searching them.

"Find anything?" Pelfrey asked him.

"Just these," Green said. He passed three red passports up to his partner.

Pelfrey swore as he looked at the passports while his partner patted a few more pockets.

Rory leaned in to look, "You're kidding? Some of these guys have diplomatic passports as well?"

"Doesn't make sense, does it?"

"No, it doesn't."

Green handed up a two more as Flynn and Esposito returned from the front of the building. "The rest of the place is empty," Esposito said. "There's an office area up front with some filing cabinets and computers."

"Good work," Pelfrey said. "We'll check that out once we get everything secure back here."

Rory wandered back to look at the work area with Cassandra sticking close to him. He approached the long workbench where the drug runners were working when the team had first entered. Sitting on the floor near the bench were a number of large electric motors and casings that were in various stages of disassembly. There were various parts laid out and strewn across the workbench and Rory looked them over. Using both hands, Rory picked up an electric motor rotor. He was surprised - it was a lot lighter than he had expected for its size. One-quarter of the part was pulverized into a white powder that sat on the bench. Setting the part down, Rory moved the powder around with a finger.

On his left, Cassandra leaned over, "What is it?"

"I'm not sure."

Pelfrey and Green appeared beside them. "I sent Flynn and Esposito over to the freighter," Pelfrey said. "What have we got here?"

"Rory's not sure," Cassandra said.

Green moved around to Rory's right, "Hold on." He stuck a finger in the powder and licked it. An eyebrow rose.

Cassandra noticed, "You know what that is?"

Nodding, Green said, "Back home we used to call it the white lady - among other things."

She looked to Pelfrey

"Heroin."

"Heroin? Really? Are you sure?"

"I am afraid so," Green said. He picked up the motor part and examined it closer, smelling it at one point, "It smells like they've mixed the heroin with a small amount of plaster of Paris. They've used just enough to mold the heroin into this shape and some-one with some artistic talent painted it to look like a real part."

Cassandra crossed her arms, "You mean someone would also be injecting plaster of Paris into their body?"

"Not really, no. They would have a make-shift lab somewhere and use chemicals to extract the heroin for street sale." Green shrugged, "I'm not sure they care if they hardened someone from the inside out anyway."

"That's cold and cruel."

Rory pointed down the long workbench, "They've done that molding and painting trick with a whole series of parts. You can tell they're not real parts right up close. But if someone like me was doing an inspection, I'd never notice it. I'd be looking for a powder in bags or bricks. I wouldn't be expecting this at all."

"I agree," Pelfry said. "And it's highly unlikely a customs in-spector would catch this either. These guys created an entire mo-tor from molded and painted heroin. It's ingenious."

"I think it's more than ingenious," Cassandra said. "They've created a criminal enterprise right under our noses."

Everyone else turned and saw Cassandra looking up. They did the same - suddenly realizing the extent of this operation. The entire warehouse was filled with two-story high shelves holding large crates. Of electric motors. There were hundreds of them.

Green let out a low whistle.

Just then Constable Flynn came walking in, stopped and hooked his thumbs in his belt, "No one is on the freighter. What are you guys looking at?"

Pelfry gestured to the shelves, "Motors. Hundreds of them."

Flynn nodded and stuck a thumb over his shoulder, "Yeah. The cargo hold on the freighter is filled with crates of them from top to bottom. Must be a million of 'em."

Chapter 47

"**THIS IS ONE BIG MOTHER** of a drug bust," Detective Delroy Green said as he looked at the others. He took his cell phone out of the holder on his belt, "We need to get narcotics in on this."

Pelfrey nodded, "You're right. Why don't you stay here with Flynn and Esposito and get that started? I'll take these folks back to the convention center to meet up with MacKinnon. He said he was going to head down there once he was finished at the airport."

Green nodded as he hit speed dial, "I'll call MacKinnon after and let him know what went on here and that you're heading back."

Pelfrey started turning to Rory and Cassandra and then he said to Green, "And you better let the office know you're going to need a number of paddy wagons."

Giving Pelfrey a thumbs-up, Green began talking into his cell phone

Now Pelfrey turned, "Okay folks, we can–"

Rory had been looking at the rows of shelves and he turned to look at Pelfrey and Cassandra - both men ended looking at each other.

Because Cassandra wasn't anywhere to be seen.

Pelfrey groaned in frustration, "*Now* where did that woman go?"

"I saw the lady heading up towards the offices," Constable Esposito said.

"And you didn't think to stop her?" Pelfrey asked him sternly.

Both Esposito and Flynn lifted their hands up in mock surrender.

"Like they could've stopped her," Rory said as he shook his head. He turned and began to jog up toward the office area.

Pelfrey was right behind him with Green following a little slower as he talked into his cell phone.

Esposito and Flynn told the detectives they were staying behind to guard the prisoners - in truth, they wanted nothing to do with the feisty redhead.

Rory opened a door and walked into a large office space. There was a slight musty smell, mixed with the odor of ink and old paper.

Cassandra was looking at papers on one of the desks in the office area.

"I would tell you to stop doing this," Rory said as he walked up behind her, "but I imagine you wouldn't listen."

She never looked up, "Pardon?"

Rory just shook his head as he looked at both Green and Pelfrey in frustration.

Green was looking down at Cassandra's legs.

Rory went over to Cassandra and placed his hands on her shoulders, "You should let me know when you're going to do something like this, okay?"

Cassandra turned her head a little, "I heard them say it was empty."

Rory shook his head, "That doesn't - never mind. What are you looking for?" He stepped beside her and looked down at the papers in her hand.

"I don't know," Cassandra admitted. "But if this is all part of what that Soto guy set up, I thought I might find some answers."

"Answers about what?" Pelfrey asked.

"About why my husband and my children were killed," Cassandra said. She threw the papers she was looking at down and moved over to another desk.

Rory looked at the two detectives. Each of them wished they could give her an answer. Each man began looking over the desks and the paperwork on top of them. They opened desk drawers and some filing cabinets. Most of the paperwork had to do with imports and exports.

Green flipped through a stack of papers, "Most of these have to do with motors being shipped out of the Port of Buenaventura in the Valle del Cauca region in Columbia."

"Same here," Pelfrey said. "And they have the name of the export company in Bogota, Columbia. The powers that be can have this followed up. Might be the start of a major drug bust in Columbia."

"Why would they leave a paper trail leading back to them that was easy to trace?" Rory asked.

"The paperwork may be falsified," Green replied, "happens all the time. But it still gives the narcotics people a good lead to follow-up on. Maybe they can trace it right back to a real big source, make a real blow in the heroin trade down there."

Cassandra called out to them, "Why would this place be list-ed as a Port of Entry for Canada?" She had entered a small glass office on the right-hand side of the building and was standing be-hind the desk, looking at some papers in her hand.

All three men looked at each other, not sure what she was talking about. They moved as one quickly to the small office and went inside.

"What did you find?" Pelfrey asked as he moved around the desk to look at what Cassandra was holding.

Cassandra handed him the paperwork, "This warehouse and the dock facility is being designated as a Port of Entry." She ran her fingers under a few lines on the top page.

"By who?" Rory asked.

"By the federal government," Pelfrey said as he glanced over the paperwork. "Canada Border Services Agency to be specific."

Cassandra crossed her arms, "A Port of Entry is the spot where you enter a country and go through customs. It could be a border crossing or an airport or, in this case, a seaport where car-go is unloaded and enters a country. But we already have the Port of Toronto authority designated to do that here."

"Why would they need another one?" Pelfrey asked as he read through a few other pages in his hand.

"What would a Port of Entry do specifically in this case?" Rory asked.

"It's how a ship would enter a country and go through cus-toms," Cassandra explained.

Green perked up, "Customs?" He began digging through his pockets. He pulled out an identity card and swore, "One of those Shotta's back there had this on him. I wondered about it."

"What's a Shotta?" Cassandra asked him.

Pelfrey looked over at his partner, "It's a term used in the Caribbean for drug dealers and other criminals. I keep telling him to use English. What did you find, Delroy?"

Green held up an identity card, "One of *them* is designated as a Canada Border Services Agency officer."

His eyes wide, Pelfrey asked, "Are you sure. One of those drug guys back there?"

"Ya mon."

"How exactly would that help them?" Rory asked.

Cassandra gave them the answer, "As an officer of the CBSA, he would be able to clear that freighter back there through our customs. And if this place *was* designated as a Port of Entry, he could work right here and clear any ship that docked back there. He could use these computers to file all the paperwork electronically and *no one* would be any wiser."

Green held his hands out wide, "Dis is hell an powdahouse. They could buy the biggest freighters that can come up the seaway and load it to the gills with the white lady. They could smuggle millions and millions and millions of dollars worth of her into the country and we would *never* know!"

Chapter 48

DETECTIVE GREEN TALKED on his phone as the others continued to look through what they had in the office area of the old industrial warehouse. Cross conversations went on discussing what they found and the possible implications to Cassandra and her family but there were no illuminating revelations. Constable Flynn entered the office from the back and stood with his thumbs in his belt, waiting to be acknowledged.

Pelfrey looked over at him finally, "How's it going back there?"

Flynn jerked a thumb over his shoulder, "We got a dozen officers back there now. And three paddy wagons. I got a couple more coming from the 5th. I mentioned to the Desk Sergeant about how many we got and he's bringing in some guys off-shift. But it's going to take some time to process them."

"That's good work. As long as it gets done. What about the freighter?"

"I got six guys working on that. It's going to take some time to do an inventory of all the containers."

Green hung up on his call, pocketing the phone, "I got me some computer people coming down here." He swept an arm around the room, "We got to get all these computers looked at. It's going to take a while to get it all done."

Pelfrey frowned, "That seems to be a consistent theme."

Green shrugged, "A so di ting set." He grinned when he saw Pelfrey shaking his head.

"Okay," Pelfrey said. "Flynn and Esposito seem to have a handle on everything here. Maybe we should head back to the convention center."

"That sounds good to me - going back I mean. But I was hoping for them to come back at the convention center with us. I may have some other things they could help me with."

Pelfrey nodded, "I have no problem with that. But maybe they can wait for the computers guys? I want them to know everything happening so they can keep us up-to-date."

"That is okay," Green said. He looked at Flynn, "They should be here in a half-hour. After that, take a vehicle and Esposito meet me back at the convention center in the command room. Put someone here you can trust in charge and have them report to you. You get any flack, you call us. We still want to keep this tight."

Flynn gave him an affirmative nod, "You can count on us."

"Good," Pelfrey said. He turned his head, "Mr. Steele? Mrs. Glynn? We are going back to the convention center."

"What about all this?" Cassandra asked. She held a thick sheaf of papers in hand.

"We have a team coming down. No worries," Green said.

Cassandra grimaced at the thought of leaving.

Rory put a hand on her arm, "Let them sift through everything with a fine tooth comb and we'll know if they come up with any more answers. We need to get some rest and something to eat."

She reluctantly agreed, letting the sheaf of papers drop to the desk.

"We'll use the front entrance," Pelfrey said, and he led the way outside to the SUV still parked on the street at the front. They stowed their weapons, jumped into the SUV and headed back to the convention center.

Green snapped his fingers and looked over at Pelfrey, "Sorry. I never did get that chance to call MacKinnon."

"Okay," Pelfrey said. He pulled out his cell phone and made a call as Green maneuvered through the traffic.

"MacKinnon. You're on speaker."

"Cam, it's John. You're on speaker here too," Pelfrey said." I'm with Leroy and Mrs. Glynn and Mr. Steele. We're headed back to the convention center."

"Okay, good. Sepulveda is here with me. How'd it go at the warehouse?"

"Big shootout," Pelfrey said, "no one hurt on our side. But a lot on their side. You were right. They were smuggling heroin into the country. It was a huge operation down there. They mixed the heroin with a small amount of plaster of Paris into fake parts for electric motors. They were painted and look pretty real. The entire motor was being imported and once they were here, they were disassembled and the parts were hammered and broken down into the heroin powder. They had an entire freighter of motors they were ready to unload."

"Any idea of the total value of heroin?" Sepulveda asked.

Green leaned slightly closer to the phone as he drove, "No idea at this point. A simple guy like me can't count to a gazillion.

But there's more. Several of the men we captured at the warehouse also had *diplomatic* passports. Looks like they traveled in and out of the USA, Britain, and Europe over the past three years."

Sepulveda cursed under her breath, "More diplomatic passports?"

"And one of the guys had credentials identifying him as a - get this - as a customs agent," added Pelfrey.

MacKinnon's voice rose an octave, "Really? These guys were covering all the bases. How in the world were they able to manage that?"

"We're not sure," Pelfrey said. "But they were trying to set up that warehouse as a port of entry. That way their own customs agent, working out of the front office in the warehouse, could clear the freighters coming in. At least, that's what it looks like right now."

MacKinnon blew out an audible breath, "Why am I not surprised? Well, at least we shut them down. We'll work on the rest of it later."

"What do you want us to do next?"

"You said you're going back to the convention center?"

"Yeah."

"Okay. We'll head down there to meet up with you in the command room. Leroy, I sent you a copy of a list of politicians Mrs. Glynn gave us. They should still be at the convention center–"

Cassandra leaned forward in the back seat, "Did you get any more information on them?"

"No, Mrs. Glynn, we haven't had any time. But I don't want to wait any longer. Someone has taken out Soto and his men but we still don't know who. I want to check those guys out as soon as possible and see if any of them are personally involved in the shootings. Once you get back, I want you and Mr. Steele to stay safe in the room until we figure out if there's anyone else who may still come after you."

"Do you think there's still someone else out there trying to kill me?"

"It looks like everyone who was chasing you has been eliminated. And with the loss of that warehouse, we've busted a massive smuggling ring. I imagine any drug dealers left in Soto's crew are hightailing it out of the country and would have little interest left in you. But I want to be safe until we know for sure. Better safe than sorry. All right?"

"All right," Cassandra said. She sat back in her seat, pushed her dress down between her knees with her hands and stared out the side window.

Chapter 49

THE RIDE BACK to the convention center in the Chevrolet Suburban SUV was a little more comfortable with Green adhering more to the rules of the road than on the trip down. He parked in the first spot closest to the back doors and they all headed inside to room 91. The rich scent of fresh coffee quickly filled the room as they each sat with a steaming mug and refueled on sandwiches and donuts.

Rory broached a subject with Pelfrey, "With all the evidence compiled, when are you folks going to clear Mrs. Glynn's name with the public?"

Cassandra stopped chewing, listening.

Pelfrey rubbed his forehead, thinking, "Well...I guess that will be up to MacKinnon. But I don't see it taking much longer. And then I imagine we will continue to look into your family's accident, Mrs. Glynn. I know Detective MacKinnon and Detective Sepulveda have all the paperwork on their accident as well as a number of the other ones. Detective Green and I will do everything we can to help them figure out what happened and why."

Detective Green nodded as he sipped on a coffee.

"Thank you, Detectives," Cassandra said. "I really appreciate all your help and I can't wait to get back home and hibernate for a month."

"I can imagine," Pelfrey said.

A knock came at the door. Rory was the closest so he moved across the room and checked through the peephole to see who it was. It was Constables Flynn and Esposito. Rory opened the door.

Constable Esposito came part way into the room. "We're back. What now?"

Green set down his coffee and got up, heading for the door, "Okay. You two can come with me. We have another task."

Pelfrey got part way out of his seat, "Do you need me for anything?

Motioning for him to stay sitting, "No need, you can wait for MacKinnon and Sepulveda." He glanced at Cassandra, a smile on his face, "Just try to stay alive until we get back, man."

Cassandra had caught the glimpse and she glared at Green.

Green made a face.

Pelfrey laughed, "Now who should stay alive?"

The glare turned to Pelfrey who sobered up.

As Green gestured to Esposito to get going, Rory asked him, "Do you mind if I go with you?"

Green raised an eyebrow, "Want to stay safe do you?"

Cassandra frowned as she stood up, "I heard that."

Green made a scared face to Rory this time as he stepped through the open doorway.

Rory wagged a finger at Cassandra, knowing what she was about to do, "Not this time. You need to stay here with Detective Pelfrey. There are too many reporters out there. Green and the constables can't do their work if a crowd of reporters goes crazy after spotting the subject of an intense manhunt."

Cassandra's frown deepened.

"Thank you. We won't be long." He blew her a kiss.

The deep frown turned to a scowl as Rory let the door close.

Green shook his head at Rory as he started down the hallway, "You a crazy man. Me not wanna be you when you come back."

Constables Flint and Esposito laughed as they trailed behind.

Rory glanced over his shoulder at the two, "I could tell her you two put me up to it."

They glanced at each other, and Flynn pretended to shudder, "I'd rather do ten with the crazies in Kingston Pen." There was laughter all around as they continued down the hallway.

"Where are we going?" Rory asked.

"We need to check out the politicians," Green said.

"But...there's like two or three hundred staying here," Constable Flynn said in surprise.

"You got somewhere to be?" Green shot back over his shoulder.

"Uh...no," Flynn said, realizing he had spoken out of turn. "But...I'm just sayin'...maybe we need more officers...."

"Yeah, he's just concerned is all," Esposito added. He bumped his partner with his elbow and made a face.

Green shook his head and smiled at getting a rise out of the two constables, "Don't worry, man. We're only concerned with twelve of them."

"The members of Estrada's federal cabinet?" Rory said.

Green nodded, "Yeah. Something might pop if we just concentrate on those guys for now. There has to be some kind of connection we can find."

Rory nodded his head in agreement as they reached the closed double-doors of the York Room.

Detective Green placed his hand on one of the door handles and looked at Rory, "Maybe we can find the right thread to pull that unravels everything. Right?"

"Let's hope so," Rory muttered.

Green pulled the door open and moved inside.

Rory followed right behind with Constables Flint and Esposito stepping in right behind him.

The room was very large, with hundreds of people sitting at various tables around the room. A loud buzz filled the air. People were milling about, talking and laughing. You could hear glasses clinking around the room and the aroma of olives, pigs-in-a-blanket, deviled eggs, cheeses, cocktail wieners, dumplings, and bruschetta was mouth-watering.

A young blonde woman approached them, looking over Rory and the two constables critically as she addressed Green."Can I see your credentials, please" This is a private function–"

Green held up his police shield, "All the credentials I need, young lady. What's your name?"

"Oh. Uh...Melissa. H-how can I help you?"

Green gave her a piece of paper, "That's better, Melissa. I need to talk to these twelve men."

Melissa took the list in hand and looked it over, "What's this all about?"

"I'm the one who asks the questions," Green told her sternly. "I ask, you act. Now, can you get these men for me or not?"

Green pointed towards the far side of the room and took two steps, "Or do I need to go up to that microphone and call for them one by one?"

Melissa moved, holding her hands up to stop, "No, of course not. No need to do that. That will get me in trouble–"

"Not as much trouble as me arresting you for impeding an investigation, Do I make myself clear?"

She shook her head, "Uh...no." She seemed to look for some help and then said, "All right, I can do that. But it may take some time for me to find them in here. We have a seating arrangement but they have a tendency to move around."

Green looked around the room and considered the situation, "Okay, I understand. Do you have a daily schedule or itinerary for each of those men?"

"Yes, of course," the young blonde said, "that's part of my job. Just give me one moment please." She went over to the right and talked to several other young ladies who were gathered around some tables at the back. They immediately began to look through a large number of brown envelopes. A moment later, she came back to Detective Green and handed him ten large envelopes. "These are the complete itineraries for each person on the list. Let me know if there's anything else I can do for you."

"Thank you," Green said as he handed the envelopes back to the constables, "I'll be back if I need anything more from you." He held up a stern finger up in front of the young blonde's eyes, "And not a single word of this to anyone. Do you understand me? Not your boss, not anyone." He pantomimed handcuffing and said 'click'.

The young blonde swallowed and nodded quickly yes.

Chapter 50

THEY ALL EXITED the York Room and Rory suggested they go over to the little coffee shop instead of going all the way back to room 91. The quartet took a secluded table towards the back and split up the envelopes, looking through the itineraries of each member of the Prime Minister's cabinet. Each packet contained a picture and a small biography of each person.

"Looks like these guys have got every minute of the day covered," Flynn said.

Esposito nodded in agreement, "Yeah. It looks like every minute of their day is set to a schedule. Interviews, appearances on television programs, meetings with supporters, lunch meetings...."

"You're right," Rory agreed. "If they kept to these schedules they wouldn't have a chance to get involved with what was happening here today. I imagine a lot of them are going to be on camera as well, solidifying their alibis."

Green shook his head slowly and did some thinking. Then he leafed through the folders in front of him and pulled out the publicity photos of each politician. He gestured to the others, "Grab the pictures from your folders and give them to me."

In a few moments, Green had them all laying in three rows of four on the table. He leaned on an elbow, straightening a few pictures as he rubbed his forehead, "What am I seeing that I'm not seeing?"

Flynn and Esposito leaned forward, looking at the pictures. They glanced at each other and gave subtle shrugs.

Rory watched them all and wondered why he had bothered coming along. This was getting them nowhere.

After ten minutes of his touching photos and mumbling to himself, Green's cell phone rang. He pulled it from the holder on his belt and looked at the screen, "It's the precinct." He hit a button and set the cell on the table, "Green. You're on speaker."

A deep voice came from the other end of the call, "It's Javier."

"Yeah, what's up?"

"I ran those twelve names on the list you sent me." Javier hesitated, "Do you know who these guys are?"

"Yeah, I do," Green snapped. "What did you find?"

"Nothing. No criminal record of any kind. And no juvenile record either. Not so much as a parking or speeding ticket for any of them. These guys all seem to be straight up dudes who go to Sunday school."

"What would you know about Sunday school, Javier," Green kidded him.

"I heard about it on the playground," Javier said. "Anyway, I got nothing for you bro. You need anything else?"

"No. Thanks, Javier." The call ended and Green shook his head in frustration.

"Squeaky clean politicians?" Rory said.

"Yeah. How often does that happen?" Green said sarcastically.

"So what now, Detective Green?" Flynn asked.

Green shook his head slowly and whispered, "I just need a thread, man. There is something wrong here. A squeaky clean politician I'm okay with. But with every one of the politicians we're looking at being clean as a whistle? No, no, no. *Something* is wrong. And there is something that my brain says is right there in front of me. I just can't find what it is."

Flynn and Esposito looked at each other.

"Go grab some coffees for us," Green said to the two constables. There's a Tim Horton's just on the corner."

Flynn and Esposito nodded and headed out.

Green narrowed his eyes and cocked his head. A moment later, he reached up to the third row, picked up a picture and set it down in front of himself.

"You see something?" Rory asked him, leaning forward.

Green just stayed quiet and pensive as he looked at the picture of one single politician. He narrowed his eyes and cocked his head the other way, studying the picture like a bug under a microscope.

Rory stayed quiet, not getting in the man's way or breaking his thought process.

After a few more minutes, Green looked at the remaining pictures. Moments later, he reached out and picked up one. This one he stared at and then tapped it against his chin, thinking.

"Detective Green? What is it?" Rory asked.

"I'm not sure," Green said quietly as he set the second picture down beside the first.

Rory looked down at the detective's left wrist. He had noticed a silver bracelet when Green had reached across for the pictures. It had a tiny caduceus engraved in it - white diamonds on each side - and it reminded him of a medical ID bracelet worn by people with life-threatening allergies–

Green must have noticed him looking because he lifted his arm off the table and twisted it back and forth, rattling the bracelet, "A reminder to stay alert."

"What's your allergy?"

"Drug dealers."

"Pardon?"

Green's face lit up as he touched the bracelet, "It is made to look like a medical ID bracelet. But it is really a tracker. I wore it undercover in case my cover was blown and they buried me in a shallow grave somewhere. This way my body could be found. It would save my family going through the ordeal of not knowing, like what happened to us back in Jamaica."

Rory grimaced, "I can only imagine what that would be like."

"Not ever knowing is horrible." He shrugged, "It also has the capability of recording conversations but you had to have someone close to receive the signal. It was an idea the brass had but I said it would never happen. Too dangerous for undercover work around crews always suspicious of every single thing–"

Just then, a man appeared a few feet away from the table. He was wringing his hands. "Mr. Steele? I'm Mr. Kaluza, the Manager of the Convention Center...?"

"I remember you."

Kaluza gave him a nervous smile, "Very good. I saw you come through the lobby earlier with the police officers. Is Detective Pelfrey nearby?"

"No, he's not."

"Oh. It's just...I may have some more information for him. Is he in room 91? I could go there–"

"Is it important?" Green asked.

Kaluza shifted nervously on his feet, "I think it could be. But if–"

"Mr. Steele, why don't you take him back up there so he doesn't get shot?"

Kaluza's eyes went wide.

Green winked at Rory, "You can check on Pelfrey to make sure he is not in the deadman yard on account of your woman."

Rory shook his head, a smile evident, "She's not my woman."

"Too much for you, eh?" Green gestured to him, "Go. Check on them. It's better than staying here and watching me. I'll let you folks know if I find anything more down here."

Rory nodded.

Detective Green went back to studying the two pictures he had picked out.

Chapter 51

RORY SLIPPED HIS KEY CARD into the door lock of room 91. Opening the door just enough to stand where he could be seen, he gestured to Cassandra to get out of sight as he said, "Detective Pelfrey? I brought Mr. Kaluza, the convention manager to see you."

With a huff, Cassandra got up and headed for the bathroom.

Pelfrey got up, shielding her departure as he walked over to the manager, "Yes sir, what can I do for you?"

Kaluza was wringing his hands tightly, "Hello, Detective Pelfrey. I understand you were looking for video of the hallway for room 92 across the way?"

"I was. But it appears someone erased the entire day. Your security staff couldn't come up with anything else."

"Yes, they informed me of that fact. But what most people didn't know - including most of my security and staff - is that I had some extra cameras installed at a number of exits. We were trying to catch someone taking a lot of expensive equipment from the convention center. We kept it quiet since we didn't know who was involved."

"Okay?"

"There is another surveillance camera installed at the exit that looks down the hallway towards these rooms. It was installed up in the light fixtures, so no one would notice. We did catch our thieve, but we hadn't taken the cameras down yet. It's been running for the last few days."

Pelfrey looked at Rory for a moment and then he said, "Thank you, Mr. Kaluza. I'll have a forensics team go down there to talk with you about securing the footage. Don't let anyone near that control board."

Kaluza nodded affirmation at the instructions and turned to leave.

Cassandra came hustling from the bathroom, her high heels clicking with determination across the floor, "Mr. Kaluza? Could you hold on for a moment, please?"

Stopping and turning immediately, Kaluza looked at the woman approaching - his jaw dropped and he lifted a hand, pointing a finger.

"She's under protective custody," Pelfrey said firmly. "You tell anyone who you saw and you're in trouble."

Kaluza glanced at Pelfrey, his finger still pointing at the woman in the news.

"Do you understand me? I'm serious."

Finally nodding woodenly, Kaluza was still mute.

Rory shook his head at Cassandra, "You see what happens when you don't listen?"

"I don't care." She looked at Pelfrey, demanding to know, "Why aren't we going to look at the video now?"

Pelfrey considered her for a moment and then took a deep breath, "Do you really want to see your friend going down to the room? The man who killed her is dead–"

Kaluza's jaw dropped again.

Sighing, Pelfrey said, "You never heard that."

Holding his hands up, Kaluza said, "No, of course not."

Pelfrey looked back at Cassandra, "What I'm saying is - we can secure the video - but there won't be any trial since the man is already dead–"

"Maybe not. But I'd like to know for sure. Right now, we only have a *theory* as to why Larrise Abbatiello was killed. Isn't that right?"

Rory pursed his lips as he exchanged a glance with Pelfrey. A moment later, he said, "Actually, she's got a point."

Pelfrey's eyebrows pushed together as he gave it some thought, "But what good does it do now? Like I said, there won't be a trial because everybody is dead–"

"Please," was all Cassandra said.

"You're *sure* you want to see it?"

"Yes."

Chewing on his lips, Detective Pelfrey finally relented and nodded.

KALUZA LED THEM BACK to the video room. He had his head of security call up the specific video before he turned to Pelfrey and pretended to zip his lips. Then he and the security man left.

Pelfrey sat in front of the console, with Rory and Cassandra taking up a standing position behind him, watching. He set the controls to fast-forward the video and began running it, stopping at spots where people appeared in the picture. All of the figures turned out to be convention center cleaning staff or someone who was just passing through, going to or from the back entrance. They moved through a portion where three men and a dark-haired young woman walked down the hallway. The three men went into room 92. The woman paused and looked up and down the hallway before she entered as well. Before Pelfrey could stop the fast forward a single woman showed up coming down the hallway.

Cassandra spoke loudly and pointed, There. That one. That looks like Larrise Abbatiello."

Pelfrey stopped the video and backed it up bit by bit to where the figure first appeared.

Rory and Cassandra got as close as they could behind him.

"Can you zoom in?" Rory asked.

"I think so," Pelfrey said. He looked down at the board and manipulated a few buttons. The camera immediately zoomed in.

"That *is* Larrise. That is her," Cassandra said.

The video showed Larrise Abbatiello crying, holding a handkerchief to her eyes from time to time. She moved down the hallway, looking at the various numbers on the doors. When she came to room 92, the door was partially open and she went inside. She came back out very quickly, turning back to the door and apparently apologizing for the intrusion. She headed back down the hallway in the direction she originally came from. A few minutes later, two figures in black leather jackets came out of room 92. They headed down the hallway in a hurry after Larrise Abbatiello.

Rory placed a hand on Cassandra's shoulder for comfort, watching her closely, "At least we know for sure."

Cassandra nodded, a shaky hand to her lips, trying to hold back tears.

"She just accidentally followed Soto and his men into the room," Pelfrey said, "and Soto sent his men after her."

Rory shook his head, "No, I don't think so."

Cassandra looked at him, "What do you mean?" Her back straightened, a little heat in her voice, "Are you suggesting she knew them–?"

Holding his hands up, Rory "No, no, no. That's not what I'm saying. I don't think Larrise followed Soto and his two henchmen into that room.."

Pelfrey shook his head in confusion, "But we just saw her."

"No. Only *one* of the men coming down the hallway - before Larrise Abbatiello shows up - was wearing a black leather jacket. There was also a woman, right?"

Pelfrey looked at him and then at Cassandra. He turned back to the console and backed the video up again. He stopped the video where the three men and the woman first appeared coming down the long hallway. He let it run at normal speed. As Rory had said, only one of the men wore a black leather jacket. The other two wore expensive, tailor-made suits.

The woman was in a dark pantsuit and trailed behind the last man, checking over her shoulder a couple of times as she walked.

Pelfrey froze the image and then zoomed in for a closer look at the four individuals.

The only noise in the room was a sharp intake of breath from Cassandra.

The man in the black leather jacket was one of the men who had followed Rory and Cassandra from the beginning, Cesar

Santana. The other man everyone in the room recognized. It was Prime Minister Martin Estrada.

It was Rory who stated what they were looking at, "It looks to me like Larrise Abbatiello was killed - not just because she saw Neron Blanco Soto in that room - but because she saw Neron Blanco Soto with Prime Minister Martin Estrada."

Pelfrey cursed as he stood up, "Looks like it. The dirty son of a−"

Cassandra's voice was filled with venom, "And now I have confirmation on why they killed my husband...and why they wanted to kill me."

Both Rory and Pelfrey looked at her, not sure what she meant.

"What do you mean?" Rory asked her.

"They killed my family and then I put a kink in their plans when I ran for my husband's seat. They were able to replace me - but no doubt I had public support and if I went after them - it would have put a glaring spotlight on what they were trying to do."

The two men listened and watched.

Cassandra pointed at the screen, "That other dark-haired man going into room 92 with Prime Minister Martin Estrada?"

Pelfrey leaned closer to the screen, Yes...?"

"*That* is Demario Gomez, the retired hockey player. Gomez is the one I was dumped for in the riding election. When I got angry and went up to Larrise's room - I gave them the perfect opportunity to eliminate me - all to make sure *Gomez* was the one they could run as the candidate in a damn election! And they've been trying to finish the job ever since."

Chapter 52

DETECTIVE GREEN CONTINUED to stare at the pictures of the two politicians he had in his hands. The coffees that Flynn and Esposito had brought back were long gone. He reached over and took the packet of information that went with the second picture he had and browsed through it again. After a few moments, he looked at the two constables, "Do either of you know Staff Inspector Ray Shaughnessy?"

Constable Flynn nodded, "Isn't he that old retired guy who hangs out and helps out in big cases?"

"That's the one. He took out a P.I. license after he retired and Ray consults for us now. He still holds the title of Staff Inspector Retired. Is he down here?"

"Yep, he is," Esposito said. "At least, he was earlier. The Superintendent set up a small trailer out there as a command post and Shaughnessy was helping. It's been all hands-on-deck since this started.."

"Would you mind seeing if he's still there and ask him to come and see me? Tell him Greenie said it's a big man ting."

"A big man ting?"

"Yes, a big man ting. Just go, he will know what you mean."

"I'll go with you in case he's not there and we gotta look," Flynn told Esposito and they left in a hurry.

Green took out his cell phone and hit speed dial. "Hi, Javier. Would you run a couple of those names again for me? Yeah. Dalton Kirk Watson and Tedmon Rylee Colbert." He read off the dates of birth for each name. "Yeah. I know you did, I'm just pulling at straws here, man. I need you to check on and run any relatives you can find. That's right, man - *relatives*. Thanks."

Ten minutes later, the two Constables came back into the coffee shop, followed by a tall, burly, white-haired man in a crumpled brown suit. His jowls shook as he moved.

The burly man held out a beefy hand, "Hey Greenie, how's it hanging?"

"Not bad," Green said as he ended his call and shook the man's hand, "I figured you'd be down here instead of playing with the grandkids."

Shaughnessy puffed as he sat down, "Nah. They're too hard on me. They run around too much. Criminals are much easier to deal with."

Flynn and Esposito sat down and Green told them, "Ray here spent nearly 50 years in the job. He taught me everything I know when I was on narcotics with him." Green took two pictures, flipped them around and placed them in front of Shaughnessy, "Which is why I wanted you here. Anyone look familiar to you?"

Shaughnessy dug out a pair of reading glasses and picked up the pictures. He looked at them for a few minutes and then waived one of them back and forth as he stared down at the table, thinking. After a moment, he said, "Yeah, that's Rylee Colbert's kid - what was his name - Teddy. We saw him when we busted Colbert - geez - that's gotta be 20 years ago."

Green looked pleased with himself, "That's what I thought. And the other one...?"

Shaughnessy looked at the picture for a few minutes and then nodded, a flicker of recognition in his eyes, "Yeah. Looks just like his grandpa." He looked over top of his glasses at Green, "How did they pop up on your radar?"

"I'm helping to work the murder case here in the convention center and had to look into a number of politicians. And it turns out, these two bozos are high ranking politicians in our esteemed government."

Shaughnessy's eyebrows went up, "These two?" He looked back down at the pictures and then nodded solemnly, "Makes sense."

Flynn leaned forward, looking at the pictures, "Who are these people you're talking about? The ones from years ago, I mean?"

Looking at the two pictures for a minute, Shaughnessy said, "Their grandfathers were two of the biggest drug runners in Canada back in the 60s and 70s. Conrad Colbert and Red Swansea. They got tied in with Pablo Escobar in the late 70s and really ramped up their operation."

Esposito looked to Green and then Shaughnessy, "Did you say Pablo Escobar? That was the Medellin drug cartel in Columbia back in the day, right?"

"That's right," Shaughnessy said, "in the early days, when he started out, Escobar would even fly a plane himself out of Columbia, smuggling drugs into the United States. Colbert and Swansea would just fly planes from the United States into Cana-

da at the start. But then they began to fly out of Columbia themselves after buying from the cartel. They'd make pit stops and
drug drops either in the United States or Canada. We busted
them but couldn't make a lot stick. They made millions of dollars
and only served about 18 years because they could afford to buy
the biggest lawyers in the country. I may be the only guy left who
was on the job when they were running their operation."

Green listened and then asked a pertinent question, "Do you
know if the family is still involved in the drug trade? I left the
drug unit about a year later and I never ran into them again in
homicide."

"Oh yeah. There were still into it when I retired 10 years ago.
Swansea's daughter married another drug runner by the name of
Nicky Watson. Their names would crop up all the time and it
would usually work back to a Colombian connection. When Escobar died, they just made deals with somebody else. Now the
grandkids never got their fingers involved into the drug trade directly but that's how their straight life was being financed. That
was all part of the master plan of Colbert and Swansea. The
grandkids were sent to school and then got involved in legiti-
mate business interests that allowed the drug money to be laun-
dered. A neat, self-contained organization."

"The problem is," Green said, "I just ran these guys. Twice.
And nothing pops up in a background check. There should be
something in the files referring to what you're talking about. Even
just a relative to relative connection. But nothing. You think it's
someone with influence must have cleaned up their files?"

Shaughnessy sat back and nodded, "It's very possible. A lot of
them over the years have tried to get on the inside to do that. Or
they hire some techie kid to break through one of your firewall

thingies and delete the files. It's tough but they've got the money to do it."

Green waited a beat, "These two guys...are Members of Parliament."

One of Shaughnessy's white eyebrows went up, "I guess being part of the government is about as inside as you can get."

Green nodded solemnly.

Flynn took one of the pictures in hand, "So - if I understand this right - we have some indications these two guys are tied into Soto and *connect* to Columbian drug running way back in the day?"

"Looks like it," said Green. "But if these itineraries turn out to be solid - and I think they will - none of these guys was directly involved with trying to kill Mrs. Glynn or any of their drug partners. Their organization would want them to stay as clean as possible."

Just then Green's cell phone rang. He punched the button, "Green. You're on speaker."

"Yeah, it's me...Pelfrey."

"Wat a guh dung? I'm here with Shaughnessy. You remember him?"

"Yes, and speak English. Hey, Ray, how are you doing?"

"Hey, Johnny, how's it hanging?"

"It's hanging good," Pelfrey said. "And see Greenie? *That's* how you talk."

"Yeah, yeah, yeah, whatcha want?"

"We just found a video of Larrise Abbatiello going into Soto's room. And get this. Just before she goes in there, one of his Soto's men brought the Prime Minister and the politician who was going to replace Mrs. Glynn in the riding election in to see Soto"

Green's head jerked back, "The Prime Minister of Canada? You sure?"

"Yes, definitely," Pelfrey said, "I don't know what his involvement is yet, but it looks to me like someone was knocking off candidates to be replaced by their own."

"What the-! What do you want us to do?"

"I'm not sure," Pelfrey replied. "MacKinnon is not here yet. He's lead and I can't reach him by cell right now. What do you think?"

Green looked to Shaughnessy for a suggestion..

Shaughnessy sidled closer to the table, "Can an old guy give you guys some advice?"

"Go ahead," Pelfrey said.

"Two of the politicians Greenie was checking out have definite drug connections. High-profile, political guys like these have plenty of friends with influence. If you take these two down to the station and run them through the ringer...maybe they give up something, maybe they don't. But I'm pretty sure someone higher up with influence will step in before too long. However...if you make them do a perp walk right out of the front door of the convention center...well...you get my drift?"

Green narrowed his eyes, thinking, "I agree with him. These guys could buy a lot of influence and a whole team of lawyers. Even if it turns out we can't make anything stick, with all those cameras out front, there will be a lot of questions asked by the media. There will be investigative journalists crawling into every nook and cranny of their life."

"I agree," Pelfrey said after a moment. "Do it."

Staff Inspector Ray Shaughnessy slapped the table and then stood up, "It's settled then. Let's go shake them up before some high priced lawyer or big-time politician gets involved."

Chapter 53

DETECTIVE GREEN ENDED THE CALL and led the way to the York Room. Within minutes, Green was pulling the doors open again. The young blond was just inside the door and stepped over to him, looking a little miffed to see them back.

"I do need you to find Dalton Watson this time," Green told her. "You need to tell him he has an important message back here."

"I'm not sure if I can find him right now–"

"Look! We've already gone through this once. If you don't find him and have him here in two minutes, *you* will spend the night in jail for interfering in police business. Do I make myself clear?"

The young blonde nodded quickly, her eyes open in fear.

"And don't tell him who wants to see him either, understand?" Green added.

The young blonde quickly enlisted several other young women to help her.

Green had Shaughnessy and the two constables stand outside the doors while he stayed inside the York Room by himself. The idea was not to spook the suspects and lose the advantage.

Within five minutes, Green stepped outside the York Room with a man in his early 30s.

The man looked put out and the doors didn't close before he turned on Green, his voice a huffy tone, "What is this all about–?"

Shaughnessy stepped forward. His tone somber and officious, playing his role to the hilt, "Dalton Kirk Watson?".

Watson's attitude turned pompous, "Yes. Who are you people? Look, I don't have time for this–"

Now a tiny grin crept across Shaughnessy's lips, "How is grandpa Red Swansea? And your dad, ole Nicky Watson?"

The two names definitely caught Watson's attention.

Green put a hand on Watson's shoulder and flashed his badge. "And how about Neron Blanco Soto?"

They saw a flicker of recognition in the man's eyes.

"Who?" Watson said after a brief moment.

"He was assassinated in one of the rooms upstairs not long ago. On his knees - bullet in the back of the head. Couple of his men hit same way a little earlier. Maybe you're next."

That definitely caught Watson's attention.

Green looked him in the eye, "You have two choices Mr. Watson. One, you stay here and eventually deal with whoever shot Soto and the others. It seems - no matter who you are - the drug trade has a tendency to catch up to you."

Watson looked very nervous as he thought about it.

Green held out a set of handcuffs, "Or two...you can go with these two nice constables down to the station, where it's much safer, so we can talk. It's your choice."

Watson looked at the dangling handcuffs for a moment and then nodded. Green cuffed his hands in front for better visibility.

The two constables each took an elbow and made a show of slow-walking Dalton Kirk Watson through the lobby. By the time they were going out the front door, reporters and news crews swarmed them, recording the event for the next news cycle.

Green went back inside the room. Within another five minutes, he came out with a dark-haired, young man in his 30s.

The man looked put out as well and opened his mouth to speak before the doors closed–

Shaughnessy grinned, "Hello, Teddy. Haven't seen you since you were a kid. How's your old man Rylee these days? And grandpa Conrad"

Colbert stopped in his tracks. He definitely recognized Shaughnessy.

The grin dropped as the retired detective stared Colbert in the eyes, "Guess you probably thought I'd be dead by now. I guess it's a good thing for the country I'm not."

"What's this all about?" Colbert asked, trying to regain whatever advantage he felt his government position held.

Green put a hand on Colbert's shoulder, "Neron Blanco Soto and your family's Colombian connections. Did you know Soto was just assassinated upstairs?"

That fact hit Colbert like a ton of bricks.

Shaughnessy held out a set of cuffs. "I think you know the drill from when you were a kid?"

Green took the cuffs and placed them on a speechless Colbert. Then he took the man by the elbow, "Let's go to the station and have a talk."

As soon as Shaughnessy took the other elbow, Colbert looked at the crowd of reporters heading his way and found his voice, "I...I want to call my lawyer."

Shaughnessy grinned, "Gee, Teddy, you really did learn from your grandpa. You got the whole perp walk down pat."

Chapter 54

RORY AND PELFREY INSISTED Cassandra stay as hidden as possible from the crowd in the lobby as they waited at the back of the front desk area. Kaluza had sent a young clerk to the front doors to wait for a signal from Pelfrey. As soon as MacKinnon and Sepulveda appeared, he waved to the young man - who then brought the two detectives through the milling crowd, behind the front desk and down the hallway leading to the video room. Pelfrey made the formal introductions to Rory and Cassandra and they all shook hands.

MacKinnon then gave Cassandra some official good news, "I've already let police headquarters know you weren't involved in Larrise Abbatiello's murder, Mrs. Glynn With all the major players out of the way and the drug smuggling operation shut down, I didn't see any reason to wait any longer."

Cassandra looked immensely relieved, "Thank you, Detective MacKinnon." She looked to Rory, "Isn't that great?"

"I'm happy for you," Rory said.

A pained grimace crossed Pelfrey's face, "Yeah, that's great. But...it's still not over, Cam."

Sepulveda's face went from delighted for Cassandra to quizzical, "What do you mean, John?"

Pelfrey looked to Rory and Cassandra, who were now looking somber, "It's something we found. I guess it would be best if we showed you - because this one is going to be hard to believe."

MacKinnon and Sepulveda exchanged troubled glances.

"Follow me." Pelfrey turned and led them all back to the security video room where he had left the video in freeze frame mode. Pelfrey stopped in front of the video display - waited for MacKinnon and Sepulveda to get beside him as Rory and Cassandra stayed back, arms crossed - and pointed at the freeze-frame picture, "We finally found video evidence where Larrise Abbatiello stumbles into room 92 and sees our friendly drug kingpin, Soto."

MacKinnon nodded but still looked troubled, "Okay, good. But...I don't think we'll be needing any evidence like this for a trial. Like I said, all the main players are dead and–"

"I realize that. Just take a closer look at those three men and the woman on the screen about to enter room 92."

MacKinnon and Sepulveda exchanged a glance, moved closer and leaned over.

Sepulveda squinted, "That looks like...Prime Minister Martin Estrada?"

MacKinnon narrowed his eyes more, "It can't be."

Pelfrey's voice was firm, "I'm afraid it is the PM."

Without straightening up, MacKinnon just turned his head and looked at Pelfrey, "Okay, so...?"

Leaning closer, Pelfrey pointed at each figure in the image, "That one is...Cesar Santana. That one is...Prime Minister Martin Estrada. And that one...is Demario Gomez. He's the candidate who was going to run in Bryson Glynn's election riding. And Gomez is the one Mrs. Glynn here was dumped for."

Sepulveda looked back and forth between Pelfrey and the frozen video. It took a few seconds before she could vocalize her surprise, *"They* went into room 92!?"

Now straightening up, MacKinnon's voice was subdued, "Are you sure?"

Pelfrey nodded strongly in affirmation as he reached out, pushed a button and let the video run. They all watched the three men and the one woman enter room 92. A few moments later a woman walked down the hall to 92. Pelfrey froze the screen and pointed, *"That* is Larrise Abbatiello." He then let the video run again as the others watched her enter and exit the room, only to be followed by two men in black leather jackets a moment later. Pelfrey froze the video and looked at his two fellow detectives. He waited for their reaction.

A shocked MacKinnon processed the stunning revelations, "Larrise Abbatiello was killed because she saw the Prime Minister and his newest candidate with Neron Blanco Soto?"

Sepulveda shook her head in wonder, "It looks like they killed Bryson Glynn to get Demario Gomez elected in a stupid election!"

"I guess that's why they tried to dump you too, Mrs. Glynn," MacKinnon said as he looked at Cassandra. She was standing back by the closed door.

"I guess I threw a monkey wrench into their plans," Cassandra said in a quiet voice. "When I announced that I would run for election in my husband's old riding to continue his work, it created a problem for them."

Pelfrey's voice was filled with anger, "And they go after you just to guarantee one of their cronies gets into office."

Rory looked at the others, "Since they probably didn't control the party at first, they had to start by killing people, replacing them and financing a run for election - they have millions of dollars at their disposal to do it by hook or by crook. Once they got control, they could hand out diplomatic passports like candy, moving drugs in and out of the country."

MacKinnon grumbled, "And then they just continued on killing people, making sure they stayed in control. That's what you get with a bunch of psychos. It's a good thing we caught up with them."

Cassandra's voice was low and filled with venom, "You still don't get it, do you?"

Everyone turned to look at her.

"What do you mean?" Rory asked.

"You're missing the bigger purpose behind killing all those people, including my own husband. I said it before but you weren't really listening. The replacements they got elected are in Prime Minister Martin Estrada's cabinet. The way our system works, those people really run the Federal government. They don't answer to anyone, except at election time. And even then, they've used our own system against us. They handpick their own candidates...to run in ridings where they are almost guaranteed to be elected –"

Rory interjected, "But we know that isn't illegal–"

"According to Detective Green, those handpicked candidates are people from their own drug organization," Cassandra said loudly. "Think about it! They now have influence over every single part of our government. One had a Toronto Detective's badge. At least two of them had credentials from CSIS - the Canadian Security Intelligence Service responsible for threats to

Canada's national security. They have at least one man who is a customs officer of the Canada Border Services Agency. They're setting up their own Port of Entry, for god's sakes Who knows where they've placed their own people throughout the *entire* country. How do you think all these Colombian criminals were able to get diplomatic passports? These guys were able to move in and out of the country - through our borders - through our customs people - through our surveillance systems - at will. They moved people, drugs, contraband, and who knows what else in and out of the country at will. And they've been invisible to law enforcement - and to our spy agency - all this time."

Everybody stay quiet and listened.

Cassandra Glynn looked like she was in the daze. "They weren't just smuggling drugs," she said with some awe. "Under the direction of Neron Blanco Soto, a Colombian drug lord, these guys don't just have control of a few candidates...or a single party. They control it *all*. They run it *all*. They've actually stolen the entire country!"

Chapter 55

EVERYONE STOOD STOCK STILL. They were all stunned when they realized the truth.

It was Cassandra who demanded action, "What are we all waiting for? The Prime Minister will still be in the convention center. Why aren't you arresting *him*?"

MacKinnon frowned as he gave it some thought, "What charge do I arrest him on?"

Cassandra advanced angrily toward the detective, "What are you talking about? You saw him in that video. He was going in to see a drug dealer. A drug dealer who ordered my husband killed!"

"You're right," Detective Sepulveda said. She looked over at her partner and realized what he was saying, "But he could easily claim it was just a big donor he was visiting in that room. And that he didn't know who it really was."

"Or maybe he blames the other guy he was with," Rory said, following their train of thought.

"Demario Gomez?" Cassandra asked. "That's ridiculous!"

"Is it?" Pelfrey asked her as he realized where this was going. "Two men go into a room. Was Demario Gomez taking the Prime Minister into the room to see a large donor? Or the other way around?"

Cassandra looked with horror from face to face around her, "Why are you all talking this way? You can't just walk away from this like it never happened."

"I can assure you we're not, Mrs. Glynn," MacKinnon said, "but these guys are smart. You're right, they do seem to have control of the entire country. And you of all people should know how powerful that makes them. With high-priced lawyers and all of that political influence behind them, they can make this all go away. We have to play this smart. We have to make sure they *don't* have any way out of this."

Sepulveda nodded in agreement but looked unsure, "But...what's our next move, Cam? How do we gather that evidence without alerting them?"

MacKinnon looked at Sepulveda for a moment, then scratched his beard, thinking, "Good question." He headed for the door, "Everybody stay put. I'll be right back."

Pelfrey turned to Cassandra who had tears in her eyes, "Don't worry, Mrs. Glynn. We'll nail these bastards yet. Detective MacKinnon will figure something out. I'm sure of it."

Cassandra nodded as she pulled out a tissue and dabbed her eyes, "Thank you, Detective Pelfrey. Sorry, I can't take a chance on my makeup running and making a dangerous return to the hooker look." She indicated Rory with a tilt of her head, "You know who has a hard time controlling himself...?"

Rory suppressed a smile and protested, "Hey! It was just one kiss."

Pelfrey's eyebrows shot to the moon, "Really?"

Shrugging, Rory said, "It was necessary at the time. Just part of the job."

Sepulveda crossed her arms theatrically, unconvinced, "Uh huh. Oh, yeah, sure."

"I'll have to try that one on my wife," Pelfrey said.

Cassandra shook her head, "No, no, no. I wouldn't recommend it. It could cost you a month on the living room sofa."

"At least," Sepulveda said as she looked at Pelfrey.

"And only a cad would do it."

Rory shook his head, That's a low blow, Glynn."

Cassandra smiled as she dabbed, doing her best to keep it together.

MacKinnon appeared in the doorway. "That Demario Gomez character just checked out. His parking spot was at the back of the convention center. The front desk said he left in a big hurry. Let's go."

Sepulveda darted for the door, running after her partner, "He must be running."

Pelfrey, Rory, and Cassandra went running after them. As they crossed the lobby, darting through the people still milling about in the lobby, Cassandra did her best to keep her head down, running as hard as she could in her high heels to keep up. The sprint continued down the hallway, past room 92, to the exit.

MacKinnon out the back exit first, followed by Sepulveda.

When Pelfrey, Rory, and Cassandra finally burst through the back door. they could hear MacKinnon calling out.

"Mr. Gomez. We would like to talk with you."

A moment later - gunshots sounded - a bullet ricocheted off the frame of the back door as it was closing.

Cassandra screamed.

Rory grabbed her and pulled her to the left behind a vehicle in the parking lot.

Detective Pelfrey darted to the right, pulling his gun as he did.

Up ahead, MacKinnon and Sepulveda were also diving for cover behind vehicles.

Rory peered over the hood of the vehicle they were behind. In the distance, in the middle of the parking lot, he could see a figure carrying a briefcase. The figure turned in his direction. He was aiming a gun. Rory ducked and a bullet ricocheted off the hood of the car. Rory heard several more gunshots.

"That's Demario Gomez," Cassandra said.

Rory turned quickly and saw she was looking over the hood of the vehicle. He grabbed her and pulled her down. Another bullet ricocheted off the hood, meant for her.

"We can't let him get away!" Cassandra exclaimed as she crouched beside Rory.

"And we can't let him kill us either!" Rory stated firmly.

"Please stop him," Cassandra pleaded.

"They'll get him," Rory said, "don't worry."

Several more gunshots sounded. A bullet shattered the car window over their head, showering glass down on them.

Cassandra screamed and put her hands over her head.

"Demario Gomez," MacKinnon shouted, "Put your gun down. Now!"

Gomez fired several more shots in MacKinnon's direction.

Sepulveda was farther to the right of MacKinnon, behind another vehicle, and she yelled, "You're surrounded, Gomez. Put the gun down."

Pelfrey was further right to her, trying to circle around behind Demario Gomez.

Gomez knew it. He fired a single shot at Sepulveda. Then he fired a single shot at Pelfrey to pin them down.

Rory held out his hand to Cassandra, "Follow me. Run low so he can't see us."

She took his hand without hesitation," Close contact again, and you're going to stop him, right?"

"Just listen and stay low." They ran as a team to the left, crouching low to stay out of Gomez's line of sight. Rory moved them along behind the vehicles parked at the back curb of the convention center. Once they reached the edge of the parking lot, Rory turned them right, following behind another line of parked vehicles that would eventually get them behind Gomez. Rory settled behind a vehicle and peeked over to see exactly where he was. Gomez spotted him, turned in his direction and fired a shot that ricocheted off the trunk of the vehicle. Rory ducked and pulled Cassandra back behind another vehicle. He took a quick peek again. His movement had allowed Pelfrey to move farther up on the far side.

Gomez saw that move as well and he swung his gun around and fired at Pelfrey.

"Give it up Gomez," MacKinnon yelled, "you know you can't escape."

Gomez must've realized the same thing because he suddenly began running towards the back of the parking lot. MacKinnon was up and running, followed quickly by Sepulveda.

Pelfrey began to run towards the back of the parking lot on his side, hoping to cut off Gomez.

Rory took Cassandra by the hand and they began to run down the line of vehicles again.

Gomez half turned and he fired off two more shots.

As everyone was running there was the sudden sound of squealing tires. A black Humvee reversed hard out of a parking spot near the back of the building and slid to a stop. The driver gunned the engine and the black Humvee laid a line of black rubber as it roared ahead twenty feet and turned hard left, tires screeching. Laying more rubber, the Humvee roared down the center of the parking lot. Smoke poured from the tires as they continued to squeal, driven hard by the lead-footed driver.

MacKinnon turned at the approaching sound, holding his hands up, "Stop. Do you hear me? Stop now."

Cassandra yelled over the roaring sound to Rory, "Who is that?"

"I don't know."

Sepulveda jumped up, ignoring the possibility of getting shot as she waved her arms, yelling, "Cam! Get out of the way. Cam, don't–"

Tires screeching and smoking, the Humvee cut around MacKinnon and continued on.

MacKinnon turned - watching the black vehicle head for Demario Gomez -the detective began running again, swearing, "He's going to get away. Stop."

But Gomez didn't think so. He turned awkwardly as he ran, firing a shot that ricocheted off the left front hood of the black Humvee. He tried another shot but his handgun only clicked. It was empty.

The huge Humvee roared directly at the fleeing Gomez.

Gomez turned and ran for his life.

The big black Humvee caught up with Gomez.

Looked back over his shoulder - eyes wide in fear - Gomez yelled, No–"

The black Humvee caught Demario Gomez dead on from behind. As the big vehicle plowed through his body, he was thrown violently into the air His black briefcase shot straight up in the air and burst open. The limp body of Gomez landed one hundred feet away as the black Humvee left the parking lot and squealed into a left-hand turn. Raw diamonds from the broken briefcase rained down - bouncing and sparkling on the pavement.

MacKinnon reached Gomez first. The detective was breathing deeply as he bent down to check for a pulse. Everyone else quickly gathered around the twisted, broken body as MacKinnon sat heavily onto the pavement.

"Dead?" Sepulveda asked.

MacKinnon simply nodded yes as he sat there, his chest heaving.

Pelfrey looked frantically to each and every one, "Did anyone get a license plate?"

Between gulps of air, MacKinnon said, "No license plates that I could see."

Everyone else shook their head no.

"Anyone see who the driver was?" Pelfrey asked.

Everyone shook their head no.

MacKinnon looked up at his partner, "Did you see what he had in the briefcase?"

Sepulveda nodded her head, "More raw diamonds. That's another thing that ties him in with the others."

MacKinnon nodded his head and cursed softly, "Also a nail in his coffin."

Other police officers were now running from the convention center and a large crowd was beginning to gather.

Sepulveda put her hands on her hips, still trying to catch her breath, "What just happened here?"

Rory looked off to where the vehicle had disappeared, "I think someone just wiped out your last opportunity to complete this jig saw puzzle."

Cassandra countered that thought, "No, not the last one. There's still someone else we need to talk to."

Chapter 56

WITH THE RUSH of reporters, photographers, and videographers from the conference center to the scene of the shooting in the parking lot, Rory knew the feeding frenzy would only increase if the news hungry group recognized Cassandra. And right now, the tall, redheaded Amazon stood out like a beacon. He led her to the side of the parking lot after convincing MacKinnon to supply one of the constables who came rushing to help. Cassandra fought the suggestion to wear his cap and pile her hair up under it - she wanted to stop hiding - but she relented when he convinced her it would soon be over. He and the constable escorted her back inside - Rory was surprised the simple disguise worked - but once they were back inside the security video room she handed the cap back to the constable.headed back to the convention center's security room, along with Sepulveda and Pelfrey. Once back inside the room, Pelfrey went over to the video board. The video was still frozen to show the three men entering room 92. Sepulveda closed the door behind them.

"Why are we back here?" Cassandra asked with some heat in her voice, "we should be confronting the Prime Minister."

Rory held his hands out, "Just hold on–"

"I don't want to hold on." Her dress swished as she turned this way and that.

Pelfrey and Sepulveda came back into the room.

Cassandra turned her anger on them, "If you're all afraid to confront the Prime Minister, I'll do it. That s.o.b. was mixed up in my husband's murder."

It was Pelfrey's turn to put his hands out, trying to calm her, "Just be patient—"

Her anger was volcanic, "Why does everyone keep telling me that?"

"Let me explain. The Prime Minister is up in the penthouse suite on the top floor. The elevator won't go all the way to the top floor without the proper key—"

"Then get the key."

Sepulveda put a hand on Cassandra's shoulder, "That's what we're doing. Detective MacKinnon has gone to find Inspector Pam Calhoun. She's with the Protective Policing Services Division of the Royal Canadian Mounted Police. In fact, Calhoun is in charge of protecting the Prime Minister and she has a passkey. She can get us up there—"

Cassandra clenched her teeth, "We can't let him get away with this."

"He won't. Just be patient."

Crossing her arms, Cassandra paced back and forth.

The door burst open and MacKinnon strode back into the room. He was followed by a short woman in a black pantsuit with a white blouse and a red, ribbon tie. MacKinnon strode to the video panel, "And I'm telling you we need to see the Prime Minister right now, *Inspector* Calhoun."

Calhoun argued back, "And I'm telling you, *Detective* MacKinnon, the Prime Minister instructed us not to disturb him. We just can't go barging in there. You can go through proper channels–"

MacKinnon pointed at the screen, "Take a good look at that screen. Who does that look like?"

Calhoun looked at the screen, bent over and looked closer. She straightened up and shrugged, "So you have a picture of the Prime Minister in the hallway. He insists on going places without an escort at times against my better advice. What do you want me to do about it?"

MacKinnon pulled a picture from his pocket and thrust it at Calhoun's face, "Take a look at this picture and tell me if you see *that* man with the Prime Minister?"

Calhoun snatched at the picture, glaring at MacKinnon. Then she bent to the screen, looking back and forth at the picture, "Okay, this man...is that man to the left of the Prime Minister." She straightened up and held the picture out to, MacKinnon, "Do I win a prize, Detective?"

MacKinnon thrust his finger at the frozen image, "*That* man you just identified with the Prime Minister was identified by Interpol as Cesar Santana. His boss is the Colombian drug lord, Neron Blanco Soto. You've heard the name?"

Calhoun's face when sober immediately.

"Oh, and by the way," MacKinnon continued, "that room the Prime Minister is going into? Room number 92? We found DNA evidence of Neron Blanco Soto being in that room *himself.*"

Inspector Calhoun blinked.

Sepulveda stepped forward, *"And* we just had a shootout with Soto's men at the airport. They were smuggling millions of dollars of uncut diamonds and heroin through *diplomatic containers*. The RCMP and CSIS are still up at the airport, as we speak."

Inspector Calhoun licked her lips.

"And *that* man with the Prime Minister is Demario Gomez," MacKinnon added as he pointed at the screen. "We just had a shootout in the parking lot with *him* as he was trying to flee. He had a briefcase full of uncut diamonds. Just like we found at the airport on the wrist of one of Soto's men."

Sepulveda leaned into the Inspector's face, "And before we could capture him and talk, a big black Humvee just ran him down."

"He's deader than a doornail," MacKinnon concluded.

Now Inspector Calhoun's face went white.

MacKinnon put a hand out to move his partner back and his voice turned softer, "Look, we need to talk to him. Now. Maybe there is some explanation. But we need to find out what is going on."

Calhoun took a deep breath, considering her options. Finally, she spoke in a low voice, "We actually haven't seen the Prime Minister for a little while. He went in there with a woman he brought up from the all candidates meeting and we were trying to be discreet–"

Cassandra took a step forward."Who was she? Who's the woman?"

Calhoun's face burned with embarrassment as she looked at Cassandra, "Actually, we don't know. She was wearing a hood.

We just assumed the Prime Minister was sneaking a young lady in–"

Sepulveda cursed, "You're kidding me! Look, we need to get up there now."

MacKinnon continued his soft tone, getting more personal, "Pam, we have a number of others dead...there's a hit man on the loose–"

"A hit man? Why wasn't I told about this?"

Anger came out as MacKinnon said, "We've been chasing one killer after another since the first death and we have fake detectives and fake CSIS agents all over this. We needed to contain it."

Calhoun licked her lips and nodded understanding. She put a hand to her forehead.

"Look, the Prime Minister is either involved *or* he is in danger. We need to move now."

After a moment, Calhoun nodded and headed for the door, "Follow me."

When *everybody* followed out behind her and down the hallway, she turned, stopped, and looked at MacKinnon with a questioning look.

MacKinnon looked back at Pelfrey and Sepulveda as well as Rory and Cassandra. He looked back at Inspector Calhoun and nodded, "They're all with me."

Inspector Calhoun considered them all for a moment and then nodded. Everyone headed for the elevator with Inspector Calhoun in the lead. She spoke urgently into a microphone inside her cuff. They all entered the elevator and Calhoun inserted a special key card into the elevator keyboard. She pressed the button to take the elevator to the penthouse suite. Everyone stood in uncomfortable silence as the elevator climbed. The elevator gently came to a stop at the penthouse suite floor and the doors opened. There were several officers, all dressed in black suits with white shirts and red ties, standing in the short hallway

Inspector Calhoun acknowledged the tall officer in front, "What's the word, Griffin."

Griffin looked at the other then told Calhoun, "We haven't seen the Prime Minister at all since he went in. And everything has been quiet in there."

Inspector Calhoun nodded as the entourage followed her down a short hallway to the penthouse suite door. She pulled a key card from her breast pocket but knocked on the door first. She knocked several times, calling for the Prime Minister through the closed door. She finally looked back at Detective MacKinnon, made a decision, and inserted the key card into the lock. The light turned green and she pushed the door open. She again called out for the Prime Minister. There was no answer. She called out several times, alerting anyone inside that they were entering the suite. There was no reply and everything remained quiet. Calhoun strode into the living room of the penthouse suite. She signaled for the other RCMP officers to fan out and check in the various rooms around the suite as MacKinnon stood beside her.

Pelfrey, Sepulveda, Rory, and Cassandra waited just inside the open door to the suite.

"I don't like this," Calhoun said to MacKinnon. She looked nervously around the room, "Something is not right."

"We've been having that feeling all night," MacKinnon replied.

One of the officers from one of the rooms off to the left called out, "Inspector Calhoun? In here."

Everybody headed in the direction of his voice and entered a large bedroom. On the bed, lay Prime Minister Martin Estrada. His black suit jacket was laid neatly at the end of the bed, He was still wearing a black-and-white checkered tie. His black hair was still neatly combed. His black suit pants still held a crisp press. He looked peaceful. The only problem was the slight foam at his mouth.

The young officer had one knee on the bed, checking the pulse in Estrada's neck, "He's dead." He leaned and sniffed near the dead man's mouth.

Everyone in the room stood in a state of shock.

The young officer backed off the bed, "Unless I miss my guess...I could smell bitter almonds...."

Calhoun cursed, "Cyanide poisoning."

Cassandra's voice came from the back of the crowd, "Suicide?"

Everyone considered her suggestion. No one wanted to consider the alternative.

"Didn't you say he was in here with a young woman?" Rory asked Inspector Calhoun.

"Yeah." Calhoun turned and called out loudly, "Anyone see a woman in any of the rooms? Is there anyone else in the suite?"

There were several other RCMP officers just outside the bedroom. "No one else in the apartment," one officer said, "it's clear."

Griffin stepped forward, "We found one of the French windows open. That's the only way you could get out without us seeing. But it's a sheer drop. Or you would have to go up to the roof."

Calhoun spoke in an authoritative voice but you could tell she was in shock, "You take some officers and head up to the roof, just in case. And I need everyone out of this room. *Now.* We need to treat this as a crime scene." She began to issue other instructions to the officers in the room.

Chapter 57

MACKINNON, SEPULVEDA. AND PELFREY stepped out of the penthouse suite into the small hallway. The RCMP ushered Rory and Cassandra out behind them. They were all very quiet as they walked to the elevator doors. MacKinnon pushed the button.

Rory broke the silence as the group stood in front of the elevator, waiting, "Do any of you think he committed suicide?"

MacKinnon shook his head slowly, "I have no idea really." MacKinnon pushed the elevator button again.

"Okay. Does anyone think The Prime Minister had everyone else killed?"

Pelfrey rocked on the balls of his feet, "Could be. Maybe he was the leader or he was trying to take over from Soto. Either way, it looks to me like he figured everything was over. He took the coward's way out rather than face a trial in disgrace."

Cassandra leaned and looked at the others, "What about this woman? Do you think she killed him?"

No one answered.

Sepulveda let out a sigh of frustration, "Could be."

MacKinnon scoffed, "And got out through that window? She would have to be one of those friggin' Ninjas to get out of that penthouse suite."

Pelfrey scratched his chin, "I don't know. Keep in mind that trick the shooter did with the lasers after they took out Soto."

Scowling, MacKinnon said, "Please don't add a Ninja to this thing."

"How else would she get out without being seen?" Rory asked.

MacKinnon blew out a breath, looking for an explanation, "More than likely one of those young officers up there escorted the young lady out. Wouldn't be the first time security had to cover over for some extracurricular activities on the part of our distinguished leaders, Despite what Inspector Calhoun said, someone must have seen her face or knows who she is. They'll get a description of her and track her down. Wrap the whole thing up in a neat bow."

"Do you think she's the one who drove the Humvee," Cassandra asked, "and ran down Gomez?"

MacKinnon shrugged, "Makes sense. She runs down our last link to her as she makes her getaway." He pushed the elevator button harder, "This is supposed to be a private elevator. Where is it?"

"It's all out of our hands now anyway," Sepulveda said. "It's now in the jurisdiction of CSIS and the Mounties. And if she did it, they'll find her."

The elevator arrived, the doors opened and the small group moved inside.

"What about the rest of members of his cabinet?" Rory asked. "Maybe one of them tried to take over or was involved in the attacks on Mrs. Glynn."

MacKinnon shook his head as he pressed the button for the main floor, "No. Nothing so far. Green and Shaughnessy were able to find a Colombian connection to Watson and Colbert but nothing on the others yet. So far, every one of them has their time accounted for. They were all present at the All Candidates Meeting for one thing. And before that, every one of them was being interviewed or were talking politics with some talking head. They all have alibis for the whole time. It's possible one of them used someone else to do the dirty work, but there is no evidence of that...yet."

Rory looked at Cassandra."So, it looks like you are finally safe."

MacKinnon nodded, "He's right, Mrs. Glynn. And I want to thank you for the work you did on that list. If got us moving in the right direction. I assure you that Detective Green and Inspector Shaughnessy are still working on the others as we speak. And the rest of us will get involved. We should be able to clean them all out eventually. I promise you, we will do everything we can to root out every single one. We'll find each man's smoking gun and get them run out of office. Just the hint of a scandal with a Colombian drug connection will probably end their political careers. And I'll put the bug in Inspector Calhoun's ear about them once she gets over the shock of what happened up there."

"Thank you, that means a lot to me," Cassandra said.

Rory considered what had been said and he looked at MacKinnon, "Can you and I talk together for a moment, Detective?"

MacKinnon looked at him and gave a single nod, understanding he wanted to talk one-on-one. He discreetly glanced at the others.

Gesturing to Cassandra, Rory added, "And maybe you can find a way to get her through the press downstairs in the lobby? They'll be an aggressive mob right now."

MacKinnon took the hint, stepped forward and pressed another button on the elevator, "Tell you what, I'll be the one to give the reporters down there the gist of what happened. I'll let them know your name is cleared, Mrs. Glynn. Play this all up as a drug war gone bad and innocent people caught in the middle, blah, blah, blah. Meanwhile, how about if Sepulveda and Pelfrey here escort you out the back way while I do that. There's another exit on the southeast corner at the back of the convention center." The elevator stopped and the doors opened on the second floor. MacKinnon pressed the button to keep them open. "Mr. Steele, you can come with me to the main floor. You can have Detective Green bring the SUV around to take Mrs. Glynn home."

Rory nodded, "Sounds good to me."

"I'm glad we could help you to figure out what happened to your family, Mrs. Glynn. Now you know who did it and why. Those two men who killed your family are dead and so is their boss. It's over." MacKinnon looked at the other two detectives, "We'll follow-up on all the other accidents and check out the replacements to see how they fit in. Let the other families know what happened as well. They deserve that."

Both Detective Sepulveda and Pelfrey nodded in confirmation.

MacKinnon gave Cassandra a smile, "Now why don't you just go home and enjoy your life from here on in and let us worry about the rest of this stuff."

Cassandra nodded and stepped forward to give the large detective a grateful hug. Sepulveda grinned as she noticed her partner blushing. Cassandra then turned and stepped out of the elevator with Sepulveda and Pelfrey.

MacKinnon stabbed the button to close the elevator doors. He and Rory talked on the way down, with MacKinnon making a single telephone call to Detective Green.

Within moments, the elevator doors opened on the first floor and the two men exited to the main floor lobby. The entire place continued to be a madhouse, filled with reporters, police and convention attendees. MacKinnon turned to Rory and extended his hand, "Thank you for your help, Mr. Steele. We couldn't have done it without you."

Rory nodded as he shook the Detective's hand, "And thank you for everything you've done to help Mrs. Glynn. I appreciate it."

"You're very welcome," MacKinnon said. Then he took a look at the crowd of reporters and took a deep breath, letting it out slowly, "I hate this part." He stepped forward, holding his hands up and asking for their attention as Rory left to get Detective Green.

Chapter 58

CASSANDRA WALKED with Sepulveda and Pelfrey along a curved hallway. They only saw a couple of people pass by as they headed toward the back exit. They went past a couple of cross hallways that were equally empty and quiet. In a few moments, they started walking across a wide, open lounge area with a number of easy chairs and sofas spread around the space. There was a large grand piano on the far side and a large bar area that was empty of staff or patrons. The air smelled of stale beer, wine, cheese and crackers from some recent event.

"I guess all the lookie-lous are down where the action is," Pelfrey said.

"Yeah, every accident scene and every crime scene seems to attract the curious," Sepulveda said with a shake of her head. "I don't understand how people–"

A figure dressed in black stepped out from behind a square column, took a combat stance and aimed a black handgun with both hands.

Crack!

Sepulveda was hit in the chest and fell backward, landing hard on the floor, bouncing once.

Crack!

Pelfrey - hit in the chest as well - had his hand only halfway to his shoulder holster when he fell backward, landed on the edge of a sofa and fell face down to the floor.

Cassandra Glynn froze.

The figure stepped towards her, weapon at her side. The heavy smell of gunpowder hung ominously in the air.

Everything came to Cassandra in a flash, It was the young Latino woman with the short, black hair and dark, hard eyes she had first seen when Clarke Navarro told her Demario Gomez was going to run in her place in the election. She was in the video, the young woman who had been with Gomez and the others when they had gone into room 92 to see Soto, just before Larrise Abbatiello showed up. She was the same young woman who had stared at her outside the washroom after she had killed that man with the porcelain top from the toilet tank. Rory had said she looked like someone heavily trained in martial arts. The comment about someone needing to be like a Ninja to get out of that penthouse suite now made sense and she now knew who had killed the Prime Minister. And ran over Demario Gomez. And then there was the assassin who had killed Neron Blanco Soto, probably cleaning up for someone. Now she was here to kill *her.*

The woman raised the handgun slowly and pointed it straight towards Cassandra's head. Her eyes were firm and unwavering.

Cassandra took a half-step backward, putting her hands up, "You...you don't need to do this. It's all over. They know everything–"

The woman swept out her right foot and took Cassandra's legs out from under her. Landed hard on her back, Cassandra groaned from the pain.

The young woman stepped forward. She held the gun straight down at Cassandra's head and hissed between clenched teeth, "Usted le dieron muerte. Ahora usted se muere!"

Looking up at the rage in the young woman's eyes, Cassandra shook her head, "I don't understand—"

A blur shot through the doorway from the stairwell on the left and hit the woman in a football tackle.

Cassandra saw it was Rory.

Rory landed on top of the woman.

The gun clattered to the floor and slid.

But the woman was catlike quick, skillfully rolled with Rory and was soon on top. Pushing off, she was back her feet.

Spinning around on the floor, Rory got to his feet as well.

The woman kicked his feet from under him.

Rory fell hard. He was in pain from the blow but he maintained his concentration and returned the favor, rolling to his side and sweeping his foot out.

The Latino woman's feet were taken out from under her and she fell to the floor with a grunt.

Lifting his legs back over his head, Rory did a gymnastic kick-up to get to his feet and went on the attack.

But the woman lifted her legs, caught him in the stomach and threw him over her, rolling catlike to her feet.

Rory groaned as he landed on his back and slid. Stopping his momentum, he rolled around to his feet and went on the attack with some martial arts moves.

She countered every one perfectly as they moved around the floor. Then she went on the attack.

Now it was Rory's turn to parry her blows.

She faked a blow to his neck and when Rory put his hand up to defend, she swept his feet out from under him again, sending Rory crashing to the floor.

Rory started a roll to his left but he was too late.

The woman had pulled another weapon from an ankle holster and stood tall, aiming down between Rory's eyes.

He had no chance. Rory waited for the bullet to enter his skull.

"Hey!"

The woman turned to her right and a shot rang out.

A bullet entered the woman's left eye and exited her skull at the back, burying itself in the roof on the far side of the room. The woman fell slowly backward, crashing to the floor.

Rory looked to his left.

Cassandra Glynn was lying on her back with both arms extended, holding the first weapon the woman had dropped.

Chapter 59

RORY ROLLED OVER onto his knees and checked the pulse in the woman's neck. Then he turned and moved over to Cassandra.

She was staring, her body rigid.

Rory gently put his hand on the weapon. "It's okay. It's over. You can let go now."

Cassandra stared for a few more moments and then blinked her eyes, looking at Rory. She nodded numbly as she let the weapon go.

Rory placed it into the waistband of his pants in the back and helped Cassandra get to her feet.

"Ow! Damn!" Detective Pelfrey slowly sat up, clutching his chest.

"I thought you were dead," Cassandra whispered in surprise. "I saw her shoot you."

"Bulletproof vest," Pelfrey said in agony as he tapped his chest a couple times. "Still hurts like hell." He got on his knees and crawled over to Sepulveda. He tapped her cheeks a couple of times.

Sepulveda's eyes shot open, she sat up quickly and placed her hands on her chest, "Bugger. Man, that hurts."

Cassandra giggled in relief, "I was sure...."

"I thought I was dead too," Sepulveda said through gritted teeth. "She must've been trained by the military or some police force. She went for the largest body mass. If she would've aimed for our heads...."

Rory nodded as he used his foot to push the ankle weapon away from her hand. "That's a 22 caliber. She must be the one that assassinated the others. The weapon she used on you two is a 9 mm. I bet you'll find a silencer on her somewhere."

Pelfrey coughed, hands on his chest as he sat on his knees, "Good thing you came along when you did."

Rory nodded, "Green was having a hard time getting the SUV out of its parking spot with the zoo of people out front and I wanted to let you guys know. I hustled my way towards the back as quickly as I could. I didn't see you at the back exit so I was coming up the stairway when I heard the shots."

Sepulveda moved on her knees over to the body, avoiding the spreading blood pool. "I wonder who she is?" She began to pat the body and search it.

Cassandra told them about the times she had seen the young woman, particularly on the video. She looked at Rory, "You thought maybe she was a bodyguard for Demario Gomez?"

Rory nodded, "Yeah. I got that impression from how she carried herself when we saw her after the washroom attack. And the way she watched the hallway when they all went in to see Soto - I would even say she had military training in her past. Not that it matters now."

Cassandra's body started shaking and her voice was filled with fear, "Someone must *still* want me out of the way, so they could run a candidate in the riding,"

Sepulveda shook her head as she continued searching, the woman, "No, I don't think so. Just before I blacked out I heard her say something to you in Spanish."

"That's right," Cassandra said. "But I don't speak Spanish so I'm not sure...."

"I know what she said, but it doesn't make sense to me," Sepulveda said.

"What did she say?" Pelfrey asked. He was still clutching his chest and his voice sounded sore.

"You killed him. Now you die," Sepulveda answered.

"Who was she referring to?" Pelfrey asked.

"I have no idea," Sepulveda answered "No I.D or passport on her. Just this." She sat back with a cell phone in her hand. She looked for the button to turn it on.

Rory knelt and reached out towards the young woman's neck, "She's wearing a necklace or something." Rory pulled on a slender gold chain and a small object emerged from underneath the collar of her black top. It was a gold locket. Rory gently opened it up. There were two pictures inside. "The woman in the picture is her. The man looks familiar but...."

Pelfrey moved beside Rory to look closer, "That's Orlin Delacruz!"

Cassandra's eyes narrowed, "Isn't that the one...?"

Pelfrey looked up at her and nodded, "That's the one you killed in the washroom. They must have been sweethearts. But how would she know you were the one? Both you and Rory were in there–"

Rory gestured to his ear, "The earpiece. Remember? Delacruz had one on him."

Cassandra nodded, "Yeah, you pulled it out because you thought someone might be listening."

"Exactly. And when we were walking down the hall, she was behind those men and I saw her put a hand up near her ear like she was pulling something out. She must had had an earpiece and was in communication with Delacruz. She heard everything that went on."

Cassandra's complexion blanched as she contemplated what he was saying, "She heard me kill her boyfriend. And they're both dead because of me."

Rory stood up and put his arm around her in comfort, "You had no choice with either one."

Cassandra nodded but still looked shaken at killing two people.

Pelfrey stood up slowly, grimacing, "She must have been part of Soto's crew and keeping an eye on things for him, likely babysitting their newest candidate in Gomez."

Rory nodded in agreement, "That would explain why the first two men were shot without a struggle. Soto probably had them killed by someone they didn't expect. I bet she was the one who assassinated the Prime Minister as well."

"Okay," Pelfrey said. But why? And why kill Soto in that room?"

Rory gave it some thought and shook his head, "I'm not sure—"

Sepulveda spoke up, "I think I know." She had gotten the cell phone turned on and was looking at the screen, "And why we always seemed a step behind. She has copies of police reports and communications on key points in the case."

"How did she get that stuff?" Pelfrey asked,

"For one thing, it looks like those guys you said had CSIS credentials were coordinating with her. And the police reports - guess who sent them to her?"

Everyone turned to look at her, waiting.

"Demario Gomez."

"Gomez? How would he get that?" Rory asked.

"Wouldn't be the first time a famous sports star got a favor," Pelfrey said.

"He's right," Sepulveda agreed. "But get this. There's a trail of messages between them. Here's one of the last ones; patrón vuelta coronar billetico." She narrowed her eyes, looking at the others, "Patrón is the big boss. She must be talking about Soto. But...the rest...vuelta - that's like running an errand - coronar in Spanish is like a crown or crowning someone."

Pelfrey snapped his fingers several times, "No, no, no. Green used a lot of that kind of language when we first started working together. He said there was a lot of slang that came out of the Columbian drug cartels. They developed their own language. If you intercepted a message you had a hard time understanding the meaning. You're right about the patrón thing."

"What about the rest? Vuelta....an errand?"

Pelfrey nodded his head as he looked down at the floor thinking, "Yeah. But there was something about vuelta in the criminal context. It's like...a job you had to do...." He snapped his fingers twice again, then looked up, "A hit. Killing someone."

"And coronar billetico is...?"

Pelfrey scratched his head, "We'll need to get Green to confirm but - if I remember correctly - coronar is about a drug deal or even the drug business itself. Billetico is like the payment for a job or a hit."

Sepulveda looked at the message again, "So she's saying...she hit Soto...he's dead...the drug business is payment."

"Sounds like this woman and Gomez were working together to take over Soto's drug business. That's ballsy."

"Maybe," Sepulveda said. "He sent a reply right after. It says; 2 hot I'm out."

Pelfrey repeated the message to himself, "2 hot I'm out. Sounds like he lost his balls because we were getting closer."

"Yeah. And she sent a reply back that said; u made deal 4 pm. plato o plomo."

Pelfrey cocked his head, "He made a deal for the Prime Minister?"

Sepulveda chewed on her lip, "I'm not sure. He replied; cant if in jail." She looked at Pelfrey, "What is plato o plomo in drug slang?"

"That's where they say you take our money - or honor our deal - or we kill you." Pelfrey scratched his chin, "That doesn't make sense. Why would she threaten to kill Gomez over the deal - and then kill the Prime Minister? If Prime Minister Martin Estrada's the one making some deal to take over–"

Cassandra spoke up, "He wasn't. You're looking at it all wrong." She looked at Rory, "Tell them what you said about Gomez' reputation."

"From what I know, Gomez was always a very aggressive player. He was always playing on the edge of the rules and getting in trouble with the league. And once he moved into management, he was noted for being ambitious - and ruthless - with a lot of teams complaining about his tampering with their players." A rueful smile fell on his lips and Rory added, "He always said he would kill to win."

Cassandra looked at the others, "Think about it. u made deal 4 pm. That plato o plomo thing is a 'this for that' exchange - willing or not. The ambitious Mr. Gomez had more than my husband's riding in mind. He made a deal to help this woman and her lover to take over Soto's drug cartel - they eliminate people one by one. In return - u made deal 4 pm - Demario Gomez. becomes Prime Minister."

Rory nodded his head in understanding, "And when Gomez tried to cut and run - leaving her behind to take the fall - she ran him over. Plato o plomo. Keep the deal or die."

"Wow," Pelfry said. "Just wow."

Chapter 60

SEPULVEDA SLIPPED THE CELL PHONE into her pocket and moved to stand up, grimacing with the effort.

Cassandra moved to help her up.

Sepulveda nodded her thanks. She looked over at Pelfrey, "Tell you what, John. Why don't you get Mrs. Glynn out of here? All the players are dead now for sure. I'll wait up here in one of those big easy chairs until you can get some uniforms up here."

Pelfrey nodded as he pulled his own cell phone, "Okay, I'll call to get some men up here right away. And then we can take her out back. Green should be–" His cell phone rang in his hand. He looked at it, "Speak of the devil." Pressing a button, Pelfrey put the phone to his ear, "Wah gwann wid you todeh?" He laughed heartily and then grimaced, holding a hand to his chest. "Yeah. Okay. Okay." He ended the call, a half-smile-grimace still on his face, "Greenie says he got out into the street but the place is a madhouse and he can't get around to the back."

Sepulveda swore as Cassandra helped her get seated and comfortable.

"Sorry," Cassandra said.

Waving off her concerns, Sepulveda said, "No, it's not that. I'm just pissed that we can't get you away from here, home and safe without a big rigamarole."

"Or someone trying to kill me," Cassandra said.

"Yeah, but we should be okay there."

Pelfrey put the phone to his ear, "Once I get a team up here, I'll get Flynn and Esposito to meet us just outside the lobby downstairs and we can shield her from the press when we take her to Greenie's car."

Rory spoke up, "Can I make a suggestion?"

"What is it?" Pelfrey asked.

"Why don't we simply take her to one of those rooms Soto had taken? The whole hallway is already filled with officers and–"

"I want to go home," Cassandra insisted.

"I know. Just hear me out. If you stay here a bit longer, you won't have to run that gauntlet. And I'm sure the press has got your home staked out right now."

Cassandra grimaced, "I never thought about that."

"You wait until most of the crowd clears away - a day at most. Maybe you get Sepulveda to buy you a change of clothing - whatever it takes to get away from the red outfit they know you're in - and then you go home and carry on with your life. How about it?"

She nodded reluctantly.

"Okay, I've got a team coming up," Pelfrey said. "Now I'll get Flynn and Esposito to talk to Kaluza and make sure all those rooms stay empty and one is ready for Mrs. Glynn."

As he called, Rory took Cassandra's elbow and moved her to the side.

"What's wrong?" Cassandra asked. "I'm doing what you wanted."

"I know." Rory pulled something from his pocket, took her wrist and fastened a silver bracelet around it, "This belonged to my grandmother and I've kept it on me as a good luck charm. I want you to have it."

Cassandra's eyebrows knit together, "You're giving me a family heirloom?"

"Just until we get together again." He gave her a wink.

Now one eyebrow rose, a tiny smile on her lips, "You're pretty sure of yourself, Mr. Steele."

Rory gave her a kiss on the cheek, "Just humor me."

"That's a kiss you give your sister."

Another wink.

Cassandra opened her mouth–

"Okay, folks, let's go," Pelfrey said.

"Saved by the man," Rory said with a smile.

Cassandra crinkled her nose as she went over and gave Sepulveda a tender hug, mindful of her sore chest. Rory was holding his arm out as she turned.

"Last time for close contact. Just in case."

She smirked at him, took his arm and they followed Pelfrey to the stairs. Once they were on the first floor again, they headed towards the front of the convention center.

Flynn and Esposito met them in the hallway just outside the massive front lobby. Voices and shouted questions echoed off the walls. "The place is a zoo out there," Flynn said. "A room is ready. How about if we walk in front of Mrs. Glynn while you two cover her from behind and we can skirt around to the hallway?"

"Sounds good," Pelfrey said. "Let's go."

MacKinnon was talking to the press, holding court in the center of the lobby as they slipped out of the hallway. The place was a madhouse of shouted questions as the four men surrounded Cassandra and escorted her discreetly along the outside edges of the lobby.

They were almost there when Cassandra glanced back and asked, "Where is Rory?"

Pelfrey jerked his thumb over his shoulder, "He slipped away to the front doors. Said he was going to have Green take him home and–"

"No, no, no." Cassandra took off, her red, high-heels rapidly clicking away as she headed for the front doors herself.

Cursing under his breath, Pelfrey took off after her, the two constables right behind.

Cassandra was out the doors before they could catch her.

Rory had his hand on the passenger door of Green's vehicle.

Running for the vehicle, Cassandra dodged people, including a few reporters who tried to stop her for comments. Pelfrey and the constables warned them off as they moved after her.

Rory opened the door, turning at the sound of her high-heels clicking behind him.

"Were you just going to leave me like that?" Cassandra chastised him.

Rory held out his hand, "Let's not make a big deal out of this. I told you we'd get together before too long."

Cassandra ignored his outstretched hand and threw her arms around his neck, giving him a big hug. She held onto him tightly for a few moments and whispered, "Thank you for everything." Releasing him, Cassandra stepped back, frowning as she held her wrist up and wiggled it, jangling the bracelet, "Keep in mind you said you're meeting me to get this back."

"That's the plan." Rory winked at her. Then he gestured to the three police officers standing a few feet behind her, "Now stop making their job harder and head for your room."

"Okay."

He put a foot inside the vehicle.

"Rory?"

"Yes?"

With a glint in her green eyes, Cassandra gave him a mischievous grin. She held her red dress out at the sides, "Would you like me to go climb something for you?"

"When we get together, we'll discuss that."

He sat down, the door closed and Green drove away.

Chapter 61

A DAY LATER, Cassandra Glynn took in a deep breath and smiled. She wore a yellow, sleeveless sun dress and matching yellow pumps, the sun warm on her skin as she stood on the sidewalk, waiting for her rental car to be brought around. She had stayed overnight and was now ready to do some power shopping before she went home and put everything behind her.

"How are you, Cassandra?"

Cassandra turned and her smile faded.

It was Clarke Navarro. He casually walked up to stand beside her and put his hands behind his back, "Too bad about the Prime Minister, isn't it? I mean, one little heart attack and the whole political party starts to fall apart."

She wanted to say something but didn't, looking ahead instead.

"Although," Navarro said, as he leaned a little closer and spoke in a low voice, "my sources tell me there might have been some type of cover-up. An embarrassment to the country they say." He shook his head solemnly.

Her lips pressed together, irritated at his audacity to get closer but also angry that she had to maintain control - and confidentiality- it was for the good of the country they had said–

"And then, there's poor Mr. Gomez," Navarro continued. "Retired hockey player goes berserk because of all those concussions he suffered in his career. Suicide by cop. Tragic."

Now a muscle in her jaw twitched.

Then Navarro asked her a point-blank question, "Are you going to run for the Canadian Federal Party again?" You know, help them to rebuild and everything? There are so many people who have resigned and they *are* going to need a lot of help."

Finally letting loose, Cassandra looked at him, heat in her voice, "Not if you're part of it."

Navarro held his hands out to her in a beseeching manner, "All I did was follow party procedures, Cassandra. You know that. I did what the Prime Minister told me to do. I didn't really want to do it, but I was forced to. That's all there was to it. There was nothing personal in it."

"Yeah, right," Cassandra replied, "but you sure seemed to enjoy it."

"I'm sorry you feel that way," Navarro replied offhandedly. "But you don't have to worry. I'm no longer part of the Canadian Federal Party."

Cassandra sneered, "Somebody finally caught up with you as well, did they?"

Navarro gave her a smug smile, "Actually, no. The people I work for actually recommended I become an independent consultant."

"The people you work for? And consulting for what?"

"Well, there are always opportunities for people in the political arena," Navarro replied. He pointed a finger, "See those two men across the street, waiting for me?"

Cassandra looked across the wide street. There were two well-dressed men talking together on the sidewalk on the other side.

"The one on the left is Raymond Donald Cooper. The one on the right is Edward Thomas McNamara. Cooper is a supporter of the Liberal party. McNamara supports the New Democrats. Neither one has ever run for public office. But you know, those two men over there would make great candidates, probably even great Prime Ministers. They have both worked very hard to become very successful businessmen. And despite their last names - as descendants of *Colombian* immigrants - they make a great success story. They both would be a very easy sell to the public. You know what I mean?"

Cassandra's blood ran cold as she looked at Navarro.

"Of course, they would need the right backing. And the right support from people with deep, deep pockets, of course," Navarro added. Then he held up a finger to make a serious point, *"That,* along with the knowledge of how the system works...well...*anyone* can get elected to office. Even become Prime Minister. I just love this country, don't you, Cassandra?"

Her jaw slackened - *was he actually saying...?*

Navarro seemed to enjoy her reaction, smoothing his tie as he looked her, "Have a good day, Cassandra." Then he stepped into the street and held his arms out wide as he shouted out a loud greeting in Spanish to the two men on the other side.

One of the men raised a hand in acknowledgment.

Navarro turned in the street to look at her again, a partial smile on his face, "I wish you well for the future, Cassandra. But do me a favor, will you? Just don't run in a riding we need. Okay?"

Cassandra's mouth fell open–

Navarro glanced around to see if anyone could hear, the smile dropped and he looked her in eye, "I would hate to see *you* in a car accident. And it *will* happen if we cross paths again." Turning on his heels, Navarro headed across the street.

Her body shook as Cassandra stared at the man's back. She barely heard the cars, or the twittering birds, or the other people around her, going about their daily routine–

"Don't worry, we got it all."

Turning her head, Cassandra saw Detective Sepulveda standing beside her. "Pardon?"

Sepulveda tipped her head in the direction of Navarro, "We got everything he said on tape. Well, digital, I guess."

Cassandra looked across the street to see MacKinnon, Pelfrey, Flynn, and Esposito surround Navarro and the two men. She looked back at Sepulveda, "You've been following me?"

"Tracking you, actually." Sepulveda gestured to Cassandra's arm, "The bracelet. It was used by Detective Green during his undercover work in narcotics. It has a tracker in it. Plus the ability to record a conversation through it, but we made sure." She gestured to a van down the street, a small dish-like array on top, "It has a parabolic reflector that collects and focuses a conversation so we can record it."

Cassandra looked at the bracelet, "Rory told me it belonged to his grandmother."

"Yep."

Smiling to herself, Cassandra said, "The dirty bastard lied to me."

"Yep. It was all his idea. He figured someone else was behind the whole scheme. Someone with a big ego who wouldn't come out of the woodwork until Rory wasn't in the picture. Turns out he was right. We'll work Navarro to find the bigger fish - but one way or another, Navarro is done - he will pay for what his part in what happened to you and your family."

Cassandra shook her head, "And here I thought Steele liked me."

Sepulveda leaned her head closer to Cassandra, "Don't give up so easily." She held something out to her, "Rory asked me to give this to you."

Taking it in hand, Cassandra's eyes widened. It was a business card for the lingerie shop where they had picked up the black wig.

"Rory also gave me a message to pass on. He says - and I quote - he can't wait to continue the theme of *close contact* with you - taking it up a notch - after you've done some shopping."

Raising her eyebrows, Cassandra said, "Oh, really?"

Laughing, Sepulveda headed across the street.

Also by Eugene Lloyd MacRae

A Rory Mack Steele Novel
Betrayal
Storm
Hunted
Fire Plague
Jewel
The Echelon Mind
The Chinese President
Knights of The Golden Circle
Cruise
Mask
The Overstolz Code
City
Stealing a Country
Box Set: Rory Mack Steele Thrillers Books 1-12

The Stopper Files
Iron Pipeline
Economic Hitman

The Gunrunner

Watch for more at eugenelloydmacrae.com.